TAKE ALL OF US

NATALIE LEIF

HOLIDAY HOUSE • NEW YORK

AUTHOR'S NOTE

I first drafted this story about a plague in 2019. It took about three years to edit and redraft, mostly because I kept realizing new and bizarre things about what living in a plague is like. Life is funny that way.

I'd imagine most anyone with a disability has a good idea by now of what sort of trigger warnings are coming up. But just to clear the air before we head in: this story contains (un)dead kids, medical neglect, grief, and a bunch of raw emotions about being abandoned by the world. It talks a lot in particular about brain damage and about losing your memories and sense of self in the face of trauma and grief.

In a more zombielike sense, this also contains some pretty gross descriptions of cannibalism, decay, and eyeballs. No shame in skipping ahead a chapter or two if that's not your thing.

On the brighter side, all the dogs survive until the end, I promise. So there's that.

Best,
Natalie "Leif" Leif

HOLIDAY HOUSE is registered in the U.S. Patent and Trademark Office
Printed and bound in April 2024 at Sheridan, Chelsea, MI, USA.
www.holidayhouse.com
First Edition
1 3 5 7 9 10 8 6 4 2

Library of Congress Catalog-in-Publication Data is available.

ISBN: 978-0-8234-5661-1 (hardcover)

For Meeka, who deserves to thrive,
and for Dave, who deserved to come back.

ONE

I first realized I loved Eric a couple hours after Mr. Owens died, when me and Eric found his body rotting in the park.

It was a late summer afternoon, the air warm and the sun a tiny ball in a sky so cloudless blue you could stare into it and watch it flicker back like static. Down the road, past bushes and the chain-link fence of a development site, someone's truck radio hummed a bass line, a steady *WHUM-whumwhumwhum* rumbling through the earth. An older couple sat with their dog a ways uphill, throwing tennis balls at the tree line, where every so often a breeze would stir up a waft of stagnant lake water and dry grass.

For the most part, though, it was just Eric and me in the park, knee-deep in scratchy thorns, our hands sticky with blackberry pulp, our fingers stinging and sweet. Eric's dad had come home early in a mood again, so Eric let himself in through my house's back door, and I knew as soon as I saw him that he needed to make himself scarce for a while, so I suggested the park. It was a Tuesday, so there wouldn't be anybody else there but the truckers and the old people. A scarce-making place.

We'd grabbed whatever we could find for containers on the way out: a stained plastic salad bowl for me, a pop cup from the recycling bin for him. Eric pushed ahead, grabbing berries and thorns by the dripping, bleeding handful, while I lingered back, threading fingers through the spikes to coax out a berry or two, so of course Eric stumbled out and saw Mr. Owens first.

That was how we'd always been. Him, a bulky and square-jawed brick of a kid, gritting his teeth to get everything done quick, then me, short and mousey and epileptic, playing it safe and watchful from a distance.

Mr. Owens's body stood on the other side of a line of bushes, closer to the lake. He wore a button-up pajama shirt and matching pants, the kind that must've fit him at one point but now dangled off his joints like curtains. His hair hung in cottony wisps in front of his sunken face, his lips pulled back in focus, showing off recessed gums and stalactite teeth. All his own set, he'd told us once, owed to a lifetime of good air and bad whiskey, and he'd laughed a rasping mule laugh.

But he wasn't laughing now, being dead and all. He muttered little half-phrases to himself instead: "C'mon, now... Git it... Jus' a couple more... Damn it..." And he kept raising his hand to pick at a berry, pulling it off the branch, then he'd lose himself somewhere in the middle and he'd lower his hand again, dropping the berry to the dirt, and shuffle on to the next one.

We could tell right away he'd died on account of his eyes. When someone's dead all the way, their eyes cloud over white and dry. But when they're dead and haven't realized it yet, their eyes go full dark, pupils blown way too wide, like a spooked deer trying to stare at everything at once. Their skin goes sallow and gray, too, their lips cracked and their joints all twitching and unsure like spider legs, but the biggest tell is always in those wide babydoll eyes.

Eric saw Mr. Owens first, and Mr. Owens stared back at him. I walked up behind Eric, and I didn't see anything at first but a scrap of pajamas, so I moved in to say hi. But Eric had more wary, protective instincts, and he put up an arm, and I stopped.

The second time I looked, I saw the eyes, and it clicked.

"Oh," I said.

"Yeah," Eric said. He grunted the word out between his teeth; Eric hated dealing with dead people.

"That's Mr. Owens," I said. "I know him. We used to help him with yard work. I didn't even know he was doing bad. What do you think happened?"

"He's old. Pro'ly just fell down the stairs or something," Eric said.

I stepped closer, fascinated in spite of myself.

Sure, dead people like this happened all the time in the more rural parts of Kittakoop, near Eric's house, where people just kinda lived off old factory water and fumes. I'd seen old folks there so messed up they looked like the really cheap apples in the school cafeteria, crispy red and two months expired, with texture like old paper.

But Dad and Mom had been paying for good water filters for at least five years now, even before there was a lawsuit and everyone got warnings in the mail from one of the old paper mills. All our neighbors drank filtered water and ate city groceries, and when they died they died proper, arms folded and eyes closed in the obituaries without any fuss at all, and they only looked crispy when caked up in makeup at their funerals.

Not like Mr. Owens.

"Musta been a bad fall. He's already totally out of it," I mused.

We kept our voices low out of some kind of respect. I didn't know if Mr. Owens could hear us anymore, not if he was half as dazed as he looked, but it seemed rude to talk about him to his face. He tilted his head at us, smiling in a friendly, absent way, and we nodded back, polite-like.

I noticed his hands by then, covered in lines of reddish-black scratches and swollen marks, and I saw the top of his head seared

red with sunburn. He'd been out here for a long while. A couple more hours, stuck in his loop of berry-picking, and both would blister and bleed.

So I glanced at Eric to see if he'd know what to do. Eric usually did, in that way of broke kids who'd raised themselves and hoarded every trick on the way. He knew how to get stains out of clothes, how to throw together a meal, how to patch up a scratch and keep moving like nothing happened.

Sure enough, he muttered: "Hey, Ian. Does he have anyone around here?"

Eric didn't use my name unless something bad happened—not when he preferred *shrimp* and *fluffy* and *suck-up*—so I didn't waste time with more questions. "I think so. His daughter works at the diner. I can call them and see if they can reach her?"

"Yeah. The top of the hill pro'ly has the best reception. Go on. I'll watch him." He reached out, pressing a hand to Mr. Owens's arm, and he muttered to him in a soothing voice, all *take it easy* and *it's okay, sir,* in a domesticated hospital room tone he must've gotten from me.

Uphill, that couple kept on playing with their dog, laughing at some old-people joke, and I realized the blackberry bushes must've blocked their view, same as it had for us. Same as it had for the radio-blasting trucker across the lot, still *whumwhumwhum*ing away. It seemed rude, in a way, for all them to be laughing and playing music only a couple yards from Mr. Owens's body. Disrespectful.

At the same time, it seemed wrong to ruin their moments, too. I took out my phone and hurried around them instead, looping a half circle across their part of the hill and toward the top. They didn't look twice, even as I hit the top and crouched to catch my breath, lungs aching and medical bracelet jangling on my wrist like a reminder to breathe.

Guys like Eric could run and shove and deal with dead people. Guys like me stayed safe and made phone calls.

Up here, I could see nearabout the entire park. The long stretch of gravel lined by chain-link fence, where tin-paneled shacks and rusted trucks sat idle for a construction project that had been going on as long as I could remember. The tree line, thick with dead grass and blackberry thorns matted together like hair. Beyond them, the shallow algae bog we all agreed to call a lake. And beyond *it*, the cinder block backs of the gas station and the mall and the antique store.

Nearly the whole town.

My phone's screen fluttered at a few bars, which would have to be good enough. I dug through its call history until I found the diner's number from last Friday, when Mom and Dad went out and left my little sister and me a twenty for burgers.

On the other end, a woman's voice picked up, crackling with static. "Hilltop Diner, what can I getcha?"

I recognized that drawl, and I perked up. "Mrs. Bailey? It's Ian."

Her voice brightened, sharp and eager. "*Ian!* How are you, kiddo? How's little Emma doing?"

"I'm fine. We're fine. Look, um, is Ms. Owens working today?" My voice came too fast, pushed out in little huffs of breath from lungs still tight in my chest, and I wasn't sure how much of that was nerves and how much of that was part of being *sickly*.

Behind me, the couple wrapped up their fetch game. They crouched by their dog, scratching his ears and back while the dog whapped its tail against the grass hard enough to send blades fluttering.

"Nah, she's off the next two days. Won't answer her phone for anything, either, knowin' her. But, oh! That nice girl Monica is here. She lives nearby. I can ask her to drop off a message for ya?"

Damn it. The one day I needed help, and of course the only other disabled kid in town would *happen* to be there. Monica always jumped at the chance to look oh-so-useful and nice, waving her cane around like a cutesy Victorian orphan, and I bit back a smudge of petty envy. Ever since we were kindergarteners, every time I tried to do something useful, Monica was there, being way more useful, way more helpful, and twice as *inspirational.*

"That—yeah, if you can. Tell her...um. That Ms. Owens needs to go to her dad's house." An understatement. I winced, glancing back toward the bushes. "He's not...doing well."

"Oh? Do you know what's going on?"

"He's—"

I cut off then, as I heard something wet and heavy thud below the hill, like a rock hitting water. It sounded *wrong,* too loud and too sharp and too *meatlike,* too close to where I'd left Eric alone with a dead guy, and my throat went dry at the sound of it. Even the oblivious old couple glanced up, their dog's ears perked and legs braced wide.

"Ian?" Ms. Bailey asked, her voice crackling distortion at the edges.

"Yeah, I'm here," I heard myself say. "Look, I'll call you back, okay?"

"Okay, kiddo. What—"

But I'd already hung up by then and started racing back down the hill, never mind the aching lungs and jingling medical bracelet. The couple—dressed too warm for the weather, both with clear brown living-people eyes—watched me go, but their dog kept jumping up on their legs and panting, a low whine in his throat, pulling their attention away. With a dog like that, they'd find the body soon enough, I figured; in a town with maybe five hundred people, things always rolled around again to those who waited. Even dead things.

For now, though, I needed to make sure Eric was okay.

I reached the bottom of the hill and kept going, around the bushes and thickets of weeds, past where Eric had been standing and wasn't anymore. Farther on, and I spotted a flash of his blue shirt and faded jeans, blackberry-stained, and I saw him standing by the bog we all called a lake, and I let out my breath in a relieved rush. He kept his hands tucked deep in his pockets, his thumb doing a nervous flick across the top of the old lighter he'd stolen from his dad. His shoulders were drawn—a workman's shoulders already, broad-set and rigidly straight as the military buzzcut his dad gave him every summer to keep the lice away.

I stumbled to a stop by him, skidding my sneakers across mud and reeds. Normally you could hardly tell the water from the grass this close—the algae across it spread out in a film, so the only way you knew there was water ahead was by how too-smooth and too-green it was compared to the ground. But something had broken up the film, rippling out in waves, and for once I could see a dark hole of clear water in the middle of it all, staring at us like a massive eye.

Mr. Owens wasn't there.

I looked up at Eric. He watched the water.

I'd known Eric for nearly ten years by then. Since my family moved to Kittakoop, West Virginia, even; since I'd walked into daycare, a scrawny blond kid with a pale face and a medical list a mile long, and he and Monica had been the only other kids my age. I'd watched him grow from a chubby, angry little boy, throwing crayons and kicking shins, to a solemn teenager with farmer's hands and a dark sense of humor.

I'd never once seen him look the way he did then. He seemed tired, yet serene. As if he'd found peace, somewhere in the water pooling around our battered shoes.

"It's gonna be okay, Ian," he said in this soft voice I hadn't heard before, something paternal and sweet. "I took care of him. Thanks for calling."

And I realized then what happened to Mr. Owens.

I stared into the eye of the lake. It rippled and wavered, the algae already shifting to cover up the gap.

A few more hours, and it'd be like Mr. Owens had never been pushed in at all.

"It happened quick. He didn't feel anything, I promise." Eric didn't look at me; he kept his eyes locked on the water, on that disappearing eye where Mr. Owens wasn't. Then he added, softer: "He didn't even get a blister."

That struck me. Eric wasn't wrong—the hot summer sun couldn't reach him down there, couldn't touch his skin enough to blister it further. And he wouldn't tear himself up on the thorns, either. Soon enough the bloat and rot in him would bob him back to the surface for that old couple to find, sure, but not before he'd breathed in enough cold lake water to drown that last part of him and turn his eyes white.

I wondered if it felt like a relief. If some part of him, baking and bleeding out in the open sun, wanted nothing more than a cool dip in the lake. And I wondered if Eric knew that, muttering up at Mr. Owens with that hospital-soft tone.

Eric hated dealing with the dead, but he'd still given Mr. Owens a last moment of peace.

I reached out and I found Eric's hand, and I gave it a squeeze. He squeezed back, not thinking about it, and both of us watched the water until it went still again, until the mosquitos picked up buzzing and the warblers darted overhead, rustling branches and scattering leaves.

Life has a funny way of moving on like that.

We walked back to the park, gathering our blackberries to go home. Up the hill, that old couple was still picking their way downward, their dog sniffing and whining at the end of his lead. Below the hill, that truck kept sounding out its steady bassline, *WHUD-whudwhudwhud* like a heartbeat.

Nothing changed. Not really.

Except that when we passed that old couple, Eric and I both nodded at them in the way you did in town when you saw a dead person, a flicker of eye contact and a grimace that said *watch out over there*, and they nodded back like *thanks*, bracing themselves in case it needed putting down like a rabid dog or a lame horse.

Except that Eric had already put Mr. Owens down, and he'd done it with caution and compassion and a low hospital voice, as gently as he could.

A kindness his dad would hate.

But I loved Eric for it.

I'd loved him for a long time, since we'd met at daycare as wide-eyed kids, overwhelmed at the world and itching to rebel against it. The word *love* itched at my winded lungs with every step back, begging to get said, rattling the bars of my rib cage with a violent self-importance that was anything but sickly.

Nothing changed, but we did.

TWO

The itch to say *I love you* rattled inside me for the rest of the evening, around a tasteless taco dinner and mindless homework attempt, and all through a long night of waking up dry-eyed and sleepless every half hour.

I finally cracked around eight a.m., when Eric *might* be awake, and I sent him a text to meet me at the mall like I had something important to tell him.

What I was going to tell him, *how* and *when* and *where*, I had no idea about.

Eric, I love you. I don't mean like a friend, I mean more than that. I want to . . . date you? Kiss you? Marry you?

Eric, I am IN LOVE with you. I don't care if you're a boy. I get if that ruins our friendship for you, and you want to leave forever and never look back—

No, that ain't true, I wouldn't get it. I don't want to lose out on spending lazy summer days together like this. So if you don't love me back, let's both pretend I never said anything. Got it?

But . . . if you DO somehow love me back, maybe we could kiss? Just once, real quick. No one would have to see, promise.

I buried my head in my hands, scrubbing against my eyelids until my vision flared red. None of those sounded right. Even in my own head, I sounded hesitant and slow, the sort of person you could only love out of a strange sense of pity.

All this seemed like a bad idea, now.

Too late for that, I guessed. I'd already made it to the mall. I'd already sat down on the edge of the fountain, on plaster that smelled like chlorine and mildewed coins.

And he was already settled next to me, drinking pop out of a water cup, waiting for me to confess whatever big damn secret I had.

Once upon a time, the Kittakoop mall was somewhere important. It was built that way, with a long, wide hallway and a dozen off-shoot stores, with lush potted plants along the walls and speakers piping synth-pop Muzak overhead. Maybe it was built with the expectation that we'd grow into it, like little kids in hand-me-down clothes.

Nowadays, though, it sat half empty, its big hallway caked with dust in the corners and that same handful of Muzak songs cycling through static. The plants still looked nice, though their plastic threads had frayed at the edges and the glue showed through in spots. Half the stores stood empty, their security grilles drawn and their insides a dark mass of cardboard boxes, while the other half cycled through brands every year or two: first a hair salon, then an insurance company, then a Chinese takeout place. Only the clothing store seemed to stay every year, a single corporate mass keeping the mall barely alive.

Every so often a person or two would mill past us, their footsteps echoing across the tile, and I watched them for the sake of something to do that wasn't trying to find words. My eyes flickered from them, to my hands, to the scattered coins rippling under the fountain's shallow pool behind us. The air-conditioning rattled, too cold and stale, cutting through the faded purple jacket I'd thrown on.

Beside me, Eric pulled out the battered lighter he always fiddled with when bored or restless. He lifted a tanned arm, exposing an inch of bare skin under the edge of his tugged-up shirt...and opened an eye to watch me.

"What?" he asked.

"It's just..." I took a deep breath, let it out again. "It's nothing. Never mind."

And it could be nothing. It could be nothing, and we could both go home, and soon enough it'd suffocate under the weight of all that nothing, and the world would keep spinning round, and it'd be fine.

That'd be the safest option, too. No one could blame me for being too safe. We'd moved to West Virginia in the first place to be safe, because I'd had a grand mal seizure on the kitchen floor and suddenly the city was too full of strobe lights and flashing signs and alarms blaring **DANGER, ALERT, EMERGENCY**, everything the doctors told me to avoid.

I could imagine just about all those signs now. They sat on any path toward talking about my feelings, blaring and bright and not giving a whit about the medical alert bracelet on my wrist that said **EPILEPTIC**.

"It don't seem like nothing," Eric said. He flicked the lighter, *flick-flick-flick*, and I bit back an itch to slap it out of his hands and remind him that *you don't even smoke, you just like looking at the fire.*

DANGER, went my brain.

"Well, it is."

"You called me all the way out here for nothing?"

DANGER. ALERT. NO ACCESS.

"Yeah. Guess I must've forgot what it was. Probably wasn't important. You want to get takeout or something instead, while we're here?"

"Uh-huh. And now you're changing the subject. Come on, fluffy."

DANGER. EMERGENCY.

"I told you, it's not a big deal. I'll tell you later, promise."

"Wait, which is it? 'I forgot' or 'I'll tell you later'?"

DANGER, DANGER, DANGER, DANGER.

"It's both. Neither? Look—" I couldn't get that flashing siren out of my head, and I squeezed my eyes shut. "I just don't want to ruin things—"

"Ian—"

"I don't want you to think I've just been creeping on you, but ever since I realized it's been hard to stop thinking about it—"

"Ian—"

"I can't hardly think right now, even, I—"

"Ian, stop." Eric pressed a hand to my arm. "What the hell?"

I stopped, but that siren didn't, and I realized with a start that it wasn't in my head. High overhead, next to the skylights, tiny lights flashed sharp white, casting the mall kiosks and plants into searing silhouettes. An alarm warbled in and out, and the speakers crackled, that soothing Muzak drowned out by a distorted recording.

"State of—Evacuate—warning—please—from the building—This is—" a man's voice echoed, thundering across the hall.

It kept on, but all I could really notice were those lights. They flashed over and over, searing neon, and as I stared at them I felt the taste of sour copper and spit gather in my mouth, along with a dizzy floatiness somewhere behind my eyes.

No, I thought. Then: *no, no-no-no, not again.*

I couldn't hear Eric's voice anymore, but I saw him hold up a hand: *stay here.* I saw him stand up, and I mouthed the words, *help me*, at the back of his head. His shirt flared a sickly reddish-orange, smearing across my vision as he moved—him surging forward in bursts of feverish white light toward the exit, me fainting backward into the fountain, and that siren still screaming, screaming, screaming over both of us.

Then I hit the water, and the back of my head cracked hard against the tile, and everything went from a carousel of electric colors to brilliant white. I tasted copper and chlorine, mixed together in a mouthful of cloudy red bubbles, and... it was funny.

Under a foot of stale fountain water, the alarm didn't sound so loud. It drifted into my ears from somewhere far away, along with echoes of **EVACUATION** and **BUILDING** and **STATE**... and, over it all, somehow, still that gentle shopping mall Muzak, crooning gently on. Even the light didn't seem so bad, distorted by ripples.

I wondered, absently, if this was how non-epileptics got to see alarms: as distant, casual things, acknowledged and ignored, the kind of things they could look directly at and then away from without once wondering if it'd be the thing that killed them.

It seemed nice.

I watched the light sparkle like stars as I choked down another lungful of water, listened to buzzing synths and happy drumbeats as my vision faded from white to pooling black, and it did seem so nice. I sank into it like Mr. Owens did, letting it settle into my aching joints and racing heart and overwhelmed head.

And it all went dark.

I can't remember what happened after that, except in fragments.

Someone pulling on me, yanking me out of the water. Eric's voice, frantic and shouting and stumbling all over itself. A rush of cold air against my face, the taste of old pennies against my teeth. Trying to breathe, failing, panicking. Throwing up mouthfuls of pinkish water onto the floor, the splash of it against cement. Taking thin, reedy breaths I coughed back out, burning in my throat. Dropping, curling up on my side, lights still too bright, fluorescents buzzing like wasps. Running footsteps.

The hallway—a potted plastic fern—sticky dark blood against my fingertips, too much, everywhere—the cool comfort of a shadowed corner, the black slab of an **OUT OF ORDER** vending machine—a pounding in my head, needles and hammers against my skull—sinking into a corner, burying my face in my jacket hood—shaky legs and a bone-deep tiredness—

And a long, long quiet.

The worst part about seizures was never the seizure itself. I fainted through those, or otherwise got so fuzzy-headed that I forgot them before they were over.

Nah, the worst part was always *afterward*: waking up disoriented on a floor somewhere new, head full of cotton stuffing and a sour burnt taste in my mouth. Shaking pins and needles out of heavy limbs, checking if I'd pissed myself again, feeling up and down for all the new bruises and cuts and aches I'd have to carry home. If I was really unlucky, there might be a couple onlookers or a cop there, too, gawking and throwing out questions like *what the hell happened to you?*

No watchers this time, at least. Hadn't pissed myself, either, somehow. Or I had, and falling into old fountain water made it hard to tell. I decided to pretend I hadn't.

When I finally felt stable enough to lift my head—with the pounding and nausea faded into something just south of excruciating—I pushed myself upright. The siren and flashing lights were gone, and the peppy Muzak, too, leaving a silence deep enough to bask in. I savored it for a second, then, all at once, I remembered being pulled out of the water. I remembered Eric's voice, shouting noises that didn't settle into words but damn sure settled into fear.

Of course. Eric always knew what to do. After years together, he'd become a natural at noticing the signs of a seizure, getting me situated in a safe place, and shooing away anyone who wanted to rubberneck. He must've run back from the entrance as soon as he saw me flailing underwater like an idiot.

So I raised a hand and forced a smile, in case he was lurking somewhere close.

" 'M okay," I rasped. "Still here. Thanks for the save."

No answer. I squinted around, raising a hand to shield my eyes from even the faint skylights of the mall.

"Eric?"

Eric wasn't here. Neither were any of the other shoppers we'd seen milling around. The mall sat dim and empty, a wide swath of shuttered storefronts and drifting dust motes. The only lights I could see were the skylights letting in shafts of hazy afternoon sun...and the vending machine beside me, its face glowing with shadows of cola cans and water bottles. Its motor hummed somewhere inside, and the fountain kept burbling on down the hall, but everything else sat quiet and dead.

Dead. At the word, the back of my head gave an angry throb, and I cried out and pressed a hand to it.

It felt sticky and somehow *soft*, like a baby's head where the bones haven't quite shaped all the way yet. I pushed at it and it hurt in a dizzying way, a little button I could press to knock myself out of my senses for a bit.

My hand came back bloody. Not just a smear, either, but a whole handful, welling into my palm and leaking between my fingers as I stared.

One mercy of waking up post-seizure: I always woke up too tired to know if I should be scared yet. I could get up, get my bearings, and tidy up most of any mess before I came to enough to panic about it.

So when I saw the blood pooled in my hand and felt it trickling down the back of my neck, I didn't scream, even when I realized in a vague way that it'd be a good time for it. I got up instead, swaying with vertigo, and staggered down the hall past all those grated storefronts and toward the nearest bathroom. A family bathroom, it turned out, one of those kinds with a single room and a baby changing station and a toilet that only came up to my shins.

And a mirror. I caught myself against the sink, smearing blood all across its pretty white porcelain, and I looked up at myself.

And I realized I was dead.

The eyes gave it away first, as they always did. I'd always had a round face and a scrawny build, as if after years of health scares my body had given up on growing somewhere around age twelve. It'd been what made me and Eric match—him pushed to grow up too soon, me stuck behind, and both of us meeting in the middle, where we were supposed to be. But now I had big black doll eyes to go with all that, nestled above purple shadows in a milk-pale face like a ceramic figurine, and that doll-me in the mirror seemed as shocked by it as I did.

Everything else came with its own flavors of wrong, too. My hair hung in blond fluffs over my forehead, dry in the front, plastered to my neck in chlorine-dark blood-clumps in the back. The jacket I'd thrown on hung waterlogged on my shoulders, all my careful iron-on patches of skulls and monsters and other cool things—slapped on in a desperate attempt to seem at least a little badass—were dyed pinkish-orange from the water. Even my shirt fit wrong now, its collar tugged askew and sleeves rolled up somewhere between falling and thrashing back up.

Just like Mr. Owens, I thought. *A little less out of it, a lot less sunburned, but otherwise we could be cousins.*

And all of a sudden, I started laughing. I laughed way too hard, coughing it up and wheezing it back down, and I pressed a red-smudged hand to my face just to keep it steady.

"Holy shit," I breathed. "I really messed up, now." Another laugh. "What a stupid way to die."

I couldn't stop laughing. Because it really *was* funny, in that awful-funny way. All the ways I could have died—hell, all the things that had tried to kill me already, from seizures to allergies—and I died in a foot and a half of rusty fountain water.

This shouldn't have even happened. I did so *good*, living in the fancy side of town and drinking filtered water and eating organic food... except mall fountains didn't have water filters, did they? Mall fountain water wasn't clean enough to drink from or to die in. It didn't matter if I'd lived like a rich person expecting a quiet death—I'd died like an old country man with a lungful of used fountain water.

Like the letter from the government warned about: `Sorry. Our mistake. Here's three hundred dollars. Buy a water filter. Eat uncontaminated food. Consider moving. Push your neighbors into a lake.`

Or maybe I'd already been doomed like this. Maybe I'd contaminated myself with some school water fountain, or a drink from a vending machine. Maybe I was always gonna die stupidly and wake back up mad about it.

I didn't even get to see what the alarm was about; it could've been a fire, or a terrorist attack, or a tornado, or anything else that would've killed me with some sort of dignity. Maybe I could have even been a hero, rescuing a dozen orphan kids before collapsing from smoke inhalation.

Eric would've found it funny, if he was here. Only Ian Chandler, fifteen-year-old walking crisis, could fail an evacuation so hard he died. Only Ian Chandler could get so flustered at being gay that he slipped on a tile and cracked his head open and let all the brains spill out.

Only Ian Chandler could die in a mall fountain before he'd even tried living first.

I kept laughing until I teared up, until the tears started streaming down my face between chuckles, until I curled up on the floor and I laughed and I laughed and I screamed myself hoarse.

THREE

Sooner or later, I got back up, mostly because I couldn't think of what else to do. There was only so long I could lie on the floor feeling sorry for myself before I started getting sore and restless, and my head still ached something fierce.

I decided after a minute or so to keep looking for Eric. If I went straight home, Mom and Dad would lose their minds with worry, and Emma would take it harder still. She already had enough to adjust to with middle school and other girls—a dead older brother hanging around until his limbs fell off and his brain rotted out wouldn't exactly earn her new friends.

Eric probably wouldn't have a *great* time with the news, either... but he was a tough guy. He'd deal with it better than anyone.

I hoped.

Anyway, I figured if I was already dead it wasn't like I had to worry too much about bleeding to death, but I also didn't want to figure out what would happen if I ran *out* of blood, so I grabbed big fistfuls of those brown paper towels and jammed them against the back of my head, pulling up my hood to hold them in place. They crunched as I moved, and I could already feel them soaking through, but they'd be better than nothing until I could find something more medical.

Outside the bathroom, the mall sat as empty as I'd left it. It felt eerie in a way I couldn't quite explain—I'd never seen an empty mall before, and it felt, deep in my bones, like I wasn't supposed to be here. Like I'd missed some vital rule everyone else already knew.

I guessed, technically, I wasn't. What was it that warning alarm said? *Something-something danger, something, evacuation, please leave the building.*

An evacuation. From what? I wondered about it as I walked down a random hall, hands tucked deep in my pockets and hood rustling around my ears. A fire? That seemed most likely, but the mall wasn't that big, and I couldn't see any smoke or smell anything burning. The weather through the skylights seemed too nice to be a flood or tornado or anything like that, either. Maybe someone pulled out a gun and tried to cause a panic?

Up ahead, I could see a couple kiosks, a line of benches...and, beyond them, a set of glittery glass exit doors, their silver edges reflecting sunlight off the roofs of a dozen parked cars.

I frowned. Would people leave their cars behind if they were running from a shooter? I didn't know. Like any other kid, I'd been through a million active shooter drills—lock the doors, get under the desks, stay quiet. But none of them ever mentioned what to do with *cars.* I had to figure, though, that if people left their favorite SUVs behind, that meant they planned to come back, right?

They wouldn't leave *me* behind, right?

Before I could get too close, something rustled in one of the kiosks and I jumped, startled for the hundredth time in fifteen minutes. I caught a blob of white and red, bright against the dull light, and I squinted, stepping closer. Another straggler? Maybe they'd have a better idea of what I'd missed.

Closer still, and the blob focused into a woman in a Dairy Queen apron, leaning against the kiosk counter in the little gap between the register and the pop machine. She stared up at the flickering back-lit menu like she'd never seen it before, her head tipped back and her ponytail limp and half undone against her shoulders.

"Hey!" I called out. My voice echoed out, too loud in the emptiness, and I grimaced, trying again a little quieter. "You got stuck back here, too, huh? I know how that goes. D'you wanna head out together?"

No answer. She turned, grasping a cleaning rag and tilting toward the cola machine, and I caught sight of her eyes.

They were black. Black and way too dry and grayish, like she hadn't blinked in days. She reeked, too, like sweat and grease and sharp vinegar, smeared in stains around the armpits and neck of her uniform. Every step she took came with a little squelching noise, her legs gone swollen and purplish black from the knee down.

A dead lady. And by the looks of it, one who'd been dead for a few days now, her blood turned to gunk and blooming under her skin like bruises. She stared at me and only half seemed to even notice, whatever thoughts she had left gone faded behind moss and rot.

"Oh...never mind." I sighed hard and stepped out of the way, letting her get back to her work.

Everything happened too slow in Kittakoop. For as long as I could remember, the traffic barely existed, the summer days dragged along, and even things like dying took a while to settle in, too steeped in routine and tradition to notice itself. A person would get up, go to work, and go to bed in the same house their grandparents owned, in the same factory their grandfather worked at. And when they died, just out of habit, their body would get up, go to work, and go to bed, until it got too slow and too sunken to keep itself going, seeping syrupy black gunk like an old machine. Then someone would guide them behind a woodshed, real gentle, and take them out of their misery.

It was the least we could do for a neighbor.

The Dairy Queen shuffled on, grabbing a paper cup from a wobbly stack and pressing it to the ice cream machine against the back wall. Ice cream poured out melty and thin, and I watched as she scooped in fixings at random: cookie pieces, brownie pieces, raspberry pieces. She blended them together to a frothy brown-pink, then handed the cup across the counter at me, and I blinked.

"Huh? Oh, thank you." I took a spoonful—the candy and berries tasted weird together, a little sickly sweet, but not bad. Better than the burnt copper-chlorine aftertaste of drowning, anyway. I leaned against the counter while she went back to wiping the machines down like nothing happened between us.

And both of us dead people spent a while in quiet together.

She hadn't stopped cleaning by the time I finished my ice cream, so I lingered awhile, digging at the dregs and watching her scrub at corners and along grill spokes, until the quiet got too loud and I couldn't not speak up.

"You don't have to keep doing this, you know," I said.

She glanced up at me, then back, still wiping away. I gripped my cup tighter, fingers digging into cold paper.

"I mean it. You're dead, no one cares anymore. Your family shoulda' gotten you by now. And maybe they didn't, but you can still go home if you want. Or go on vacation. Anything. The clock's all zeroes."

Again she gave me that blank, dry stare. She stared too long, mouth agape, then started turning back real slow to the ice-cream machine, and I gripped my cup so hard it dented under my fingers.

"Are you *listening*?!" I cried. "Ain't there *anything* else you wanna do with yourself before you're all the way gone? I know this is what you've *been* doing, but it can't be like you signed up for this job thinking you'd do it forever, right?" Sticky ice-cream syrup spilled over the sides of my cup, smearing down my hands. "You must've wanted to do something better at some point. You fell into this, but you can still climb out! It ain't too late!"

She kept staring. My head pounded, and the words rasped in my throat, edged with desperation. For who, I didn't know.

"*Please* do something else. Anything. Go see a movie. Leave town. Tell a friend you love them." My voice wavered. "Tell them you always loved them. Tell them you want to grow old together. Tell them that even if they think they're a dirt-poor mess with a mean dad, to you they're the best thing that ever happened, anywhere. Tell them you're both gonna get over everything that makes you feel sick and angry and tired all the time, and you're both gonna get out someday and become something great. Tell them that before you *die*."

She stared.

"Please do something. Please." I stepped forward, meeting her eyes with my own matching set, hers too dry and mine too watery. I grabbed at her collar with a free hand, as if I could force her to stop turning away again, working again. "Please—"

The light shifted, a long sunbeam yawning across tile, and I heard the low thud of footsteps ahead. A voice spoke up, blunt and sharp and girlish.

"What're you doing?"

A girl about my age—maybe younger, with a heavy oversized army jacket on that made it hard to tell—stood in front of the door, her hands deep in her pockets and her ruler-straight hair haloed by glass reflections as the door swung back closed. She hunched into herself like one of those homeless people outside town by Sheetz, withdrawn and desperate, but there wasn't any desperation in the way she glared straight at me.

I dropped the Dairy Queen's collar, and my cup to go with it. The cup hit the tile, dribbling ice-cream slush, and the Dairy Queen pulled away toward her precious cleaning rag. I stepped back, suddenly way too aware of my hands, my breathing, my posture.

"I just... I dunno. I wanted her to wake up, I guess."

"Won't work. She died." The girl stepped closer, glancing up and down at the Dairy Queen. "No obvious wounds on the outside. Still kinda young. So probably a stroke or an aneurysm. Thirty thousand people in the United States have a ruptured aneurysm each year." She spoke in a low monotone, as if reading off a hidden sheet of paper, but I still found myself grimacing back.

"That's... really creepy to think about." My eyes still felt too damp, and I scrubbed at them with a jacket sleeve, trying to pull myself together. It was one thing to cry at a dead body, another to do it at a stranger staring up at me with intense brown eyes. "Anyway, I *got* that part. I can see her face. I just felt bad about it. Is that okay?"

The girl watched me, then tilted her head.

"Is it?" she repeated.

"What?"

A pause.

"You died too. From a head wound, right?" she asked. Moving on, too quick.

"I—yeah?" I pressed a hand to the back of my head, where the paper towels squished together. "Yeah. A little bit ago. It still hasn't really hit me yet."

"Oh." She still spoke in that bland monotone, but as I watched, her eyebrows knitted in concentration, and when she spoke up again I heard forced emphasis. "I'm... *so* sorry. For your loss. It must have been *awful*."

For some reason I preferred the monotone. Less painful. So I waved a hand, shooing it away like a cloud of gnats.

"It's okay. You don't gotta try." She sagged in obvious relief, and I pushed on to a better subject. "Do you remember what *happened*? I heard alarms and a message about an emergency, but now it's off and everyone's gone . . . ?"

She'd stopped staring at me, I noticed; instead, she glared somewhere over my shoulder, at the plastic fern behind me. Like keeping up that steady eye contact took too much out of her. "It's obvious. There was an evacuation, and they left us behind."

They left us behind.

Something in me went cold at that. Like the ice cream I'd eaten had soaked its way into my bones. I remembered Eric pushing his way to the exit, a blur of red fabric fading away while I died only a couple feet behind him, and I swallowed a mouthful of icy spit.

"What? No. I don't know where *you* were, but I was with my best friend, and he wouldn't do that. He's always looked out for me." My shoulders itched where they'd been grabbed at hours ago, like evidence. "He pulled me out of the water. He *saved* me." My head throbbed. "M-mostly."

"He did? Where is he now?" She tilted her head, birdlike. Behind her, the Dairy Queen slowed her cleaning, lingering in one spot with her head tipped down. Too gone to listen but eavesdropping anyway.

"I . . ." Another swallow. "I don't know. I'm looking for him. Something must've distracted him."

"From you dying."

"*Yes*. Maybe?" I didn't know. All I could remember was that smear of red shirt cotton, those hands yanking me out, and the silence. "Look, even if he *did* leave, it's not his fault. I was having a seizure, and neither of us saw it coming—they can be *really* random, sometimes, I swear—"

"You were having a seizure?"

"A short one, yeah—"

"You were having a seizure and he left you to die."

"It was an *emergency.* Maybe he noticed something we didn't, or he got hurt...? I don't know what he was thinking, so I'm trying to find him so I can ask—"

"He was thinking you were a *burden.* A disabled, expendable *burden.*" This time, she didn't have to force inflection to her voice. It rasped out through her teeth, echoed in how her fists squeezed against the hems of her jacket.

I stopped. Started to speak, but the words squeezed tight in my throat. Trailed off. Tried again.

"He wouldn't. He's never said that. He's always helped me out," I said.

"When it was *easy,* maybe. They always help when it's *easy.*" Her words came out low, bitter. "They can hold open a door for you or explain a joke and get to feel *so* proud of themselves over it. But if they have to try harder than it feels good to do, you're a problem they didn't ask for."

"Who is 'they'? Who are you *talking* about?" I could hear the defensive edge in my voice, and I hated it.

In response, the girl spread her arms wide, sweeping them across the mall, and I got what she meant.

Them. All of them. Everyone who'd left us behind.

And I didn't know what to say back. I stood there in a long quiet, my throat too tight and my head pounding, thinking about that red smear of jacket and the exit doors, until she spoke up, softer this time.

"When times are good, we get to ask for help. Get to linger behind. But in an emergency, it's survival of the fittest, and no one ever saw us as *fit.*" She spat out the words. "We survive when there's enough for extra, and we die when there isn't."

"He wouldn't do that," I repeated, and even as I said it, it sounded pathetic. A weak objection to an obvious fact: whatever he might've done to try to pull me out, he'd vanished afterward. Gone ahead with everyone else.

I wanted him to love me back. Not just pity or humor or anything else you'd give to a burden, something you'd drop as soon as things got to the point of *emergency* or *survival of the fittest.*

Something you'd leave behind to die.

I swayed on my feet. All this seemed too much, too soon. Yesterday my biggest worry was working up the courage to confess, mixed with all these little things, like picking up Emma from her friend's house or learning to cook. Maybe that was part of how being dead felt like: standing in the same mall I'd been at a hundred times, realizing that all of it suddenly looked unfamiliar and didn't fit anymore.

Behind me, the girl spoke.

"I can kill you, if you want."

No inflection. No tone. I stared back at her. She stared somewhere over my shoulder, glaring at that plastic fern. Her hair hung in straight wisps in front of her face, flat and speckled with dandruff.

"What?" I asked. Weakly, again. All of me felt as weak and raw as a newborn.

She held a knife. When had she pulled out a knife? It sat firm in her grip, a wicked serrated bowie knife with a wooden handle. It was pockmarked and scratched all over, well-used.

"It'd spare some trouble, at least," she said. "He left you because you died. That can't be fixed. You died quick and young, so you've got a while before your body catches up. But by tonight, your body will start to rot. Your mind, too. You'll forget things. Minor things at first, then the parts you care about. By tomorrow, your senses will dull. Your joints will swell and your tissue will decay. Then, moving will become harder. Your blood—"

"Okay, okay! I get it. It'll be slow and miserable." I held up my hands. "I get it. Please stop. I get that it's awful. I don't want it."

"But it doesn't have to be."

She stepped closer. Close enough for me to smell her jacket, sawdust and detergent and hay, like the inside of a hardware store. Close enough for me to see the holes in her jeans, to see the dirt crusted onto her boot laces. Close enough for that knife to gleam.

"I can stab you. It wouldn't be hard. One strike to the back of the skull would destroy the brain stem. All self-awareness and body functions would be severed. It would be quick and simple, same as your original death."

Like pushing Mr. Owens into the river, I thought. *Quick and cool and soothing to all the sunburned parts.*

Is that what Eric would want? What he was hoping would happen, when he left me back here?

"It... would be," I said, slowly.

"Merciful," she said.

"Yeah."

"An ease of a burden."

"Better than rotting over the next few days, probably." I laughed. It wasn't funny. "Wow. You'd do that for me?"

"I don't care. It's fine."

Too close, now. We stood there, me facing her and her facing that stupid plastic fern, her knife held tight. She walked around behind me, but I still saw the edge of her knife out of the corner of my eye, glittering everywhere that wasn't marked with scratches. A well-cared-for, well-used knife, in good hands.

Its tip pressed against the back of my head and I felt the paper towels squish, felt that sharp and dizzying hurt, like stinging static against my brain, and I imagined it like getting a booster shot at the doctor's, a quick sting and done, the right thing to do, the best thing to do, and I'd be dead and gone and—

And I hissed in a breath and drew back, squeezing my eyes shut.

"*S-stop*, stop-stop-stop!" I cried.

The knife sank back down. I pressed my hands to my head, shaking.

"Stop, stop it, I don't want to die, I *don't*. I don't care if I rot or lose myself later, I just—I don't want to die, not right now, please." I was babbling and I knew it, a river of nonsense pleas spilling out, and I gritted my teeth to keep them out.

Behind me, the girl—still so goddamn monotone—nodded.

"Thought as much." She tucked the knife away, slipping it into some hidden inner pocket of her jacket. "They want us to be noble sacrifices for the greater good, but we can't be. Even if living is rotten and painful and slow, in the end, even burdens like us want to live."

My stomach churned, and I bit down harder. Worst part was she wasn't *wrong*; no talk of rotting or falling apart could make me scared enough or noble enough to want to die here and now. Not when I could still drag it out a little more.

"I hate you," I breathed.

"Likewise," the girl said. "My name is Angel."

I turned. She held out a hand to me, small fingers edged with bright white calluses. I hesitated, all that hate and fear and disgust turning circles in my gut, and tucked my hands deep into my pockets instead.

"Ian," I muttered back.

If she'd gotten offended, she didn't show it. Angel looked at the Dairy Queen instead, who'd slowed to a stop, watching us with that dry, shallow stare.

"Want me to kill her?" Angel asked.

"What? *No*. Why do you keep...?" *Asking me about stabbing people*, I wanted to say, but I reconsidered. I'd been the one shaking the Dairy Queen's collar and ranting at her; maybe Angel assumed we knew each other. Maybe we did, in the distant cousin way of two mutually dead people.

"If you don't want to rot, you need to keep your body thinking it's alive," Angel said. "Give it air. Give it blood flow. Give it food that won't make it sick."

I glanced toward my ice cream cup, still dribbling pink in lines between the floor tiles, wafting a smell of clotted milk and raspberry syrup, but Angel shook her head.

"The only thing that don't make a dead body sick is a dead body. It's instinct. Last thing your flesh remembers is how to eat parts of itself to survive. Put in something new, it might realize something's different—that it can't digest like it used to anymore. Put in something familiar, it'll keep eating what it thinks is itself, forever."

Back to the Dairy Queen, both of us staring now. She stared back like a caged pet, black doll eyes blown wide, not understanding.

"I'm a vegetarian," I muttered.

"Want me to kill her for you?" Angel asked again, like she hadn't heard.

And this time I didn't answer.

The dead didn't eat people. They weren't vengeful or desperate like ghosts in an old house. Hunger meant want, meant need, meant growth, and the dead were too tired to be desperate. Like the Dairy Queen in a dead-end food service job, working the counter long after an aneurysm should've sent her home, because...

Because why?

Because she was too tired to do anything else?

Because she'd never known another, better job?

. . . Or because it made her happy?

Maybe I had to imagine her happy, if she couldn't talk to me, herself. Maybe she liked the swirl of ice cream and the rustle of condiments. Maybe she had friends on staff who called her by name.

Maybe even in a dead-end job in a nowhere town, a part of her wanted to live.

Could I bring myself to kill her if she seemed, even a little, like she was living?

"I ... no. It's okay. She can stay," I muttered. "I'll... eat later, maybe."

Angel raised an eyebrow, but she kept that knife tucked away. She shrugged and started walking, farther into the mall, and as she passed, I saw a faded hiker's backpack on her shoulders. It jingled with cans and boxes—survivor rations, I guessed, from a girl who would hunker down and weather this evacuation for as long as it took. A girl who intended to survive.

I hesitated, watching the Dairy Queen watch us.

Then I hurried over to one of the rest areas, grasping a bench by the armrest. It was light, metal carved in thin little curves and whorls like the skeleton of a bigger bench, and I dragged it over in a scraping, stuttering line to the Dairy Queen's kiosk. I pushed it around behind the counter, jamming it askew in the entrance.

That done, I grabbed a paper cup from the stack and leaned over toward the soda machine, pouring a sputtering cup of water. The Dairy Queen watched, unblinking, until I shoved the cup into her hands.

"Here you go," I said. "I can... I can take over the register for a bit, if you want to go on break."

It took the Dairy Queen a while to process, confused by this interruption. She held the cup of water like a little kid, both wrinkled, bloodless hands around it.

But she knew what a *break* was, and she'd been working for days. So when I stepped back, she dazedly settled down on the bench. And some part of her rotting brain clicked with that, because she leaned back into it and drank from her cup. Her hand moved, fingers grasping an imaginary cigarette.

I stood beside her, letting her settle off her swollen legs and tilt her head back. Letting the bone-deep aches she'd ignored all shift settle in.

And when she let out a slow, easy breath and didn't draw one back in, I rested a hand on her shoulder until it went cold beneath my fingers, until the flutter of her heartbeat rested its way to a stop. Until she hacked out a mouthful of dark oil and it went still on her lips, without any breath rustling it back.

And she died on break.

Which meant the same thing as Angel suggested—she'd still *died*—but it felt different, somehow. *Letting* her die, not *killing* her. Going through the motions of her life, instead of interrupting it with a mercy kill like some know-it-all god.

Maybe that's what Eric was hoping for, too. Maybe he'd seen me bleeding out and he'd wanted me to hang on back here as long as I could. Maybe that meant he loved me, too.

I hesitated there, watching her neck, her shoulder, her skin, all that *flesh* Angel had said to eat... and I shuddered and pulled away, instead.

At some point I'd probably get desperate enough to try it. For now, though, it seemed way too weird to take a bite out of an ice-cream lady. A messed-up punch line to a respectable moment of peace.

So I hurried on instead, fueled by nothing but melted ice cream and a cautious determination to keep trying.

FOUR

Anyone else might've made small talk while we explored the mall, but Angel didn't seem bothered to try. She let me tag along behind her, leading us in a zigzag between stores. I lingered back as she peered into the takeout joint—**Teriyaki Town**, its sign read, in swooping, faded orange letters. Inside sat rows of dusty tables with chairs stacked upside down on top, pressed up against walls lined with sun-bleached mountain posters. Angel pushed ahead to the front counter, then behind red curtain strips and into the kitchen, and I winced as she clattered pots and pans.

"Is it really okay for us to just... *break in* like this?" I stepped closer, leaning over the register until I could just see her hunched, gremlinlike, over a cupboard. "I mean, it was an evacuation, but they left all their stuff. They'll probably be back soon." Over the register hung a clipped-out newspaper picture. An older couple stood in front of the storefront, their arms around each other, their smiles grainy and blurred. "The people who run this place seem nice."

Angel stopped then, and raised her head to look at me, expression flat. She'd pulled an industrial-sized white bucket into her lap, its edges—and her fingers—smeared with chicken grease.

"All things left behind are ours," she said, simply.

"Not sure that's how it works, but—" I cut off, then, tilting my head. Faintly ahead, footsteps echoed across the floor. They tapped against the floor in a slow, sharp off-pattern. *Step, clink, step, step, clink.* Like someone dragging a metal pole.

"Oh jeez—Angel, someone's *coming*."

She shrugged, shifting her backpack off her shoulders and next to the bucket. "Let them. We were here first."

The footsteps got louder. Closer.

"That's not what I mean, Angel—what if they're a cop looking for—for stragglers, or military, or they have a gun—Angel, I don't want to get caught—"

"Do you think they're going to kill you for it?" she asked, and I couldn't tell if she was sarcastic or not.

"I think we're gonna get in *trouble*," I argued.

Closer. I could see someone's shadow now, flickering across the wall. Angel *still* didn't seem bothered, too focused on pulling plastic food containers out from the mess of cans and boxes in her backpack. Like this was normal for her. She didn't even try to stop the rustle and clang as she worked, as loud as an alarm screaming, *we are here*.

So much for not getting in trouble. I shuddered out a breath and stepped outside by my own damn self, hands raised, right as someone came striding up.

"Look, I'm *so* sorry, please—" I started, and stopped.

The figure wasn't a cop or a soldier or anyone else old enough to fear. Instead, I saw another girl, maybe a year or so older than me, with coily black hair tied in tight puffy buns. She had a mask on, the thick paper medical kind, and a faded brown shirt covered in warm-colored swirls in an artistic impression of a horse. Turquoise bracelets jangled on her wrists near her chipped blue nail polish, hands wrapped around a cane wrapped in what looked like spirals of pink duct tape.

Like Angel, she had a backpack on. Unlike Angel, she had a

wrinkled notebook to go with it, pressed tight to her chest as she blinked up at me in surprise.

I blinked back. I knew her.

Monica Delaine.

Of course.

Of course, she'd still be alive. Of course, she'd have a notebook. Of course, she'd be more prepared than me.

I shoved those feelings down as she stared, determined not to look dead *and* immature.

"Um?" she said.

"Oh, uh," I said back.

Great start. My face burned. "Sorry, I thought you were, like—I don't know, a cop or something."

"Oh! Oh." She brightened. "Yeah, no, I was just..." She gestured around her, like that answered everything. "Getting supplies together around town."

Behind me, Angel—when had she made her way out of the kitchen?—cut in.

"Barely worth it. This mall is half empty." She shook the container in her hands, chicken sloshing against its lid. "Hi again, Monica."

"Oh! Hey, Angel." Monica waved back, the notebook fluttering in her hand.

I glanced between them. "Wait, you two know each other?"

"Sort of," Monica shrugged. "We were in summer school—AP Biology, I mean, not that that's important—when the sirens went off. Normally I'm supposed to stay back and wait for a teacher with a mobility device, so I did, but..." Her grip tightened on the cane. "I guess they forgot?"

Angel snorted a dry laugh, but Monica—apparently used to this—looked right past her.

"Aaanyway, by the time I wandered out of the room, everyone was gone." A pause. "Except Angel. I spotted her stealing from the vending machines."

I couldn't help it; I laughed back. "You really wanted a candy bar, huh, Angel?"

Angel stared. "We won't be able to survive alone without water. I took what bottles I could before they could be stolen."

Oh. "Right. That makes sense. Sorry for, um, doubting you."

Angel didn't react, but Monica waved a hand. "It's okay. I did, too. But Angel knows more about survival than I could ever guess at. So if she chose not to chase after the evacuation trucks, I figure I won't, either."

"Yeah, about that." I raised an eyebrow at Angel. "Sounds like Monica and I both got stuck waiting on other people. But why did *you* get left behind?"

"Didn't get stuck. I chose to stay." Angel glared into that Tupperware container like the chicken grease was personally responsible. "Too suspicious. There's no obvious disaster happening. No news online about it. Only alarms and National Guard vehicles outside, with government workers saying to follow them out of town and not ask questions."

"So you didn't go," I finished.

"The day I leave my home to follow the government is the day I die."

"I get it. Sure, sure." In truth, I was thinking about those people who'd stay in their homes during hurricanes until the waves crashed down around them, glaring at lifeboats and calling them *government handouts*. I glanced over at Monica, trying to say, *you're SURE she's not a crazy conspiracy theorist?* with my eyes, and Monica fluttered her hand—a soothing, peacekeeping motion.

"It *is* weird, though," Monica added. "I've been updating my Instagram as I go, but so far no one's said anything about it, besides a couple comments like 'weird' or 'I don't know'." She shook her head. "Best I can figure is maybe it's a local gas leak or oil spill, or... something with the dead, maybe?" She blinked. "Er, sorry, no offense meant, um—" She squinted. "Ian, right?"

I brushed a hand over the back of my head, like I didn't even care if she remembered my name or not. "Mm. And it's okay, I'm starting to get used to it. Kinda funny, even!" I insisted, too fast. "I just sort of slipped and fell in the middle of everything. Bad luck, I guess."

"Really bad." Monica lowered her voice, into that sympathetic tone people used around babies and the dying. "I'm so sorry. Is there anything we can do to help?"

I started to say *no*, to say *everything's fine*, and reconsidered. "Well..." The paper towels squished against my fingers, too warm and too soft. "Do either of you have a first aid kit? So I can get this stitched up a little...? If that's not too gross or anything."

"It's only flesh. I could do it," Angel said.

"On second thought, no. I don't trust you around the back of my head."

Angel raised an eyebrow, genuinely confused—as if she couldn't believe I'd ever doubt her—but Monica cut in.

"I can do it. It's fine."

"You sure that's okay? I can try doing it myself, too, it's not a worry—" I started, but she shook her head.

"I'm a farm girl. I've seen more body fluids than a midwife has, probably." She gestured to the floor, and I took the hint; I gave a thanks and sat cross-legged, my back to her.

I heard a close rustle that I guessed was her sitting down as well, then the tap of her cane and the fabric *fwip* of her backpack zipper. Unlike Angel, her backpack didn't clink with cans and boxes, so I turned my head to peek and saw a stack of clothes, all in vibrant shades, and... an eye shadow kit?

She grasped my head, turning it forward again like a barber at a shop, but too late.

"Is eyeshadow good for survival?"

"*Mental* survival, yeah," Monica retorted. "There's a lot—a *lot*—of things going on right now I can't control. But I figure getting to look cute doesn't have to be one of them."

"Hey, everyone has their own methods. I get it," I said. "It's a nice color."

"Thank you."

She tugged at my jacket hood, and I heard an *eugh* under her breath as the paper towels shed away with it in clotted clumps. Still, she kept going. I heard the rustle of plastic, then the snip of scissors, clearing away the last of the paper mess.

I sat as still as I could while she worked—first peeling the towels away, then wiping at my head with something cold and stingy that I guessed was an alcohol wipe. I bit my lip and squeezed my eyes shut, bearing through it, until I felt her settle back and reach for the thread.

Beside us, Angel—apparently not interested in stitches—went back into the teriyaki place. Every so often she'd come out with another bucket or a handful of spices, laying them out in tidy rows and stacks in front of the store. Then she'd glare at them as if she could, with enough willpower, fit them all into her backpack.

Once she started stitching, to distract me maybe, Monica spoke up again.

"So... this seems like what you *needed*, but... is there anything you *want* help with?" she asked.

I smiled. "You mean like 'last rites' or something?"

"Last rites, friendship, whatever you want to call it."

"Fair 'nough." I thought it over. "I want to find my friend and ask him what happened while I was out." *If he abandoned me or if he loves me.* "And I mean, obviously I wanna make sure my family's okay, but... now that I think about it, they probably went with the evacuation like everyone else."

"Gullible," Angel muttered, still crouched by an industrial bucket of beef.

"They would've wanted to *be safe*," I argued back. "I have a little sister. My parents would've looked out for her first. So I'd have to see if there's still a way to catch up, somehow . . . ," I trailed off.

"If they even accept the dead," Angel said.

". . . What?" I asked.

She kept watching the buckets, not answering, and a part of me suddenly wanted to shake her. To force her to look at me, to say *something* beyond cryptic, trolling sentences. I breathed instead, steady and slow.

"What Angel means," Monica cut in, "is that, if it's something to do with the dead, they might not want to risk taking you. As far as I saw, they haven't accepted *any* of the dead."

My mind flickered back to the Dairy Queen, left behind at her counter in a never-ending shift. Right. In a morbid way, it made sense: if they hadn't even lingered behind to get Monica a mobility aid, why would they bother evacuating people who were already doomed?

In an emergency, it's survival of the fittest, and no one ever saw us as fit.

"Maybe not," I muttered. "Maybe they won't accept me. Maybe no one I knew will look at me the same way ever again." My throat itched, and I swallowed past a growing lump. "But... I still want to see them, even if it's just to say goodbye."

Monica waited a second, then spoke up, in that same gentle voice.

"There's another option," she said. I turned to her, and she nodded before nudging me back to facing forward. "When I was little, my mom and I once made an emergency evacuation plan. If I ever needed to run away and meet up somewhere, for any reason, there was a special spot in front of the hospital near our house where we could find each other. A little grassy knoll. We used to have picnics there, whenever I finished checkups. It always made me feel safe." She trailed off. "You'd probably know it."

I did, too. I remembered every piece of the Kittakoop Medical Clinic—too small and too country to be a real *hospital*, but small enough for each section to feel intimate. Like the parking lot and front yard, full of patches of rocks and too-green grass, wide entryways and lines of still ambulances. I remembered waiting for a ride home under the entrance sign, looking over and seeing another family with a picnic blanket unfurled in the shadow of a tree, hearing cicadas and the hiss of soda cans and laughter. Something fun, in the middle of a place full of invasive tests and unanswered questions and long, painful waits.

And I remembered wanting to invite myself over, but never knowing how to speak up. Not as I got older each year, as I moved from the awkward boldness of a little kid to a teen too uncomfortable in his own skin to push it onto someone else. Especially not someone I wanted to seem better than—someone I could never admit that sort of weakness to.

Still... it'd seemed so cozy. And eventually they'd stopped appearing, and I moved on with the sinking feeling that I'd missed my chance.

"You think she's waiting for you there now?" I asked.

"I *know* it. Even if everyone else in town—everyone else in the *world*—left us behind, she wouldn't. Not ever. And she wouldn't leave *you* to die alone, either. She'd fight it with everything she had. So if we find her, I promise she'll help you find your friend." I felt something sting on the back of my head, a sharp tug, and then a snip of the scissors. She leaned back, and I heard the smile in her voice. "There. That should stitch it."

"Oh, hey. Thanks!" I poked at the spot with a tentative finger. It still ached, dizzying and sore, but it didn't feel like it was pouring blood, and it didn't knock me out of my senses to prod at anymore. A wound, but not an open one.

Before I could get up, though, she nudged my shoulder, pushing me back down.

"Bandage, too," she said. "You don't want to crack it open all over again."

"Got it." I settled in place. "So is that where you're headed next? That's at least a good ten miles away from here. You're just gonna walk by yourself?"

A papery rustle, then the *krt-krt-krt* of backing paper peeling away.

"That's the plan," Monica said. "After I get enough supplies for a hike, anyway." She pressed a cotton pad to the back of my head, then leaned forward so I could see her watching me. Even with the mask over her mouth, I could see her eyes crinkling in a smile. I smiled back, sheepishly, and wondered how many of those smiles I'd missed. "There. You're all patched up, Ian."

"Thank you," I said, and meant it. I didn't feel *clean*—not when I could still feel sticky clumps of blood in my hair and see them staining the sleeves of my jacket—but I felt worlds better, anyway. "I know it's dumb—not like it's gonna kill me or anything, at this point, but..."

"But it feels wrong to leave it open, right?" Monica suggested.

"Yeah. Getting patched up helps. So... thanks again, farm girl." I didn't mean to stare, but I couldn't help glancing at her cane, anyway, as she pushed herself upright with a low groan. "You *sure* you're okay with walking ten miles?"

"Not like I have much of a choice. It *should* be okay. If I'm lucky, pollen count will be low. Don't really want an allergic reaction in a town with no ER." She tapped the side of her mask, trying to play it off as casual and not really managing it.

It wasn't *exactly* reassuring.

Angel interrupted then. She seemed to have made her peace with the industrial buckets, focused instead on stacking them in a wobbly tower.

"Could just steal a car," she told the buckets.

I winced. "Angel, *no.* Look—stealing food is one thing, I guess. We need to eat. But we don't *need* to hijack someone's car—"

"Monica just said there wasn't a choice. I gave a choice."

"Not if the choice is *stealing*! Look, I don't know what *you* do for fun when the world isn't ending, but I never stole anything in my *life*—" I ran a hand through my hair, hard, like pantomime could make it make sense. "That's wrong. You get me, right, Monica?"

Silence.

"Monica?" I turned and I saw her looking thoughtful, a hand pressed to her mask.

"I'm not sure. It *would* be nice to drive. And we'd give it right back, obviously," she said.

"What? No. No, no, no—we're not stealing a *car*—"

"No," Angel said. "I would be stealing it. You two would only get in my way."

"You're *not* stealing it. How could you even *think* about that?" I cried.

"Like this," she said.

And she pushed the tower of industrial buckets over. The bottom one wobbled and the top two collapsed, cracking against the tile and spilling raw meat everywhere.

For a moment, I only stared.

Then I started shouting. Monica joined in, both of us yelling over the other.

"What the *hell*, Angel, why did you—"

"—That's so much wasted food, Angel, that's so much waste—"

"—All over the floor—"

"—Can scoop it back up? Ten second rule—"

"—Just made a huge *mess*, what is *wrong* with you—"

"—Probably worked really hard to get that—"

Angel grimaced, slamming her hands over her ears and hunching into herself, then shouted loud enough to drown us both.

"SHUT UP!"

We shut up, though the mall echoed with our voices for a couple seconds still. Angel drew a breath, then opened an eye to glare at us.

"We're *surviving*," she spat in a rough and angry whisper that was somehow worse than her usual monotone. "*Both* of you got left behind 'cause you were waiting on someone else to tell you what to do. Full of righteous insecurity"—she nodded at me—"and polite indecision." A nod at Monica. "Scared to be rejected. Scared to ever be a burden or a regret or say no. Even after everyone's said you're too much of a pain to keep alive, you're scared to prove them right." Her hands tightened at her sides. "You're cowards. For once in your *goddamn lives*, will you just let yourselves *be a burden* and *destroy something*? Will you take up some *goddamn space*? With me?"

And I didn't know what to say to that. Unlike our shouted words, her hissed speech didn't echo off the walls; it faded as soon as we heard it, so it might as well have not gotten said at all. But it lingered in other places, like the sour taste in the back of my throat or the uneasy pit growing in my stomach.

No. Not uneasy. Not discomfort, or confusion, or anything delicate as that.

I felt *angry*. Angry in a raw, exposed way, as if by calling out all those secret inner thoughts, she'd stripped all the skin off me and left the irritated nerves hanging out.

As I watched, Monica stepped forward, looking as angry as I felt. Her cane hit the tile and I heard that off-pattern from when she'd first walked up, all *step, clink, step, step, clink*. Slow, yet somehow graceful. Like she'd spent hours making sure her footsteps still swished like a model and tapped so pretty.

She stopped in front of Angel, her cane gripped tight in both shaking hands, and for one long second I knew she was gonna whack Angel upside the head. I didn't even know if I should stop it. Maybe, in some traumatized way, that was what Angel expected—for me to hate her and for Monica to hit her and for both of us to act as hurtful as the people who'd left us behind.

Instead, though, Monica shifted at the last second, and she slapped her cane into the side of that last upright bucket. It *exploded* open, its lid flying away, and pale white chicken thighs sloshing onto the floor. She whacked it again and its side cracked, splintering white plastic shards and pink grease. Again, and again, until she finally stepped back, her face red and her shoulders heaving, her cane dripping pink.

"Fine. *Fine!* Is that *taking up enough space* for you, Angel?" she cried. "Is that what you wanted? Mindless, pointless *destruction*?"

"Yes! *Yes!*" For the first time, I heard genuine excitement in Angel's voice. She bounced up and down on her heels, her hands flapping on their wrists like butterfly wings. It seemed *cute*, cuter than I'd expected; Monica must've thought so, too, because I heard her laugh.

"Oh my god. Wait. That *did* feel good, actually. I didn't expect that. I've...never actually done anything like that before. Ian, did you *see* that?"

She glanced back at me, but I grimaced, my hand gripping my other arm.

Hitting buckets was a waste of food. It seemed pointless, and worse, like it'd make a huge mess for someone to clean up. It seemed like *looting*—the sort of thing Dad would see on the news and shake his head at, cursing the world for being full of opportunistic punks and criminals and people who caused problems on purpose.

The sort of thing I'd die before I risked.

(Or was that me being full of righteousness again? Like, if I could do everything else in the most morally perfect way, I could justify my existence.)

That sick feeling in my stomach rose up again, clawing at my insides, and I moved closer, and I thought about how it felt to live selflessly and die anyway in two feet of stagnant fountain water. I thought about how it felt to fall in love with a boy with a military haircut and swallow it down out of fear of rejection, even as he left me to drown anyway. I thought about eating chalky pills while Mom and Dad argued over moving across the country to somewhere less bright, somewhere safer, somewhere where the medical bills wouldn't be half as ridiculous.

And I thought, then, about zombies coming back from the dead, and hey, aren't they supposed to be feral, anyway?

I thought that as I grabbed a bucket, grasping it tight, and I carried it away—not toward the Teriyaki Town, probably owned by two old people doing their best, but back a couple yards, down the hall and toward the fountain.

That stupid, overwrought, overdone fountain. A half-circle pool of water against a chest-high wall, covered in bathroom tiles and trickling water from rows of spouts. Too stupid to kill anything.

I *threw* the bucket, and it crashed against the back wall of the fountain, scattering plastic chunks and meat pieces into the water. But it still stayed mostly whole, so I grabbed the biggest hunk and flung it again, whipping it against the tile until pieces chipped off.

“I hate—this stupid—*fountain*!” I screamed between throws. “I hate it, I *hate it*!”

Behind me, the JCPenney—the only store in this place to stay alive through rows of other closings, the only place that kept on displaying seasonal outfits and **BOGO SALE!!!** signs through every slow year—glittered, its windows reflecting water droplets. I grasped the bucket and heaved it at the store’s wall—too soon, my fingers skidding on grease, and it hit the window, and oh, how the glass *shattered*. It shattered and fell through the window frame in big sheets, which hit the **BOGO** signs and shattered further into pieces, all of them shining rainbows and water specks. Inside somewhere, an alarm went chirping off.

And for the first time in what must’ve been years, my stomach felt a little better. I huffed in breaths all thin and sharp, and I stared at the ruins of what I’d done.

Behind me, Monica and Angel walked up. Angel licked chicken grease off her hands, absently, while Monica still looked red-faced and dazed.

“Holy shit,” I breathed. “I broke a window.”

“You did,” Monica agreed. “And a good piece of that fountain.”

“I really hated that fountain,” I said.

Monica reached out, patting my shoulder.

“I know,” she said. “I heard.”

Angel looked up at us both. (She seemed so *small* up close, hunched in her coat and standing barely up to my chin.) “Are you two criminal enough to steal a car yet?”

Her monotone had come back, and the contrast made me give a winded laugh.

“I think I am, yeah,” I sighed. “Monica?”

“I don’t know how to feel about the fact that I’m starting to love doing crime,” she muttered. “But... I want to try.”

That really was the whole of it, wasn't it? I didn't know how to feel about that anger in me, or how good it felt to take up space and be a rejected mess on purpose for once. I didn't know how to feel about being dead or being heartbroken.

But I wanted to try figuring it out. I wanted to try doing everything I'd never let myself do while alive. And if that meant doing it as a messy, rotting, undead corpse . . .

Fifteen years too late, a couple hours too late, and a town-wide evacuation too late, I wanted it.

Whether he loved me back or not, I'd find Eric. And I'd find out why he'd left me behind—find *whatever* reason he thought was good enough to run away and let me die. And then once he'd given it, he'd see too late that I was the restless sort of dead, too stubborn to stop, and *I'd bite his limbs off.*

FIVE

The sun shone bright on the horizon outside, glittering between trees and off the rooftops of cars in hazy heat lines.

I closed my eyes, letting it sear red across my eyelids as we stepped through the mall exit. Out here I could smell overgrown grass and ditch weeds, the rubbery aftertaste of asphalt and the crispness of late summer air. Crickets chirped in the thickets, hopping from stalk to stalk, and lazy clouds drifted overhead.

The last time I'd been out here, I'd been too focused on confessing to notice anything else. I'd kept my shoulders hunched and head down, trying to glare words into life as I texted Eric.

Since then, I'd died, been abandoned, come back, missed an evacuation, and made new friends.

These really were the longest days of the year.

The first thing I noticed as I opened my eyes back up was how quiet it'd gotten. Kittakoop always was a sleepy town, with barely more than a main road and a gas station to its name, but it had enough people to make a steady rumble of life: traffic drifting by, people chatting on the sidewalk, sometimes someone's radio, or barking dog in the distance.

I didn't notice any of that now, and the absence of it rang in my ears and flickered like shadows at the edges of my vision. No cars passed on the road ahead or down the larger road a couple blocks back. No dogs barked. No people.

Just...this. The crickets, the birds, and our own footsteps, crunching on the parking lot, as the three of us stood where people should be.

And then, somewhere in the distance, something else. I strained my ears, trying to listen. For a long while I didn't hear anything, then it came again, once more: a low, steady whisper of a noise, fading in and out like radio static, echoing from the hazy peaks of the mountains.

Beside me, Monica and Angel milled outward, between lines of cars. Monica slowed, glancing back at me, and I caught her gaze.

"Did you hear that?" I asked. My voice sounded loud and flat out here, without tiles to echo off or background noise to soften it out.

"What?" she said.

"It sounded like . . ." I thought it over. "A voice? From up north." I tipped my head, listening until my ears hurt, but it didn't come back.

"Probably the evacuation team," Angel muttered.

"I hope they're okay. . . ." Monica squeezed the straps of her backpack, then shook her head. "No. I'm sure they're okay. And we can catch up with them as soon as we find Mom." She turned her head to both of us at that, like a big sister looking after kids.

"Right," I said.

Neither of us believed it. I felt it in the sinking unease in my bones, and I saw it in how Monica gripped her straps harder, how she glanced too quickly back at the cars, as if looking for a distraction.

Stay focused. Find Eric, find Monica's mom. Figure out where to go from there.

"Really is a lot of cars left behind for an evacuation, though . . ." she muttered. I watched her run a hand over the side of a hatchback, fingers tracing lines in the dust gathered at its window edges. "You'd think most people would drive out. . . ."

I wandered past a dented minivan, and through its back window I spotted a kid's car seat, still strapped in place and empty.

“You’d think,” I muttered back. “Angel, you said there were National Guard trucks outside when you looked, right?”

She muttered something like “mmhmm” from where she stood, leaned halfway into the passenger seat of a station wagon with one hand pressed against the door for balance. After a moment of shuffling, she popped her head back out, and I waved.

“Can you tell us more?” I prompted.

She nodded. “They had lines of trucks. Mostly ACMAT, of course—” she pronounced it as a word, like *ackmat*, “—as that’s the most versatile production line. I noticed an ACMAT VLA truck stocked with people in the back. Soldiers and civilians. Couldn’t discern ranks from my distance. It looked like they were forming a caravan.”

She went on, adding something about the model of truck and their use as an adaptable transport, but I couldn’t make out the words.

Because when I turned the corner, scanning up and down parking lot rows, I spotted another truck. A pickup truck, mottled white, with a wire rack on the roof and something like a generator in the back, edged with rust.

I recognized it, in that vague, textbook way I recognized a lot of things from out of town. Trucks like these were all over the place farther east: patrol trucks, for picking up radio interference along the National Radio Quiet Zone.

Everybody in West Virginia knew about the Quiet Zone. Hard not to, when it took up half the state. High up in the Allegheny and Blue Ridge Mountains sat the clearest possible spots for reception in the United States, and so in the middle of them sat the U.S.’s best telescopes and military bases, camped in a miles-wide square where anything that might interfere with their signals got banned. No cell phones near the observatories. No Wi-Fi near the observatories. No microwaved pizza rolls near the observatories. Only military and scientific broadcasts, a hundred secret codes and data projections a day, beamed up toward the stars.

For my parents, it'd been a selling point, back when doctors were still trying to figure out why my brain sometimes turned on itself like a rabid dog. A chance to get me and Emma away from any flashing lights or 5G radio signals that might be scrambling our heads, into the cleanest air in the U.S.

Now? Looking at it sitting idle as a dead bug gave me a sour taste in the back of my mouth.

The patrols weren't supposed to drive this far out from the Quiet Zone.

The National Guard wasn't supposed to show up and order everyone to follow them in a caravan, leaving all their homes and cars and booster seats behind.

Eric wasn't supposed to leave me to die.

Everything about this was *wrong*.

It took a long time, after it went quiet, for any of us to speak. Monica—organized, resolved, the unofficial leader of this quest—cleared her throat.

"Well, if there's a lot of cars left behind, that just means more choices for us, doesn't it?" she said, forcing a sharp cheeriness into her words. "What kind of car do we want?"

"Does anyone have a screwdriver and some wire strippers?" Angel asked. Casually, like she was asking for a napkin.

Monica went pale. "I...no. I don't. Sorry. I had a tool kit on the checklist, but...I couldn't find one at the mall. Just food and clothes."

"Then whatever one has spare keys somewhere." She tugged open the door to a van, glancing under its sun visors and in its glove box before slamming it shut again with a frustrated grunt.

For lack of a better idea, Monica and I tagged along behind Angel, watching her stalk down the aisles and glare into windows. With every failed attempt she hunched into herself more, her hair hanging over her eyes, so I took the opportunity to gently interrupt.

"Hey, Angel. You know how to hot-wire a car? That's pretty cool."

She looked back, wary at first—as if hunting for a trap somewhere in my statement—then straightened up.

"Doesn't everyone?" she asked. "It's not hard. Push a screwdriver in the ignition. Connect the ignition wire to the battery wire. Spark the starter motor wire. Only hard part is reading the manual for each car to make sure it's the right ones." A pause. "Also, not getting electrocuted."

"Yeah, that last part seems important." I glanced into another car, this one filled with empty fast-food bags and crumpled napkins. "How did you learn to do that?"

She didn't answer for so awkwardly long that I almost asked again—but before I could, she spoke up, her monotone somehow flatter than ever.

"Dad."

That was it. She pushed on, turning the corner to another row. As I tagged behind, Monica caught up, and I whispered at her.

"'Dad'? Is her dad a car thief?" I asked.

She shrugged back. "Maybe? It would explain a lot. I won't question a good thing, though."

I wasn't sure how to feel about that.

We passed another row of cars, creeping to the very edge of the parking lot, before Angel held up a hand for us to stop. Monica and I stood around as she lingered in front of a battered pickup truck, one with short bucket seats in front and a rolled-up tarp in the back. It looked well cared for, but still a relic of the 90s, from its rust-red paint job to the cigarette discoloring inside.

Still, the driver's side door opened with a creaky lurch when Angel tried it, spilling out a waft of dust motes and stale air. She climbed inside, settling herself on the very edge of the driver's seat.

As we watched, she dug into her pocket, pulling out a knife—not the bowie knife from before, but a tinier pocketknife, with a blade the size of a pinky finger flicked out from the handle. She considered the ignition for a moment, thoughtful...then drove the pocketknife into it, hard. Out, and again, and again, wriggling and nudging it, until she'd driven the knife all the way down to its cracked red hilt.

Then she turned it—and, to our shock, the engine spluttered, coughed, and turned over, purring out fumes from its exhaust and rattling the cabin. She looked back at us, and I saw the tiniest, tiniest smile on her face.

"I found a key," she said.

Monica still seemed stunned, but I broke down laughing. For once Angel's monotone voice worked in her favor, giving her line a flat humor that didn't match the manic way she'd driven the knife in. That didn't match *any* of this, really.

She'd found a key. We had a truck.

I hurried over to the passenger side, sliding on in, but Monica didn't follow after. Instead, by the time I'd clicked the seat belt, Angel shifted to the middle seat and Monica slid into where she'd been. I blinked as Angel bumped against my side, settled in with her hands wrapped around her backpack.

It smelled like cigarettes and kerosene in here, a little too warm and a little too cramped and a little too dusty, mixed with the sawdust waft of her puffy army jacket. (How was she not roasting in that? My own jacket, thinner and comfortable in the air-conditioned expanse of the mall, pressed warm against my back.)

"Oh. Hi, Angel," I said.

"Hi," she said to the dashboard.

"Didn't expect you to sit there. Is Monica driving?"

"Yes."

Monica spoke up. "Angel doesn't know how to drive, so I volunteered."

I opened my mouth. Closed it. Stared at Angel. She stared at the dashboard.

"You can *hot-wire a car*."

"Yes."

"And you can't drive one?"

"I don't want to." Her hands tightened against her thighs. "It feels too big. I don't know where anything is supposed to be. Directions are... difficult. Rights and lefts. They're difficult."

I didn't know exactly what she meant, but I could tell from her fists and her expression that she didn't want anyone to talk about this particular topic. "Hey, it's okay. If you don't want to, you don't have to. You did enough with starting it."

"Ian's right," Monica added. She reached up, adjusting the rearview mirror and letting it wink fragments of sunlight back. "I can take over from here. Where're we going first?"

"Um," I spoke up—and sank back in my seat as both of them looked at me, all open expectations and wide eyes.

What right did I have to ask them favors after they'd done so much for me already, just for the sake of being nice?

But still... I took a breath, and the air tasted like dirt and cigarette smoke and fast-food wrappers. Like Eric.

I hated how much I missed him, even when I was furious with him.

"Can we... stop at Eric's house, first?" I asked. "I can give directions."

"You think he went home?" Monica asked—gently, like I was a toddler struggling my way through mouthing sounds for the first time.

"Yes. Maybe. I'm not sure." It sounded stupid aloud, and I bit my teeth against it. "He has a dog back home. Charlie. He wouldn't have wanted to leave without her. So if we're lucky...maybe we can still catch him?"

Something mean in me scoffed at that. A little voice going, *Kinda pathetic, ain't it, to think that he'd let you die but save his dog?*

But Monica nodded, and Angel echoed her, nodding back...then leaned against my side and closed her eyes.

The decision was made. Okay, then.

I watched Angel, but when she didn't stir, I settled back down, resting a hand absently on her arm. Understandable. I'd spent half the day unconscious, and I still felt like I needed a nap, too.

Monica pulled us out of the parking lot in a rush of exhaust and a crunch of tires on asphalt, then turned us toward the main road. The vents on the dashboard coughed up tepid-cool air-conditioning, clearing out the cabin's stagnant air. I leaned back against the passenger side window, pointing out turns I'd taken a hundred times before, away from the mall and deep into the trees.

Toward the dead part of town.

SIX

As usual, a shift in the road let me know when we got close—the asphalt became thin and cracked, our truck's tires lurching across potholes in a steady stop-and-go motion. Monica drove slow and cautious, easing her way over them like an old lady unsure of her own weight, but Angel barely stirred, huddled against me in a pile of dusty coat fabric.

"This is the turnoff." I nodded toward a stretch of dirt just past a light pole and a rusty mailbox. Houses stood to either side, squat white buildings with faded siding and identical gray roofs, but Eric's home stretched farther back from the road, down toward where the grass thinned out and the trees bunched together to make scraggly line patterns against a thin blue sky.

Monica bit her lip, but she didn't say anything as we pulled in, even when we got close enough to see the house—also flat, also white, but with a line of chain fencing dug out on one side and a big American flag draped off the porch like a rug left out to dry. It smelled like baked dirt and hay, a dry rural smell that wafted everywhere in town but always seemed to settle here.

We heard Charlie before we saw her; her wild barking echoed in the air, hot and possessive, along with the thunderclap of her running toward us. She crashed against the fence, sixty pounds of golden retriever mutt, the *krsh-krsh-krsh* of the chain-link fence dancing beneath her paws as she howled.

It was *then* that Monica spoke up; she gave a tiny *yip* of a noise, startled enough to grasp the wheel and push against the brakes, as if Charlie was another car out to take over her lane. As if we weren't already crawled to a stop, halfway up Eric's driveway. A mean and petty part of me wanted to laugh at her, but it wasn't the time or place for that, so I put a hand on her arm instead, sympathetic-like.

"Ha . . ." Monica forced a smile. "She's cute. Really... *big*, huh?"

"Yeah... I should go first," I said. "Charlie knows me."

Monica didn't answer, but she didn't object, either, when I pushed open the passenger door. Getting out from under Angel took some work—I slid my arm away from her head, rustling pins and needles out of it as I laid her down easy against the seat. She grumbled under her breath, but either didn't wake up or chose not to move as I got out.

Charlie recognized me right away, despite the dark dead eyes and the smell of gunk underneath my skin; I could tell because her tail started whapping back and forth, a flag of raggedy peach fur and flying pieces of thistles. The barking didn't so much stop as change in pitch, higher now, and her paws scrabbled frantic patterns against the chain-link fence.

I stopped in front of the gate, grasping at its rusted flip-lock. It wriggled like a loose tooth in my grip.

"Hey, girl," I breathed. "Easy. *Easy*. Enough. It's just me."

When I pushed the gate open she scrambled toward me, jumping up to smear muddy prints across my jacket and jeans as I flailed back. She sniffed my shoes, then my legs, then my shoes again, licking her nose and huffing massive dog breaths as if she couldn't figure out what that fascinating new corpse smell was.

Eric's dad had put her in one of those big choke-chain collars, the kind with little barbs on the inside all tangled in her fur, but I never could bring myself to grab it even when she was too excited to listen;

I reached for a scruff of her neck instead, right as she jumped back up to sniff at my jacket, too.

"Whoa, down! Down. Easy. Stay."

As usual, Charlie didn't seem great at orders—she stared up at me with blank brown eyes, head tilted but tail *whap-whap-whapping* away, and as soon as I moved my hand she jumped again, barking in excitement.

It took three more pushes and four more *STAYs* before she either got the idea or lost interest, bounding away to grab her favorite toy in a spray of dirt and cotton stuffing. I let her go, nodding toward the truck—all *it's okay, she's calmer now.*

Monica eased the driver's side door open, but she still hung back close to it, ready to scramble back in. Angel didn't leave the car at all, even as I gave an uncertain thumbs up back. Once Charlie didn't immediately maim Monica, though—mouth too full of toy fabric to even bark anymore—she stepped closer, hand tight around her cane handle. I kept a hand on Charlie's neck, just in case; I might not like Monica, sure, but last thing we both needed was for Charlie to barrel into the kid with a bad leg.

"Any sign of Eric?" Monica asked.

I looked around. The stretch of yard Charlie lived in seemed the same as it'd always been: stretches of dirt and clover peppered with holes and drying turds, worn footprints leading up to a squat back shed Eric and I had converted ages ago into some kind of doghouse—though it seemed more like a chicken coop, its floor coated in hay and the cotton-fluff pieces of a dozen dead toys.

Beyond the shed, though, I couldn't see any lights through the house's side windows. No other cars in the driveway or in the yard, either, aside from the rusted-out skeleton of a van out in the weeds.

Charlie licked at my shoe, too fascinated by my new corpse smell to even investigate Monica, and I let go of her neck to scritch behind her ear.

"Nothin'," I reported. Then, mumbling to Charlie: "He didn't come back for you, either, huh?"

"Maybe inside…?" Monica suggested, sounding about as eager to investigate as I felt.

"Yeah. Maybe." I let go of Charlie's ear, letting her get back to tearing apart her toy and rolling in the dirt, as we headed for the back door.

Eric's dad almost never remembered to lock the front, but sometimes he did and sometimes he slammed it shut so hard that it jammed in its frame, its hinges bent all askew. We'd gotten used to letting ourselves in through the back ages ago, slipping open the screen door and nudging it shut behind us before Charlie could nose her way in and cause a ruckus. If we were lucky, we could creep through the laundry room and up the stairs to Eric's room without his dad even knowing we were there.

Now, though, I didn't bother creeping. I let the screen rattle closed, the sound echoing across the cement walls of the laundry room, and nothing so much as peeped in reply.

Inside, it smelled like mildew and a dozen generic brand detergent bottles, stacked upside-down in rows across the shelves to let the last dribbles of each settle at the top. Mismatched socks and towels sat on the washer, piled next to a jar of loose change and a puff of multicolored lint—mostly polo shirt navy and denim blue, but with some of Eric's red jacket threads in there, too.

Damn it. I wanted to stay mad at him, but the more we wandered into his quiet, empty house, the more I could feel that anger souring like old milk into a curdled lump of worry.

"Eric…?" I called out, and the voice echoing back at me came back shaky and softer than I wanted. I tried again. "Eric!" Hell with it. "Mr. Braun!"

"Mr. Braun!" Monica echoed. "Hello?"

No answer. Monica and I shared a worried look, then pushed on, through the laundry room and into a thin hallway, up a set of wooden steps that creaked and popped underneath us like living things. Monica's cane thumped against each, guiding her way forward while we both gripped the handrails tight.

Upstairs smelled less like detergent and hay and more like bare wood and mold, a sour musk that seeped up from the gray-beige carpet and down with the dust motes flaking off the ceiling fan. Everything was tinted some shade of nicotine brown, giving it a haze like one of those old noir movies.

I didn't go up here often these days. I used to, back when we were little kids and the whole world was ours to run screaming through. But somewhere around puberty Eric had gotten self-conscious, shutting his door and jamming laundry in the bottom crack to keep it shut, and that was the end of that.

Even now, I took a second to prep myself, weighing how pissed and worried I was against how illegal it felt to force my way in. '*This is an emergency*' won, if by a smaller margin than I wanted to admit, and I shoved against the doorframe, forcing his laundry pile back against the wall with a dull *whud* so we could both tumble inside.

It'd changed since I'd wandered in last. Three years of growing older showed in Eric's new posters on the wall—the bike from *Akira*, all sorts of different Spider-Men, a skeleton girl with massive bone titties, a **NO TRESPASSING** sign that looked freshly stolen from someone else's yard. Someone, probably his dad, had put up one of those metal Jesus fish near the window, but Eric had taken a lighter to its edges, turning the metal warped and orange-rainbow tinted. His bed sat unmade in one corner, a bare mattress with mismatched shoes and a giant woven blanket thrown on top—the art fair kind, with a wolf pack howling at the moon printed on it.

While Monica poked around, nudging empty energy drink cans

aside with her cane, I took a second to breathe it all in, letting the dust and wood smell settle in my lungs.

God, Eric's room was *so cool.*

Focus. I couldn't let his badass decorations distract me from being angry—though Monica apparently didn't have the same idea, because as soon as she reached the back wall, she called out, "*Awww,*" loud enough for me to snap out of it and glance over.

Next to Eric's bed, crammed up against the dirt-smudged window, sat his old dresser, a little more chipped and faded, but still the same hunk of mismatched wood I remembered from childhood. But somewhen back, the piles of dishes and melty candles that used to sit on it had been cleared off, making space for... I couldn't say what. It looked like an Amazon box, with a stack of notebooks and folders beside it.

I stepped closer. Peering over Monica's shoulder, I could make out a few things I recognized: on top of the notebook pile sat the line of pictures he and Emma and me had taken at the mall's photobooth, ages ago—in the two-month window before the booth got graffiti on it and was wheeled out again, anyway. Eric glowered at the camera, chest puffed and shoulders hunched in a stained **Kittakoop High** T-shirt, while I stuck my tongue out and made "rock on" finger signs in a Godzilla shirt that didn't fit me anymore, and Emma held out her press-on pink nails and batted her eyes like an influencer girl.

It seemed kinda embarrassing, now; all of us baby-faced and trying way, way too hard to look cool. Monica smiling at it like a cake in a pastry case didn't help, either, and I reached to flip it over and shove it under the notebook pile.

Except... the pile seemed weirdly similar, too, looking closer. The notebook on top, for one, was Eric's old Math notebook—the one we'd passed back and forth during slow days, taking turns doodling on it until the whole thing was a mess of smudged ink. My drawings were wobbly and quick, spiky monsters and random Pokémon and that cool "S" with the pointed tips. His were black and painstaking, fiery pentagrams and super-detailed motorcycles and somber anime guys . . . and that cool "S" with the pointed tips.

"I didn't realize he'd kept this," I muttered, half to Monica and half to myself.

Underneath it was a folder full of all the scrap paper we'd shared in History, bad jokes and doodles that grew into a huge back-and-forth role-play thing—him writing about a loner race car driver chick with a car powered by damned souls, me writing about her pit stop mechanic who was also a samurai. An entire year of story planning, gathered up in torn patchwork.

And in the box . . .

In the box was a magpie hoard of everything I'd ever given him.

Most of them weren't mine to begin with—my mom and dad had told Eric a long time ago that he was always welcome at our place, but when he didn't come over, they sometimes sent me with snacks and fresh clothes and money, Red-Riding-Hood style. Empty granola bar wrappers lined the bottom in a crust of dried crumbs, along with the packaging to a set of socks Mom had insisted I bring over.

But some things *were* mine—like that same Godzilla shirt, left behind at his house years ago, or the walleyed bootleg crab doll I'd won from a claw machine and given to him. They sat in a rumpled pile in the middle, covered in granola dust.

"I gave these to him," I breathed. "All of them."

"Huh. He must care about you a lot," Monica suggested. "He wouldn't even throw away a wrapper you gave him."

I grimaced at the idea, even as it made my chest flutter and my heart hurt. Farther down in the pile, past the role-play notes and the doodles and the crumbs, sat a magazine—rumpled, torn at the edges, likely shoplifted from somewhere. I only caught a glimpse of oiled muscle, dark chest hair, and men in tight boxer briefs before I slammed the pile back down on top of it, face burning.

"I *don't get it*," I blurted before I could think too hard about *anything else*. "If he *cared* this much, why did he leave me to—" I couldn't bring myself to say *die*, "—to *get like this* in that stupid mall fountain while he ran away? Why did he act like I was a *burden*?"

My voice cracked across the words, and I gritted my teeth hard. Being furious at him was easier; it hurt, but in a somehow helpful way, burning away the stress and heartache and leaving dumb determination in their place. If he hated me, I could hate him right back twice as hard.

I didn't know what to do if he cared about me. If it was an accident, or a mistake.

Monica put a hand on my shoulder, but I stepped away, back from the dresser and closer to the other wall. I didn't want her to care about me, either—not when I wanted us to still be petty and competitive.

She didn't understand, anyway. She was still alive.

In the long, passive-aggressive fight to see which of us was most sickly and sweet and deserving of pity, I'd finally won.

Eric had left his phone charger behind, hanging from the wall outlet in a tangle of white plastic and electrical tape. I glanced at it for something to do that wasn't fishing through Eric's hoarded memories anymore.

"I should charge my phone a little before we head back out," I heard myself say.

"Okay," Monica agreed—soft, agreeable, like always. I realized then she'd never actually tried to pick a fight with me, had she? Not in the years and years we'd known each other.

Trying to be better than her, sicklier than her, more helpful than her...that'd always been in my own head. I wasn't sure if she'd even noticed we were fighting.

Maybe it would've been easier if she'd had. If she'd been more like

Eric, we could've just roughed each other up in the schoolyard one day and gotten it all out of our systems and walked away as friends. Maybe we could've had a picnic together, laughing and bonding over all the annoying hospital stuff we'd gone through.

"I'll...go make sure Charlie has food and water," she suggested. "I don't want her left totally alone."

I nodded, or maybe I didn't, and Monica left, one mismatched footstep at a time. Once she was gone, I plugged my phone into Eric's wall charger, sitting by it in a slump against the wall, right beneath the **NO TRESPASSING** sign and next to a box of memories and underwear magazines Eric had been collecting since puberty hit.

It took my phone a minute—waterlogged, cracked, low on battery—to catch itself up to the new cable. But all at once it flickered to life in my hands, and with it came a dozen buzzing new messages and alerts, spilling down the screen.

Missed call - MOM, 12:03 p.m.

Missed call - DAD, 12:05 p.m.

Missed call - EMMA, 12:10 p.m.

New message: DAD:

Ian are you still @ the mall w/ Eric???

Theres an emergency alert going on. Idk details yet but theyre talking about evacuating the down

*town, sorry

It seems veryy serious...... Please pick up !!!AS SOON AS!! you get this message!!!

ALSO.... If you see emergency vehicles DONT PANIC, follow their instructions & well meet up with you and Eric as soon as possible! I love you....!!!

Missed call - DAD, 1:32 p.m.
Missed call - MOM, 3:12 p.m.
2 new voicemail messages.
New message: DAD:
IAN, ITS BEEN SEVERAL HOURS..... WHERE ARE YOU??????

Update: your mother & Emmamama are here.... Confirmed theyre evacuating the town. We're O.K. & safe but were on our way out...... Well circle back to find you as soon as were allowed to leave... But call us back PLESE........

Are you okay???? Are you hurt????? Youre not in trouble but you need to call back !!!AS!!! SOON!!!! AS!!! You see this!!!!!

We love you very much!!!!

Missed call - MOM, 3:20 p.m.
New message: MOM:
Ian, you need to charge your phone.

We're waiting for you at the evacuation site near the exit to Charleston. Look for the orange tents. Ask Eric to drive you.

Be safe. Love, Mom

New message: EMMA:

heyyyyy nerd heads up if ur dead im taking ur stuff lmao

mayb call mom & dad at some point they are freakin ooooowt

look at this dumass cat also: [LINK]

New message: DAD:

Almost forgot...!!! Your mother has your medications.... There's spares in the bathroom cabinet so Dont forget them..!!! Drink water as well..!!!! Everyone is worried about you IAN.......!!!!! Love, Dad

4 new voicemail messages.

New message: MOM:

Please pick up the phone. I love you. Please let us know you're safe.

My heart hurt, thumping against my ribs with beats it didn't need to make anymore but hadn't realized yet. It begged me to reach back out (AS!! SOON!! AS!!! I saw this message!!!) with a bunch of apologies, to at least patch one thing where I could here.

Don't you realize they're worried about you?! it pounded. *Don't you know Eric keeps all your precious memories together in a box by his bed, down to the empty wrappers?! Don't you get that Monica always wanted to be your friend, and she never even noticed you were competing with her?!*

You're surrounded by so many people in your life who've always cared about you. This whole time. They love you even when you're angry or petty at them. And you love them, too.

That means the only person left to be angry with is yourself.

I set my phone down, nestling it in my lap so I could hug myself instead. My fingers dug in tight against my arms, digging red lines against skin that had gone a little more dry since this morning, a little more pale, a little closer to dead.

Please let us know you're safe.

I love you.

Later, I promised myself, I'd text Mom and Dad and Emma and apologize. Before I rotted away totally. They deserved that much—to know that their son was dead and wouldn't be coming back.

"*Please let us know you're safe,*" Mom wrote, but I couldn't even tell her that, could I?

I couldn't tell him anything at all.

For now, I'd treat Mom and Dad like one of Monica's picnics. Like a little bubble of safety just outside the hospital, a grassy hill dotted with sunlight, where parents sat with a basket of Dairy Queen and sodas and waited for their sick kid to come out so they could laugh about it all and hang out together. And as long as I never came any closer to it, as long as I never said anything different, it'd never leave and the sun would never set and that parent would keep believing their kid might be okay forever.

SEVEN

When I left Eric's house a few minutes later, wiping my eyes dry and squinting at the sun, the first thing I noticed was Charlie standing at playful attention, her head lowered and her front paws stretched forward. She had a tug toy in her mouth, muffling her growls.

The second thing I noticed was Angel gripping the other end of the tug toy, standing ruler-straight and growling back.

I blinked back and forth at them as the door swung shut behind me.

"Having... fun?" I asked.

"No. It's important to show dominance in front of dogs so they respect your authority as a leader," Angel reported between steady monotone growls.

Charlie's tail fluttered in the air. She jerked her head, twisting the toy, but Angel held firm.

"Yeah, she seems, uh, *terrified*."

"Perhaps. But establishing authority through fear is a well-known historical method of leadership." Angel shifted her grip, keeping the toy straight as Charlie worried and yanked at it.

"Fear and tug toys."

"A leader must use tools their subjects can understand."

"Oh, obviously. Keep up the hard work." I put a hand over my mouth, stifling a dumb little grin behind it—I wasn't sure how seriously Angel was taking this tug-of-war, and I didn't want her to think I was making fun of it or anything.

Fortunately, Monica chose that point to wander over from the shed, dusting her hands off on her jeans and leaving hay-colored smears behind. Her forehead was shiny with sweat and half her face was covered by one of those white respirator masks, but her eyes were bright and happy.

"All right. I set out enough food and water for a couple days, but we should come back if the evacuation haven't returned by Tuesday. She's a Labrador, I think, so she might make herself sick if we leave out too much food at once."

"Oh yeah," I remembered, "she used to be real bad about food as a puppy—she'd try to eat the entire bowl, throw up... then try to eat the throw up." I grimaced at the memory. "That's a Labrador thing?"

"Mmm. They don't really get 'full' in the same way as other dog breeds, so they have to be fed in rations. Like horses, in a way." That bright farm girl cheer in her eyes softened then. "There must be a lot of farm animals out here that aren't being cared for right now. I... don't know what to do about them all."

I hadn't even considered the idea. Standing out here in Eric's empty yard, though, I suddenly remembered every other animal I'd seen around here. Were the horses in the fields south of us being cared for, or had their owner been evacuated, too? What about the dog owned by the old couple in the park? Cats, cows, sheep, chickens...?

Before I could get too in my own head about it, Angel let out a yelp, and I turned in time to see Charlie tossing her toy around in victory while Angel rubbed at her reddened hand.

"Oh jeez. Are you okay?" I asked.

"Fine," she grunted in a tone that was anything but. "I hate this. Are we leaving yet?"

In response, Charlie shoved the tug toy against Angel's hand, tensed and ready for another round, and I bit back a laugh.

"That—yeah, sure, we can go. Thanks for the detour, guys." Then, to Monica: "Maybe your mom will have a better idea of how to split up and hit every farm around here?"

I couldn't see all of Monica's face with the mask on, but she nodded, which I took as approval.

Angel didn't stick around to chitchat; she'd already started moving back to the truck, bored of this conversation, and I hurried to catch up, pausing only a minute to give Charlie a pat and check the gate latch.

"We'll come back for you, girl," I murmured, hand buried in the sun-warmed corn-yellow fur on her head. "Keep out of trouble until then, okay?"

She bapped the tug toy against my other hand, which I took as a yes. Or close enough, anyway. I wasn't sure if she was even trained enough to know what 'trouble' was—but she stared up at all of us with the bald, open love of a dog, without a doubt in her mind that we'd come back well before she ran out of food and we'd be ready to play again.

I decided, then, that I'd stay alive at least long enough to come back here eventually. Even if I woke up tomorrow and my brain was rotting and my limbs wouldn't move... I wanted to make sure we looked after all the pets left behind in Kittakoop. They'd been left behind, too, after all, but they didn't even have the thumbs to open gates or the language to understand where the rest of the world had gone away to. So it was up to us, the other left behind guys, to make sure they ended up okay.

Once we left the rural part of town and got closer to Main Street, Monica drove extra slow, easing her way around turns and any roadblocks—sometimes branches or rocks, but sometimes other cars, left askew and abandoned in their lanes.

Next to her, and with Angel once again huddled at my side, I watched the desolate scenery of Kittakoop unwind behind the dusty passenger window film, one empty Ford and black-windowed storefront at a time. I wasn't sure what I was hoping for—a light or flicker of motion from someone else still here, maybe—but every place we passed seemed hollow and empty, as if it'd been abandoned years ago and only now caught up enough to go dark.

At some point Monica clicked on the radio, shifting the dial through stations. Most of them came as static—the truck's dented antenna had seen better decades—but a few pulled through, and they all sounded... oddly normal. Christian rock. A bass-pounding pop song. A commercial for veteran insurance. Christian pop. More commercials.

We shared a wary look as she got to the end and it faded into static again.

None of the stations had a mention of evacuations. Or an alert, or even a shift in programming. Even the two local ones, warping in and out of a static haze, played on like nothing happened. The closest one got was a vague line during the station bump: a DJ going, ***"This is Tri-State Focus, stay safe out there."***

At least five hundred people gone, and not a blip.

I couldn't decide if I wanted to be sad or happy about that. Sad, because I felt left behind again by the world. Happy, because at least this meant everywhere else was still *normal.* If we drove far enough, we'd end up in Huntington, and there'd be a gas station with a living clerk and a whole host of traffic waiting for us.

And we'd ask, *did you hear about what just happened in Kittakoop? Everyone's gone.*

And they'd say, *where the hell is Kittakoop? Is that anywhere near Parkersburg or Green Bank?*

For now, I pulled out my phone, scrolling through local news websites. Summer flood warning. A donation drive for the homeless. An ad for retirement asset management. And at the bottom, a footnote: cases of the latest COVID strain reported near Huntington.

Toward the end of the article, though, an anonymous commenter had left a note, one that drew my eye and made my breath catch.

"We're not sick. It's in the mountains. It's calling the dead home."

Home? I read it over again, three times, as if that could make it make sense. What was in the mountains that might be 'home' to this guy? What did 'home' even mean?

When it still didn't form into better words, I tipped my phone uneasily toward Monica.

"Hey, Monica, take a look at this...."

I trailed off. Because she'd already pulled to a stop in front of a dollar store. One with a flat green roof, a line of chipped yellow parking poles in front... and a broken front window, its posters for store hours and the **Item of the Week!** swaying in tatters behind shards of glass.

As I watched, a shard fell off, hitting the cement and skittering away.

"Oh, huh," I said. "Someone's already been here."

"Someone's been here *recently*," Monica added. "Look at the stuff on the ground."

I looked. Next to the pile of glass dust sat a couple scattered items—a plastic hairbrush, the cardboard backing to a stolen toy, a frozen TV dinner.

The TV dinner caught my eye the most, and after a second it clicked: it shouldn't still be frozen. Not with the sun still kissing the horizon like it was, muggy and warm. But even from here I could see freezer burn on its edges, sparkling like dew.

"Huh. Good deduction," I said.

Beside me, Angel had already shifted upright, her dark eyes alert and her shoulders squared as if she'd never been asleep to begin with. Maybe she *didn't* sleep, in the way some sharks always stayed low-key ready to bite.

"They're close," Angel muttered.

"You think we should get out and search for them?" I asked. "I mean, more people sticking together ain't a bad thing."

"Unless they try to rob us. They *did* break that window," Monica pointed out.

"Ian broke a window," Angel added.

I pressed a hand to my face, flustered. "That—that was different, you wanted—I just—I think it might be worth talking to them. If we stick together and don't head too far from the car."

Monica thought it over. Her brows knit together, and her fingers tapped uneasy patterns against the wheel. Finally, she sighed, the sound rustling through her face mask.

"Ten minutes," she said. "We'll get out and look for ten minutes. If we don't see anyone, or if there's any signs of trouble, we go back."

"Got it," I said.

"Mm," Angel added.

We climbed out of the truck, Monica on one side and me and Angel out the other. I shifted my arm to give Angel space... and grimaced as a few flecks of dried blood sprinkled off, dripping from a stiff and faintly tingling limb.

Oh yeah. I'd died.

I decided to stick to the back of the group, with my hood up and my hands deep in my pockets, letting Monica lead and Angel guard. I couldn't hide every part of being dead and bloodied, at least not without a good shower and maybe a costume designer, but with my hood up I could save it for last, the punchline to a bad joke. *Three lost kids walk into town. A chronically ill farm girl, a half-feral survivor girl, and a dead guy. And one says, 'Hey, why the long face?'*

We could tell at a glance that our mystery raider wasn't hanging around on either side of the dollar store, smoking cigarettes or getting a bag of ice. Like a lot of Kittakoop businesses, the store was a squat building in the middle of nowhere, lined on either side with spindly birch trees and a flat lawn and nowhere to hide, so Monica tried the front entrance.

The automatic doors didn't *whoosh* open. She stepped forward, bumped into them, then gave a nervous don't-know-what-I-expected laugh, and grasped at their edges, pulling them apart. They rattled, crunching broken glass along their railings, their pasted ads and logos sliding away to reveal the store's insides.

And we all stopped to take it in.

Last time I'd been in this place, it'd been a mess of noise and movement: lights glaring, oldies music crooning overhead, and at least a half dozen elderly women arguing over greeting cards. It still seemed vibrant in places, mostly in the neon rainbows of cleaning supplies and party balloons. But without power and without people, it seemed washed-out and sad, too. Even the balloons floated a little lower, drifting over the tops of a dozen **EVERYTHING $1** displays.

For whatever reason, the balloons got me, and I lingered back to watch them as Monica and Angel moved on.

I'd known in an obvious way that, without anyone in town, all these things left behind would start to fall apart. We'd talked about as much when feeding Charlie.

But it didn't hit me fully until I watched the balloons. Until I thought about how they'd keep sinking out here, until they hit the ends of their strings and withered on the floor.

All the flowers in the greeting card section would dry up and shed brittle petals, too. The frozen dinners would melt and leak mold. Pet owners like Eric's dad left their dogs and cats behind, stuck behind a locked front door, wondering why dinner was coming so late today, tomorrow, forever.

I looked at my hands, already a couple shades paler, grayer than they were this afternoon.

We'd all fall apart like this.

Something rustled down the next aisle and I jumped, startled out of my thoughts. Up ahead, Monica and Angel examined bottles of hand soap, Monica with interest and Angel with suspicion. Neither of them seemed to notice the rustle, and I wasn't entirely sure I'd *heard* it, either—it itched at the back of my head, more like a feeling than a noise.

"It's calling the dead home," that anonymous commenter had said, like an in-joke only us dead people would get.

The rustling echoed again and I found myself creeping toward it, around a display of dusty candy bars and toward the canned food. Past shelves already half empty and battered, I could see the glass-gapped hole of the broken window, sunset bleeding through it in rays stretched long and orange across the linoleum. Next to it, scrawled across the plaster in jagged Sharpie ink, I could see graffiti. A promise.

ZOEY WAS HERE & SHE LIVED DESPITE IT ALL TO SPITE IT ALL

My head itched somewhere to the right. I looked right.

Slumped against a shelf of bottled waters next to the window, his hands bent in jagged angles against his chest, sat a dying body. An old man, in a cashier's apron and faded blue jeans. I could tell he was dying all the way because half his head caved into itself like a rotten fruit, sunken and wrinkled in the back, and a couple fat horseflies already plinked against it like hailstones. His hand twitched, tapping against the window glass over and over, its own insect trying to escape.

Closer. His skin looked too small. Not for him, but for everything *in* him, everything swelling and straining at the hems of his apron as he died. It looked too small in the way a spider's abdomen looked too small for a hundred eggs, and at the sight of it my teeth itched and my head itched and my hands itched and I couldn't stop looking at his *eyes*. His eyes seemed so dark, and *viscous* somehow, like a rainbow-slick puddle on the asphalt, like I could poke a hand in and it'd break through the surface tension and underneath I'd find something wide and deep as an ocean trench.

He stared back, his pupils blown so big they turned his whole eyes dark, his fingers curling and uncurling like a baby's, his mouth gaping and closing in surprise, and all of a sudden I wanted to grasp his shoulders and ask him a dozen questions, right now, in these few seconds before he went gone.

What happens when you go all the way dead? What are you feeling right now? Is it a relief? Is it scary? Is there something after death, something warm and good and homelike, or does the black nothing in your eyes go on forever? Where are you going? What happens to us? What's gonna happen to me?

But he couldn't answer, of course. None of them could answer, not when they were already so dead they'd about died all the way. Any parts of himself that could speak were bloated and rotten and turned to gunk, worn down to this, this wide-eyed stare and this gape-mouthed slack-jawed look at *something*, like the cusp of a revelation, like the déjà vu of a familiar room, like the second between a lightning crack and a rumble of thunder.

And suddenly I wanted to eat him. Before the thunder hit or the realization clicked or his eyes went white, I wanted to cut it off, drinking darkness out of his eyes so it tasted familiar next time and didn't seem so scary-infinite. I wanted to take the pieces of myself drifting away and ground them in blood and bone and solid things.

Last thing your flesh remembers is how to eat parts of itself to survive, Angel said. *Put in something familiar, it'll keep eating what it thinks is itself, forever.*

Would that help?

I crouched down by him and I itched so much, and he stared back and our matching dark eyes caught each other, reflected each other, a million galaxies shoved into impossibly tiny human bodies, and I leaned in toward his eyes, toward that tense second before it went white and he forgot everything, and I pressed my teeth against it and it burst like ripe fruit, and I tore up long pieces of flesh and coated my throat with copper and lightning, and it tasted like crisp mountain air and open skies and *life* and I drank it in and clung to it for every extra moment it could give me—

And beside me, I heard the window glass crunch again. I jerked my head up, startled as a cat, snapped out of *whatever that was* and dragged dizzily back into now.

The raider—*raiders,* I saw, a pair of kids in dusty clothing silhouetted by the sun behind them—came back. A girl, first, stepping over the window shards in a wide cowboy straddle, a shopping basket swinging from her clasped hands. An actual shopping basket, like this was one of a dozen other errands for the day.

She moved closer, and in the shade I saw she was taller than me, older than me, with a broad athlete's build and a tattered **HUNTINGTON ROLLER CITY GIRLS** T-shirt. Her hair looked like it might've been blue once but had faded to greenish-brown, tied in a loose braid over one shoulder, and her face looked square and battered. An out-of-towner, probably, from somewhere that had athletes and roller cities.

She held out a hand to her partner. He stepped through more stiffly, brushing shards off the front of his red jacket as he moved into the shade. . . .

And I saw Eric again.

My breath caught.

In less than a day, he'd changed. A deep red scratch lined one cheek, tracing under eyes gone dim and hollowed, over a chin already speckled with brown stubble. His red jacket, stained to start with, had new scuffs on its elbows and dirt on its sleeves. He stood too straight, too rigid, that military toughness his dad had beaten into him etched in every corner.

Eric, who'd left me behind to die.

Eric, who hadn't left Kittakoop, after all.

I found him.

He found me.

I loved him so much it hurt.

I hated him so much it hurt.

As I swallowed hard I tasted oil, lining my tongue and dripping down my chin. The back of my head pounded, its stitches aching, and I saw myself: a corpse, crouched in front of a dead body with my teeth smudged red, *eating* it, my skin mottled gray and decaying across my bones.

He saw me and I watched his shoulders tense, a dozen emotions playing across those distant eyes: surprise, confusion, realization, horror, revulsion... and then a deep, awful grief, the kind that twisted his face into itself, and I knew in a second that he'd never meant to leave me to die. He couldn't have, not when he saw me dead and he looked like it killed him a little, too.

For a moment we both looked wrong, me dead and him wearing all these soft and vulnerable feelings I swore he'd broken down a long time ago, shoved somewhere his dad couldn't reach.

It sounded wrong to hear him whisper, "Ian...?" all delicate, shaking in the air.

I stood up. Damn the blood, damn the afterlife, damn death and all its rotting pieces. I loved him like a dog or a soldier, alert and upright before I'd even thought about moving. I loved him like instinct.

"Eric—" I started, and I stopped, because as soon as I got to my feet he took a step back, shoes crunching over glass.

"S-stay back," he said, his voice a low, rough hum. "If you can hear me, just—stay back."

I remembered, too late, how much he hated the dead. How they smelled, how they looked, how they acted so close to normal and so *not.* So I held up my hands: *easy, easy.*

"Eric, listen. I'm sorry you saw me like this, but... I'm still me. I know this—all this—is hard to deal with—believe me, *I know*—but we can figure it out together." I felt myself babbling, but I couldn't stop it. I took another step forward, and he retreated again, eyes wide.

"No—no, no-no-no. You're not him anymore. I *killed* him. Ian's gone and he wouldn't—" He glanced at the body, its eyes hollow and its face weeping red. "He wouldn't want this."

I killed him.

Eric choked out the words, twisted with a sickly sort of guilt, and my heart ached.

"Eric—whatever happened in the mall, I'm *sure* it wasn't your fault. It was an accident." I swallowed again. "C'mon, Eric, let's just get out of this stupid town. Anywhere. We can do whatever you want. Pick blackberries or—or a road trip, or breaking windows, you name it."

Another step. He watched me in a desperate way, and I wanted more than anything to hold him close and soothe everything that hurt, and—

I froze.

Because I heard something go *shunk*, a dull and liquid noise.

Because the words caught and died in my throat.

Because I looked down and I saw the tip of a metal pole, one of those shelf supports with the notched holes and the sharp, sharp edges. It stuck out at an impossible angle, jabbing up from the floor and into my stomach. *Through* my stomach and clear out the back.

Because I heard a girl's voice, too cheerful, too close behind me.

"Think he told you to stop, little guy," she sang. "Don't worry, Eric, I got your back."

She pushed against my shoulders, shoving me to the floor, and I felt that sharp pole pulling back, resisting for only a second or two before it slid out and left a breathless hole behind.

It didn't hurt, not at first—it felt cold and empty, the wind knocked out my lungs and my chest hitching too quick against the floor. The world blurred in and out of focus, swirling and pulsing around itself, and any other words I wanted to babble at Eric dissolved on my tongue like cotton candy, broken apart into heaving gasps and pooling blood and a distant ringing hum that *wouldn't stop*.

In glimpses, I saw the girl—Zoey, I guessed, here despite it all to spite it all—raise her pole again, readying it over my head, and I saw the cashier with his head already caved in and his eyes gone neither white or black but empty, but eaten, and I saw a dozen scattered cans of green beans and corn, labels of cheery mascots laughing to themselves—

And I heard Monica and Angel at last, shouting and running across the aisles between us. I saw Zoey's face shift from excitement to skittish anger, saw her drop her pole and grab Eric's arm instead—saw Eric stare back at me one last time, not sad or confused, but angry now, disgusted in the exact painful way Angel warned me he'd be—

—I saw my hand reaching out to him, smeared red and shaking but still reaching, pleading with him to not go, please, don't leave me to die again, *please*—I saw them jump out the window, anyway, toward that sunset outside, toward a big world full of living people with futures and evacuation plans—I saw Monica running after them, face red, shouting curses I'd never heard her use before, grabbing those laughing-mascot cans to fling out the window after them, shattering glass and bursting stale food across the floor as she screamed at them to *never come back*—

Blurring, in and out. I saw Angel crouch beside me, her hair in strands in front of her eyes and her jacket hunched high, her hands on mine. I choked down a lungful of air, enough to pant out a few words.

"A-am I dying?" I asked.

"No," she said. "That would be redundant. Hold this. Keep breathing. Keep moving." She pressed my hands against the hole in my stomach, holding me together. Blood welled through my fingers, but darker than it was last time, colder than last time, thicker than last time. Like the dregs at the bottom of a spoiled carton of milk.

I kept holding on. Slowly, the ringing in my ears faded from a whine to a hiss to a whisper. Slowly, the blurring, spinning room around me settled into itself. My stomach hurt, but in a pinching, distant way, a hunger pang already used to being ignored.

Not dying. Already dead. I breathed, in and out, and my body realized in some way that it didn't need to try so hard to survive. That panic gripping my heart eased up an inch, and it sank from a rabbity race to the sluggish, resigned thudding it'd taken on since I'd woken up this morning.

Dead, but still not dead all the way. Not yet.

Angel glared up at the cleaned-out shelves, digging through her pockets. "We need more than dollar store trash to stitch this." She pulled out a wad of napkins, moving my hands aside to jam them against my jacket.

Monica strode up, her face red behind her mask and her hands tight fists around her cane. She muttered under her breath, some long-winded threat about grinding them up into horse feed if she saw them again. As soon as she saw us, though, that anger melted into anxiety, her fists loosening to grasp at her collarbone, instead. She crouched down close, taking in my smudged hands and the blood smeared across the floor.

"Oh my god... Ian, are you okay? Did they hurt you?"

I'm fine, just spilled my guts a bit—but I was already doing that, I thought, then realized that might be a little too unhelpful. All my thoughts felt useless, disjointed jumps and connections skittering around one another without forming into sentences.

"I... I'm still here. I think," I finally managed, panting out the words between slow, wet breaths. "Thanks. For the help. Yelling at them. They're gone. He's gone."

"We *said* to stick together," Angel added, halfway through shoving a ratty towel against my spine, and I winced.

"I know. I'm sorry. I thought I heard something. G-guess they *really* didn't like me." A nervous laugh. "They're not wrong, right? Dead people must be awful to like. I'm not myself anymore. Did you know that? It's finally hit me. I don't have a happy future with anyone. I won't even remember this before too long. No wonder Eric left me behind. No wonder *everyone* left. I'm so scared. I don't wanna die. What if they're right? What if I'm not worth taking with? What if—"

And then Monica pulled me into a tight hug. I twitched, startled, as her chest pressed against my blood-smeared one, and her hair brushed against my smudged cheek in little coily puffs, her cane clattering to the floor beside us.

She mumbled against my ear.

"You're worth it to us."

That was all. Beside us, Angel still had that intense, blank look on her face that she usually did, but she'd paused her focused chest compression to reach her hand out and touch mine. I blinked back gathering tears.

"I'll just die and hurt you, too, you know," I muttered.

"A hundred other things have already tried to hurt me. I'm too stubborn to care at this point," Monica replied. "We're *not* abandoning one another. Whether it's a few days or years, we'll help you survive for as long as we can."

This close, I could see Monica's glittery eyeshadow, painted over her lids and the tired bags underneath. Her nails were chipped blue around where she'd chewed at their edges, her cane wrapped in decorative pink tape. As if by putting herself together cutely enough, she could force some kind of order to the mess.

I looked over at Angel. She hunched so far into herself, her shoulders up high and her hair over her face in a slapdash attempt at cutting off all the sights and sounds and feelings in the world, but she kept both hands out, now, a single finger brushed against mine and one more against Monica, tiny twin lifelines keeping her from shrinking all the way inside herself and disappearing forever.

And me. Small, sad, dying.

But not all the way dead, yet.

And maybe that was enough. Maybe all three of us, damaged and weird and burdensome, could be enough here.

I broke down crying. For the second time today, I cried fat, messy tears, the kind with snot and whimpering breaths and desperate clinging—but unlike the first time, collapsed beside a mall bathroom mirror, this time it felt nice. A cathartic kind of cry, the kind that let it all out and in the open, the kind that left me feeling tired and drained and safe.

I felt safe.

EIGHT

We didn't have any tools or know-how to patch up all the inside bits Zoey impaled, so Angel stitched the front and back of me closed with a plastic sewing kit, sealing both ends with safety pins and a couple kitten-patterned Band-Aids. A doctor would've fainted at the job, but we figured for the dead, it'd work out fine enough.

The wound still felt more cold and numb than painful, but as my adrenaline faded, I felt a growing ache in my bones to go with the ache in my head. A dull reminder of everything that'd kill me, as soon as my lagging body caught up to itself.

Monica hadn't winced once during the stitching, though she went pale once Angel took off my shirt and she saw how gross it had gotten. At some point, itching for a distraction, she'd noticed the cashier's body still crumpled by the water bottles. If she noticed the bite marks on his face, too, she tastefully didn't comment. Just walked to another aisle and came back with several packets of white shower curtains, then pulled them over him, blanket-like, and held it all in place with a paperback bible and a couple fraying plastic flowers.

A farm girl's efficient, dollar-store burial.

"Frustrating," Angel muttered, tossing aside the empty Band-Aid box. "Like trying to knit with chopsticks."

"You did the best you could with what we have." Monica straightened up from beside the cashier, hugging her chest and pointedly not looking at any of us. "We should hurry to the hospital. They'll have better tools. And... blood bags, maybe? Is that something we need?"

"Mm. No more distractions." Angel glared at us both. "I told you. No one will help us. We don't need to hunt down any more strangers."

"Sorry," I mumbled, then yelped as Angel smacked the back of my head.

"Stop apologizing, too," she said. "Let yourself take up space."

"Okay, then I'm *not* sorry. I'm glad we didn't listen." I rubbed at my head. "At least we got some more supplies, right?"

"It's... mostly junk, but yeah." Monica held up her backpack, giving it a firm shake. It rattled. "I found a few poles and ropes for that tarp in the truck, if we want to set up a tent for tonight. It should be big enough for all of us *and* Mom."

Behind me, Angel grunted under her breath, and I didn't have to guess why: Mom. Yet another person we were blindly hoping might help us. Yet another betrayal or trap for us to wander into.

At the same time, I couldn't bring myself to ruin the one plan we had, now that Eric was... gone. If we didn't keep moving forward, it felt too much like waiting to die. Not now, not while I could still distract myself from it through everyone else's problems.

"Going to the hospital sounds like a great plan." I held up my fingers, ticking off them. "Blood bags, medical supplies . . ." I brightened. "Oh! And there's gotta be *some* kind of record of what happened in there. You don't just evacuate an entire hospital without having, like, intake forms and notes."

Monica sighed, hard. "And medications. Oh my god, I'd kill for a stash of Elavil. I have an emergency supply on hand, but... I don't really want to find out what happens if I go cold turkey on pain meds."

"Point . . ." I hummed. "Come to think of it. I dunno if it even matters now, but I'm supposed to take seizure meds with dinner."

"I want to take opioids," Angel added.

"I—what? Why?" I asked.

"See what would happen. If I'm strong enough to overpower them."

"That . . ." I glanced at Monica, who shook her head so fast her mask went askew. "Okay, no. No medications for Angel."

"Why not? We already broke a window and stole a car," Angel said.

"Yeah, but we need to draw a line in the sand somewhere, still," I pointed out. "Everything else about the hospital sounds like a good idea, though."

"It's settled, then." Monica nodded. "We'll push on. No more distractions."

"Mmhmm." I nodded along... though deep down I couldn't say *what* I'd do if I ran into Eric—into *a distraction*—on the way. I'd hoped, stupidly, that seeing him would clear things up or give some kinda closure, something I could pick up and carry with me, but all it did was make everything hurt worse.

I killed him, Eric had said.

When I'd woken up, I'd thought of him leaving me to die as an accident, the sort of careless thing able-bodied people do—running toward an emergency alert, forgetting to check on the seizing kid in the fountain water behind you, etcetera.

It... *was* an accident, right? He had a shoebox full of our memories together. He'd saved every scrap of doodles and role-plays we'd made. He cared about me.

. . . Right?

We headed out maybe an hour later, arms full of snacks and cleaning wipes and spare socks. The store didn't have any backpacks or hiking gear like survivalists wore in action movies, but I settled for a vibrant yellow tote bag with the words **SOAK UP THE SUN** across its side, tossing it into the back of the truck with the rolled tarp and Monica's tidy, labeled boxes of canned food.

Though we searched all around the building, we couldn't see any sign of Eric or Zoey outside—except, Monica pointed out, a new pair of scuffed tire marks in the parking lot near the back.

"So we're not the only ones with a car," she noted. "Wonder why they stayed behind in Kittakoop, then...?"

My gut reaction was a desperate sort of wish fulfillment: *they stayed because Eric came back for me, because he loves me.* I shrugged instead.

"I dunno. Guess everyone has their own reasons."

We settled back in the truck cab—which, with the sun down and the sky a murky gray-purple, had gone from stiflingly hot to comfortingly cool. Cool enough, at least, for me to zip up my jacket, and for Angel to snuggle deeper in hers like a baby bird in fluff. Only Monica stayed in a T-shirt, but if she had complaints, she didn't let them show. She just took the wheel and started the engine, rolling us back out of the parking lot and onto an open road, headlights cutting lines through the dark.

My stomach ached around the stitches, slow pulses like a ticking clock, a steady reminder of another second, another minute closer to dying. Had eating part of that cashier put it off for a while, like Angel suggested, or had I spilled that part out with the new hole in my gut? He'd tasted so *alive.* So real. If I *hadn't* eaten that guy, would I be dead-all-the-way by now, my weird zombie limbo all bled out onto the linoleum tile?

I didn't know. I didn't know any of it, and I hated sitting here in the truck with all my thoughts about it.

I'd found a cheap notebook and a set of pens at the dollar store, so I sat against the passenger door with them in my lap, and I wrote instead. Every so often we'd pass by a flickering streetlamp or a road sign reflecting our headlights back, and bright orange-yellow streaks would trail down the page and light up what few words I managed to scratch down, in scribbled-out notes and rewritten paragraphs.

Dear Mom and Dad and Emma ~~and Eric~~,

~~Hi, I'm doing fine~~

~~I'm doing okay~~

~~I'm not fine, but~~

If you're reading this, I'm probably gone by now. I ~~really really really~~ don't want to die, and I'm going to do my best to put it off as long as I can, but just in case, I figure I should get my will written up, right? ~~That's what you're supposed to do I think~~

First of all, PLEASE don't worry about me too much. It ~~didn't hurt~~ happened quick, and while dying is ~~REALLY~~ scary sometimes, I think I'm still happy right now. I met up with two girls from school, Monica and Angel, and we're ~~okay~~ heading to the hospital to get help. Emma, I think you'd like them. So if you meet, look out for each other, okay? ~~And look out for Eric, too. He's taking everything hard.~~ Please check up on Eric's dog, Charlie, when you get back. She's a good dog and I don't want her to be alone.

Emma can have all my stuff, except the clothes and the video games. I already promised the games to Eric, and I don't want Emma to dye my clothes black and cut them up for her e-girl fashion. ~~Maybe donate them instead, I don't know yet.~~ If anything turns out to be worth a bunch of money, Emma can have it, but she's got to split it with Monica and Angel.

I think that's it???

I'm sorry I died. It was an accident. ~~I'm sorry I don't have more stuff to write, either.~~

I love you all. I hope you're all okay.

Monica turned and the undercarriage shifted beneath us, rattling over gravel and asphalt. I snapped my notebook closed, peering through the window.

Across a long and perfect lawn, I could see the hospital, and my hands clenched against my thighs on instinct. I recognized the winding turnoff to the parking lot, the big directory sign next to the lot, even the smell of cedar bark and mountain grass in the air—and something else, a low rubber and barbecue scent, rolling in from the back. I recognized a hundred things from every time I'd been pulled out of school to come here, always with some new symptom to describe or test to take.

A small seizure this time. No blacking out, but he had muddled speech for roughly an hour and he couldn't stop drooling. We had to clean him off with a napkin.

What were the symptoms, again? Hmm. Did you lose bowel functions again, too? Did you hurt yourself this time? Strip here, and we'll examine you for bruises. Come on, now, don't look so humiliated. Your parents will buy you a toy from the gift shop at the end.

Step on this scale, please. Put on this blood pressure cuff, please. Take this medication and report back next month. Please wait. Please hold. Please stay here.

We're not sure what's causing this. It's still happening? Huh. He'll grow out of it. It might be nothing. We don't know yet. Why don't you come back again? And again, and again, and again?

On the other side of the cab, Monica's hands tightened against the wheel and her breathing went thin.

"Not a fun place to go back to for you, either, huh?" I asked.

"I keep remembering the taste of chalky multivitamins." She smiled, her eyes crinkling over the mask. "Last time I went here, they called it anxiety and told me to go home."

"Have you considered growing out of it?" I replied.

We shared a knowing laugh. Angel glanced between us with obvious confusion, stuck in the middle like a lost younger sibling, and I nudged her arm, forcing a grin.

As much as I didn't like going back to the hospital, we'd still made it. Soon enough we'd find Monica's mom—a real adult, with real experience—and she'd tell us what to do. And just like every other medical issue we'd ever had, this entire evacuation—this entire *dying* thing—would get treated.

From here, all we'd have to do is check ourselves in, say what happened, and then let someone else do all the thinking and paperwork.

That, at least, Monica and I had been born to do.

Monica pulled us through a steady loop around the building. Our headlights cast everything into long shadows and spiraling motes of dust, filmy yellow light meeting deep mountain darkness, but we took it slow enough for all of us to pick out shapes and locations from the gloom.

A single ambulance, askew in a parking bay with its door left open. A thin island of bushes and wildflowers, raised up from the lot by bricks and decorative pebbles. A couple trees. Monica lingered over those slowest of all, lights tracing every scraggly branch and trunk, until they cut through to the grassy hill beyond it and I heard her draw in a sharp breath. I did, too.

The picnic spot, that perfect shady clearing between the trees, sat empty.

No blanket.

No Mom.

No rescue.

Monica kept staring rigidly ahead, her hands locked at ten and two against the wheel, a perfect posture ruined by the violent white flare of her knuckles.

“Monica . . .” I started, my voice low—but she looked at me and I saw her smiling, a serene and patient look that didn’t match her hands at all.

“Oh well. I’m sure that’s okay. She’s probably inside. It’s late. She wouldn’t have stayed out all night.”

Between us, Angel hummed again, the same annoyed mutter she’d given at the dollar store. I bit my lip, biting back a dozen concerns with it.

“Sure. It’s definitely…possible,” I said back. “We can check, at least. No harm in that.” I pressed a hand to Angel’s arm, a gentle warning to play along for now. Angel shifted away from it, but she didn’t speak up, either.

Monica nodded, pulling the truck away from that dark and empty spot and toward the hospital’s back side. That rubber-barbecue scent came thicker now, along with more swirling motes caught in our lights, dancing around each other in rising chains and tufts.

“Of course! There’s no harm in checking. My mom cares about everyone in this town. If people in the hospital needed help evacuating, she would’ve helped.” Monica spoke a little too fast, the words edging over one another for space. “She’s probably still helping, even. So it makes sense for us to help how we can, too. They’ll appreciate the supplies we got, if nothing else—”

“We can’t help them anymore,” Angel cut in, and I flinched.

“Angel, *don’t*—” I started, but she wasn’t looking at me. She’d pushed herself higher in her seat, head craned toward the building, and I followed her gaze and I trailed off quick.

A long black swathe cut through the hospital’s brick and pillars, an ugly smear painted across pinkish brick and empty window frames. Support beams hung out of it in jagged angles like broken teeth, hanging through piles of debris still smoldering embers deep within. They blurred in and out of focus, disappearing behind clouds of dark smoke wafting up into a matching skyline, blotting out the stars. It swirled in front of our headlights, those little motes—smoke motes, not dust—skittering faster now, heavier now, and that rubber-barbecue smell leaked through the windows thick enough to coat our lungs.

A fire. A *recent* fire.

I looked back to Monica, but she'd already cut the engine and grasped her seat belt. She wrenched her door open before we'd even rolled to a total stop, stumbling out onto the parking lot with wild jabs of her cane for balance.

"Monica, wait—!" I cried, wrestling with my own stubborn seat belt and rusted doorframe. Beside me, Angel stayed still, and I braced myself for a smug *I told you so.* But when I twisted my way out and caught sight of her in the headlights' glow, I saw her hugging herself instead, staring off into the distance.

Like she'd wanted to be wrong.

I offered her a hand. She stared at it for a second like she'd never seen a hand before, then she slid over, grasping it and letting herself hop to the ground.

There wasn't a way into the hospital from the back—at least not that we could see, with everything blurred in smoke and scattered with debris—so Monica ran back toward the front, her sneakers skidding across pavement and her cane swinging wildly in one hand, a neon pink guiding baton that Angel and I tailed after.

"Monica!" I called out to no answer.

The front door, I noticed, had been propped open with a chunk of cement. But Monica wrenched it open wider still, cracking it against its hinges before darting inside. It swung back too fast, crashing against the block, and I jumped, giving the block a glare.

But I didn't touch it otherwise. The thought of being accidentally locked in here was worse than the sound the door made slamming against it.

Inside, without any sunlight or fluorescents left running, the lobby sat impossibly dark, a sheet of black oil that stank of rubber and itched as we breathed it in. I wafted a hand, cupping the other to my mouth.

"Monica, *wait*! Wait for us!" I called.

No answer. I couldn't even see her neon cane anymore, swallowed by the void. Like an idiot, I'd left my tote bag of supplies in the truck. And like an idiot again, I'd grabbed mostly food and toothpaste and wipes, anyway, forgetting things like *flashlights* or *matches*. I hadn't tried to think like a survivor beyond the fun of role-playing like one for a bit.

Beside me, I heard rustling. I jumped again, but as my eyes adjusted, I made out Angel's blurry silhouette, digging through her backpack. A few more seconds and she flicked on a flashlight, flooding the place with electric white light.

And in that flood, I saw everything.

I saw Monica first, standing with her back turned, her cane limp in one hand and her head tipped back.

Then the hospital lobby.

It was empty now, but people had *been* here. All the waiting room chairs, thick plush things with wooden frames, had been pushed against the walls with the toys and the magazine racks, leaving a massive gap of empty space in the middle. The reception desk across from us was a mess of scattered paperwork and empty boxes, laptops and tangled wires, and—weirdly—a pair of old shoes, leaning against the computer monitor. All the doors stood unlocked and open, shoved aside by masses of people leaving in a hurry.

It felt too warm in here. Warm, and smokey, and ruined.

Monica turned back to us, and even behind the face mask, she looked… empty. Those eyes, so bright and determined and lined with perfect makeup, stared blankly back at us, then away again. She wandered to the side, to a dented bead toy in the corner. The same bead toy she and I had played with as little kids, bored and stuck waiting for appointments.

I stepped closer, stretching a hand out in the air between us.

"Monica…," I started, but I wasn't sure how to finish. What could I say? What would possibly make it better? "We—we must've just missed her. But if we look around, I'm sure she must've left a message or a clue for us. We can figure out where she went, and follow her—"

"There's no point," Angel interrupted. "There you have it. How many times do you need proof? This is all there is for us: empty space and ruined things."

She spread her arms, her flashlight beam bouncing in one grip. Bluish shadows played across her face, stretching her cheekbones and the sockets of her eyes.

"No one waited for us. No one will save us."

"Shut up, Angel," Monica muttered in a low voice I'd never heard her use before. A warning voice. I couldn't see her face, not with the flashlight pointing away, but I heard the venom in her words.

"No." Angel lowered her arms, her eyes flashing even in the dark. "If we keep grasping at what we lost, we'll die waiting here. Like the school—you were willing to sit in a closet until you starved, waiting for permission to leave."

"Angel, I'm warning you—"

"You saw me stealing from the vending machines. You asked me what to do. I told you how to survive. I'm telling you now. Your mom *was never going to be here."*

"Angel—"

"We go to the *same school*, Monica. Your mom *died.* She didn't linger behind like Ian, and she *won't*. No matter how much you dress up, or wait for her, or need her help. Let her *go*."

The room went deathly silent. I took a step back, as if I could put real distance between Angel's confession. As if stepping away could stop her from blurting out the blunt and ugly truth.

She died.

She died, and she didn't linger behind.

"What...?" I asked.

I still couldn't make out Monica's face. It was hidden in the dark and in how she lowered her head, hunching it between her shoulders. I couldn't see her sparkling eyeliner or notebook full of lists, every part of herself she'd primed and organized into a pretty and lovable version of herself.

I couldn't see how hard she'd worked to be someone worth coming back for.

Then she *screamed*, and she shoved at the reception desk, heaving it sideways. It hit the floor with a wild crash, spilling paper and wires and shoes all across that empty middle space. I scrambled back, pressing myself against the wall, but Angel barely flinched.

Angel, once again offering blunt truths, pushing buttons, then standing stock-still, waiting for the snap and the punishment that always followed. And Monica once again glaring over her, buttons pushed, her eyes brimming with offended tears and her cane gripped tight. Like we'd never left the mall and were still arguing over chicken thighs and stealing cars.

And once again, Monica whiffed the shot. She dropped her cane, letting it clatter with the fallen desk, and coughed, rasping in smokey hospital air.

"Leave, Angel," she growled instead. "I want you to *leave*!"

And that must've taken Angel off guard, because for once, she didn't look so detached. For a second, she looked genuinely hurt, in the way a little kid might look hurt after touching a burner they didn't know would be hot.

"You said no matter what—" Angel started.

"Leave!"

Angel stumbled back. She blinked, hard, her eyes shimmering damp in the jittering flashlight glow. She stared at me like I'd defend her, like I'd translate what she meant into words that hurt less, but I stood confused and stupid between them, too stunned by the news to speak. So she put on that cold and emotionless mask she usually wore, then turned and ran, deeper into the burnt reaches of the hospital.

And Monica and I stood alone in the dark, surrounded by empty chairs and wafting smoke and all the open places where the people meant to save us were supposed to be.

NINE

My gut instinct was to run after Angel—she shouldn't head off alone, not with everything burnt and falling apart in here—but I made it only a couple yards before I lost track of her flashlight and got left stumbling in the dark, blind and useless.

I muttered a swear and pressed a hand against the wall, tracing my way back how I came, into the lobby with its weak starlight trickling through the doors—not enough to see by, not really, but enough to make out the shapes of things and get my bearings.

Near the toppled reception desk, I saw Monica's shadow, hunched over her backpack. She clicked on her own flashlight, dimmer than Angel's, with a flickering yellow light instead of an electric white one. Her skin looked ashen in it and her eyes looked hollow.

As I edged closer to that light, mothlike and lost and crunching over ashes, I heard her mutter to herself, voice choked and wet with tears.

"Dumb bitch."

"I'm sorry," I said automatically. "I think she was just trying to help, in her own way—"

"Not Angel." Monica scrubbed at her face, her mascara smudging across her hands and in an arc up to one plucked eyebrow. "*I'm* the dumb bitch. I acted like the *voice of reason*, but I led everyone on some... stupid, desperate goose chase. I hate that I'm like this, this—gullible, desperate... bitch."

"Hey, hey." I crouched down beside her—wincing as my gut ached at the motion—and lowered my voice to something more soothing. "Please don't hate yourself for that. We all needed somewhere to go that wasn't... y'know... sitting in a school or a mall, feeling sorry for ourselves."

She snorted a small laugh. Not much, but something.

"Do... do you want to talk about it?" I tried. Then: "Why did you lead us here if you knew your mom was already d—gone?"

I expected her to flinch at that, but either she expected the question or she'd gone too numb to get startled at it, because all she did was hug her backpack and sink to sit cross-legged on the floor.

"I don't know. I don't know. I guess... I thought that, if Angel was right and the newly dead were acting differently, and that caused the evacuation, then... maybe that meant she'd changed her mind, and she'd come back for a bit, too."

"Changed her mind on... you?"

Monica nodded. "I've always been afraid that I'll slowly start being less... *interesting* to people. Ever since I was little. I have all these—these memories of being a little kid in a hospital bed, surrounded by balloons and presents, and everyone's there—they're telling me how brave I am and how cute I look. It's so exciting and beautiful.

"But then it's like... it's like the novelty wears off, for people? They get so tired of the same thing. And I'm tired, too! I'm tired whenever the same problem comes back, tired of... of weird *rashes* and *body aches* and *meds*. I'm tired of being so *boring*. I'm tired of asking for help. But I want people to do it, anyway. Even if they're so bored they want to scream, I want them to stay behind forever." Her voice cracked; she shuddered.

"I wish she'd left with everyone else. Then I could call it an accident. But if she just died and didn't linger behind... that means that there wasn't anything interesting enough to linger behind for anymore."

"I'm sorry," I repeated. I didn't know what else to say. I fumbled through a couple reassurances, all twee and mindless in the wake of everything, and settled instead for patting her back, like she was a baby needing to get burped. "I...I don't think that's what that means. I think your mom loved you a lot, but...we don't know what makes people stay behind. Maybe she couldn't, or—or she didn't want you to see her fall apart, or she didn't drink enough unfiltered water, or a ton of things."

"Or she wasn't interested in it." The words came out congested, mumbled.

"Or she wasn't interested in it, sure." I shrugged. "But even *if* that's true, we *are* interested in you, Monica. Me and Angel both, here and now. Even when you think you're boring, I want to do the same things over and over with you." I squeezed her shoulder. "And...I think it's messed up that you were raised to believe you have to always be interesting or good enough to justify being in people's lives."

"Isn't that how it works?" she mumbled back. "We study. We work. We do good, interesting, important things. And in return, we're allowed to exist in people's lives."

"Says who? Says what? Why do we always have to *work*?" I cried. "Maybe Angel had a point. Why can't we just *take up space*? Isn't that what we're doing here, learning to be selfish and survive?" My voice echoed off the dark walls. "I don't wanna work hard enough to justify existing. I don't even wanna *work*."

Monica raised her smudged eyebrow. "Ever?"

"Ever." A pause. "Well, maybe a little, just to keep from getting bored. But like, four hours a day, *tops*." I shrugged. "That's my big afterlife bucket list fantasy, Monica. Ain't that sad? I've been thinking all day about what to put in my will. About last rites and...and what I want to tell Mom, and Dad, and Emma, and Eric. What to do before

I die. And I think the answer is...I'd take a nap. And eat a snack. And drive around to nowhere. Boring, slow, unimportant things that aren't worth it." This time, it was my turn to sniffle back tears, even as Monica laughed and I laughed along with.

"Well, dreams do come true, Ian. I drove you to nowhere." Her mask crinkled as she hiccupped. "I'm so sorry. I drove you in circles and wasted hours of your last day here—"

"You didn't, though! You *helped* me." I shifted from a crouch at her side to a more casual sit down. "We were all hoping for it to work out. And...I had fun, stealing a car with you. And wrecking the fountain."

"And getting stabbed?"

"That part, um...less so. But . . ." I pressed a hand to my stomach, to the texture of Band-Aids under my shirt. "It was nice to feel wanted afterward. *Almost* worth it."

Monica went quiet for a while, her knees drawn up to her chest and her arms wrapped around them in a soft hug. After it though, she shifted, and she spoke up.

"You know? Me, too." Then: "I saw you every time you watched us, you know. When my mom and I had picnics."

"You—you did?"

"Mm. I wanted to invite you over, but...I don't know. It's hard to assert myself like that. Easier to say that you'd come over when you were ready." She turned to me, and I saw her smile through the minty fabric of her mask, her cheeks rising up on either side and flushing pink. "I worried after my mom left that I'd never get that chance again. So I'm glad I got to know you now, at least."

I smiled back. And I reached over, slowly, to rest my hand against her own.

"I'm glad, too." I considered, then went on: "And...I'll be glad to keep knowing you, even after I get used to it and you get boring."

She shoved at my shoulder. "*God*, you really are a dork."

"And you're a dumb bitch, I guess." I laughed. "We fit so well, huh?"

"Like a couple of misfits."

"Like a bunch of left-behind rejects."

"Like mismatched socks behind the dryer?"

"Ooh, good one. Like, um . . ." I thought it over. "Like... like when you break eggs to make an omelet?"

"Like two different puzzles made with the same shaped pieces." She laughed again, a nice snorting laugh, and stretched out a leg across the open middle space. It brushed against a sheet of scattered paper, and we both glanced at it, curious. She tipped her flashlight toward it, and I squinted as the text lit up.

Most of the paperwork, spilled out from manila folders and clipboards, seemed like photocopies of the same check-in forms, identical grainy diagrams of human bodies and fill-in-the-blanks marked with *X*s and scratchy handwriting. One in particular caught my attention, mostly for the wobbly circle traced around the diagram's head. Next to it were a couple notes, too scrawly to make out more than a few words here and there.

INTERNAL PAIN – 8 OUT OF 10.
DISORIENTATION, MEMORY LOSS.
SCLERA DISCOLORATION (BLACK/GRAY).
SEMICATATONIC.

I realized with a start that I was looking at the chart—the private medical record—of another dead person.

I froze, torn between pulling away out of some kind of respect... and pushing in deeper to read everything I could.

I'd figured out a lot about the dead by now, in the way you picked up absent facts about ditch flowers or noisy neighbors every time you passed one. I knew Mr. Owens picked blackberries and mumbled to himself in almost the same way he had last year, when he was alive and too stubborn to stay at home. I knew there was a rumor that our English teacher's mom had stayed behind for a solid week and a half, before he'd called in a neighbor to put her down. I knew about decay and bloat.

But I'd never talked to a doctor about any of it. Never heard it filtered through medical terms, never had it made *formal.* I didn't know a dead person's heart rate or blood pressure, or how their MRI scans looked, or how many grams of painkiller they were prescribed after a checkup. I didn't know what the medical textbooks wrote about being dead, in Latin science terms that made it seem all abstract and organized.

Beside me, Monica shifted to her knees, fanning out a band of paperwork like a deck of cards. Dozens of identical diagrams shone up at us in the wobbly flashlight glow, hundreds of scratchy black pen notes. Heads circled. Arms. Chests. Eyes.

> CHEST PAIN.
> HEART PALPITATIONS.
> DISCOLORATION, DISCOLORATION, DISCOLOR., DISCL.
> UNRESPONSIVE.
> HYPERTENSION.
> ISOLATE TO PEDIATRIC WARD (QUARANTINE PROCEDURE).
> REPORT TO NATIONAL RESPONSE CENTER?

"Whoa. There were so many dead people here . . ." she breathed, and I realized she was right. At least every other record seemed like a dead person, more than I'd ever seen wandering around Kittakoop. Dozens of catatonic, unresponsive, *pained* people, their diagrams circled around the eyes and marked with morbid little *X*s.

I checked the dates on top. Most of them were messy and hard to read, but they all seemed similar, with the same chicken scratch 7s marking each month.

"Look. This is just recent ones, too." I pointed, tracing down the fill-in-the-blanks. "No way *this* many people died in Kittakoop and we didn't notice. Is there?"

Were there even enough people in Kittakoop to account for that? I didn't know everyone by name, sure, but I knew my neighbors well enough to know if a pile of them had gone oil-eyed over the summer.

Monica furrowed her brows together, breathing hard behind her mask. "I don't recognize a lot of the names, though. Not even a little." She flipped one of the papers over, checking the back. "So... maybe not a bunch of local deaths, but... transfers from out of town?"

"But why would they all go *here*?" I asked. "There's other hospitals closer to the city. Why not hit up Huntington and get actual care, with MRI machines and stuff?"

Monica went quiet. I watched her glance through papers, her finger tracing softly, almost lovingly across each page.

"I dunno. Dead people have been here for years, so maybe this clinic is the only one used to dealing with them?" she mumbled. "Or they *wanted* to go here . . . ?"

"Wanted to go to *Kittakoop*?"

"Wanted to go *somewhere*, anyway. It started around here. So maybe this is like... home, for them?"

Home.

My head itched and my throat went dry at the idea, the same disorienting *want* I'd felt at the dollar store. I found myself holding my stomach again, brushing pale fingers against Angel's bandage work and the metal edges of the safety pin, to the stitches and raw tissue underneath. To everything that should've killed me so far but hadn't yet, because my body hadn't caught up all the way. Because it kept pushing on like a puppet on a sting, torn apart and stitched back together.

Wanting... what?

"It's in the mountains," that anonymous commenter had said. *"It's calling us home."*

Had dozens of dead out-of-towners wandered here by themselves, full of oil and broken memories, all trying to go back to the Appalachian mountains, to go back *home*?

I thought about the dollar store cashier again, and I wondered if he'd been looking for *home*, too, in those moments before he was all the way gone. He'd been straight rapturous lying there, mouth agape and twitching like a follower speaking in tongues in church, or like a kid having a grand mal seizure on a shopping mall floor.

Black pools. Grasping, grasping. The moment just shy of a revelation, the words on the tips of our tongues, the universe just a thin oil puddle of surface tension away.

I leaned closer, sifting through all those similar intake forms, as if I could find the answer scribbled somewhere between NAME and NOTES. Past copy after copy of the word DISCOLORATION, in increasingly rapid handwriting, more . . .

And I stopped.

On the bottom of one of the sheets, a single note had been scratched out, different from the rest and terrifyingly simple.

~~FLAMMABLE.~~

And then we heard Angel scream.

TEN

Neither of us thought twice; we took off running, past the lobby and down a hallway, Monica's flashlight beam bouncing off walls and casting everything in dancing bursts of yellow glow and searing red afterimages. Floral tiles. Office doorways. Signs and directories. Smoke. So much smoke, harsh as sandpaper in our throats.

The hallway opened up into another reception area, this one with a wider curved desk in front of a wall of wooden mailboxes. Wallpaper patterns flashed by, polka dots in rainbows washed out by Monica's flashlight into vague orangey non-colors. Along one wall I spotted a walleyed Dory the fish, hand-painted, next to a school of goldfish and a blotchy bootleg SpongeBob.

The pediatric ward. I'd been here a hundred times by now. Over there sat the aquarium, burbling with pink coral. Over there, the battered *Highlights* magazines. Over there, the beaded toy Monica and I played with, years ago, tracing wire paths and loop-the-loops.

It smelled like ash. Ash and rubber and a sickly sweet smell, like old ham or spoiled fruit. Our shoes crunched over dirt and debris, grinding into the tile with every step, leaving mottled footprints. Every breath I took came in too warm, too stale, too dry in my lungs.

Still we kept going, ducking around the reception desk and toward a doorway on the right. Toward another hallway, a shorter one this time, with smudged black walls and air so thick our flashlight barely shone through it, its wavering orange light cutting in and out with dust.

In the middle of the hallway, standing rigid, was Angel.

At first she didn't seem too shaken up. She stood hunched as always, quiet as always, distant as always. So I edged forward, holding a hand out to her shoulder.

"Angel!" I called. "It's okay, we're here—"

"Don't touch her, Ian!" Monica shouted, and I froze, my hand inches away.

This close, I could see Angel better and pick out all the little *wrong* details. Like how hard she gripped her backpack strap, and how the tendons in her throat and along her jaw stood out rigid as tent poles.

I raised my hands instead, a wall between us, keeping myself back. Giving her space.

"Okay. Got it. I won't touch you, Angel. Nothing you don't want, promise." I watched her chest, hitching up and down for rabbitlike breaths, and my heart ached. "What happened? Are you okay? Hurt?"

No answer, just that same rapid breathing.

"Angel . . .? Can you hear me?"

Still no answer. She didn't even look at me, too focused on the wall ahead of her, so I tried another angle.

"I... look. I'm sorry, Angel. We shouldn't have chased you off. You were right to be upset. We made a pledge to stick together, no matter what, and we failed you. We didn't listen to you."

Behind me, Monica shifted like she wanted to speak up. But as soon as she moved closer Angel's breath caught, her arm flinching toward her chest, and Monica pulled back away. I kept my hands up, a protective barrier between them.

"Don't worry, she won't yell at you anymore. I promise. No one's fighting, and no one's mad at you." I laughed a little. "This must be really overwhelming, huh? I get it. *Trust me*, I do. But you're safe with us. So we can take a couple deep breaths together, if that's okay?"

I breathed in, even though the air here tasted like salt and left a filmy residue against the back of my teeth. My eyes watered and my lungs twitched with the urge to cough, an urge I shoved down. Steady breathing, never mind the smoke. In and out.

Angel didn't answer or move, but I swore I saw her breathing slow down a little, from a panicked hitching to a steadier draw. Or maybe I just wanted it to work? Either way, I pushed on.

"Hey, yeah. Good job, Angel. Thanks for that. Are you hurt anywhere? Don't gotta say so. Just... maybe shake your head or nod?"

For several long, slow seconds, Angel didn't move. Then, barely a twitch, she shook her head. Not hurt, and I felt that tension in my gut ease up a notch.

"Good. I'm glad you're okay. Thanks for letting me know." I glanced down to my jacket, thin purple fabric lined with edgy iron-on patches—the same jacket Angel had leaned against in the truck, the same one she'd clung to when we climbed out together, standing too close.

I held out an arm. "You can hold on to my jacket if you want. It's a little dirty, but still pretty soft. And the patches are kinda fun to touch."

Again, that long delay in any response. I waited it out, giving Angel time and space to process.

And so, after a beat, Angel reached out, a pale and shaky little hand half hidden in the oversized folds of her own army jacket. She squeezed at the hem of my jacket, running a thumb up and down the wears in the hem.

"Hey, yeah. Nice, ain't it? I like it a lot, too."

She mumbled something, but I couldn't make out the words. I blinked, moving in closer to listen.

"Startled me," she muttered, her voice raspy with smoke. "Should have prepared. I suspected it would be bad. Didn't expect the smell. The feel. I hate it—" She coughed, hard, bending forward and hacking lines of gray drool onto the floor, her hand squeezing tight against my sleeve.

I peered over, despite everything in me saying not to.

In the mixed light of both flashlights, bleeding yellow-white, I could make out a doorway in the middle of the burned-out hallway, right where the smoke hung thickest. Smoke billowed out of the cracks in plumes, smoldering and over-warm.

That word on the intake report itched in my head, repeating itself over and over. FLAMMABLE. FLAMMABLE.

Dead people are full of oil. It replaces their blood and seeps from their eyes.

Dead people are flammable.

My head itched so much. I reached a hand out, pressing it against the door, against hot wood grain that smudged like charcoal against my fingers and smelled like burning people.

How many dead people had been taken into this hospital over the past month? Dozens and dozens from across the county area, sent back to their source, back *home*, like damaged mail.

Monica hadn't recognized any names on the intake lists, but I hadn't checked them, and it scared me now. What if I looked inside this room and I found burnt pieces of Mom and Dad and Emma, the same clothes they'd worn this morning all tattered and ruined on the floor? What if I saw Monica's mom, her picnic all laid out pretty on the tile, waiting for me to join in? What if I saw Mr. Owens there, dredged up from the lake, and he stared at me and he hated me so much because we'd killed him for being a corpse and now I was a corpse but I wanted to keep on surviving?

Angel clung to my jacket sleeve, but she didn't tug me away. Monica, either; she lurked farther back, her face pale and her mask smudged with ash, and I appreciated them both for that. After too many times of being abandoned or hurt for some greater good, out here we could make all our own bad decisions.

I pushed open the door. It moved slow, scuffing against the floor and cracking on its broken hinges, shoving against something *heavy*, scattering dust and clumps of wafting ash, and I looked forward and—

I didn't remember walking inside. I blinked, and I found myself in the doorway, and as I looked I saw everything but the bodies: I saw more messy wall paintings of seaweed and turtles, bug-eyed and grinning, and I saw a long countertop with a metal sink dug into it and cupboards with laminated posters telling me to get my flu shot and sign up for the Young Adult Medical Care Program, and I saw crumbled black walls and pieces of support beams smoldering with red embers and heat ripples, and over it all I saw a big gap in the ceiling and I saw the night sky, cloudy and gray with smoke but still so wide and so nice—

Then I saw the bodies, dozens of people piled up on one another like old Barbie dolls scattered in the dirty bottom of a plastic tub at a garage sale, their limbs bent and their hair singed off and their faces melted back into toothy smiles—

And I saw the sky again, overhead, winking stars and clean air, with the wispy peaks of mountains just a couple miles ahead, so distant and so lovely—

And I saw everyone piled up against the door, a bottleneck of people scrambling to get out, limbs shriveled and darkened by the heat, but still surprisingly whole in odd ways, in the yellow scrap of a dress, in a clump of frizzled hair, in the white line of a half-lit cigarette settled in the grooves between wrinkled fingers, my bad, sorry, old habit, and habits are all we have left—

I saw the sky and kept looking at it, staring at it, focusing anywhere else—

And I saw the milk-bright eyes of dozens of dead-all-the-way people staring up at me, people who'd died together, dead enough to come here but aware enough to scream in pain and rapture as the oil in their eyes and in their bones caught fire, too fast and too bright, a searing catastrophe of too many *flammable* people crammed into one small quarantine room, so close and so far from *something, something, SOMETHING*—

My throat itched. I bent over and threw up a mouthful of thick black gunk, splattering onto the tiles. My vision went dark and *viscous* somehow, hazy, like looking at the world through a rainbow-slick filter, and through that filter the pool of gunk at my feet seemed like it was moving, twitching in on itself, and I heard a sound like a hundred scratching insects in the back of my head, a mass of something growing, grasping at my bones, and it smelled like charcoal and it tasted like rotten fruit. I stumbled back against the doorway, away from the embers and the smoke and the warmth and everything that might catch fire to a body full of gasoline.

Everything felt too bright, a seizure through the eyes of a dead person. I heaved again, another mouthful of the same sickly saturated rainbows I saw all around me, and then Angel and Monica were there, pulling me back out, and I wanted to scream at them in holy tongues, scream about *something*, jamming everything I saw into words too impossibly small for it, like a million people speaking together into screaming noise, like the universe crammed into a single dying body, like a seizure lighting up every part of the brain at once, like a cigarette spark in a room full of oil, and it all blurred together into searing whites and screaming nonsense and everything so much, I couldn't breathe or hear or see—

And finally, after a couple seconds and a hundred years, it all went soothingly dark.

I dreamed of the whispering voices of mountains.

Cracked cliffside faces, their age carved in jagged lines and outcroppings of rubble. Dry scrubgrass, clinging to the gaps between rocks, leeching thin air and scraps of rainwater. Fog wafting along the river and leaving cool dew in its wake, feeding the grass of rolling hills below. Slow, peaceful, open.

I dreamed of hiking up a path with Eric, our coats heavy and backpacks heavier, our breath swirling clouds in front of us and crisp in our throats. We hopped from rock to rock, laughing every time our boots slid or our arms pinwheeled, confident and invincible. Every time I stumbled, he reached out to catch me, and we climbed up together hand in gloved hand.

And when we hit the highest point we could reach, when the rocks got too steep and the hiking path trailed off, we looked back over the side to a beautiful view. Sunlight winked between mountain peaks, in and out, and the clouds cast long shadows across the landscape. I squinted up at them, a hand over my eyes, and the sky around them shone clear and infinite. As I reached toward it, my fingertips traced in glowing blue, I felt closer than ever to home.

On another mountain to the east of us, the Green Bank Observatory kept working away. Its telescope turned on grinding motors, pointed high, whispering lines of messages from everyone on Earth. *We're here. We exist. We're very tired and the world is cold and cruel. Where are you? Please say something back. Please give us something to reach for out there.*

And the sky reached back down, caressing it with gentle fingers, as large as stars and as small as a mote in the water, and it whispered back.

I'm here. Come home, love. Sleep, love.

I looked back. Eric was gone, but in his place sat a pile of dead people, all lying on top of one another with arms spread and smiles wide. Out-of-towners, with frizzy hair and wheelchairs and teeth shining, and out here they didn't seem so burnt. Here they seemed like family, all of us with the same eyes and same bones and the same itch inside us to climb as high as possible and drop our tired bodies into the mass at the very top.

To leave everything behind.

Friends. Family. Home. The skin on our bones and the meat in between. At the top of the mountain, we'd dissolve into rainbows glittering on oil and slip back into the water, trickling down into the mouths of a hundred unborn souls who'd die someday and wake up with an itch to climb mountain-ward.

Wasn't that something beautiful? To be a part of something so complete, so cyclical, as formlessly ideal as a martyr? We'd never again do anything as human as hurt, not in a sky as dark and infinite and writhing with life as a mountain of ants. In heaven, everyone gets what they want.

But when I stepped forward, my teeth ached and my stomach hurt, and neither of them tasted like heaven. They tasted like dirt, and blood, and the sickly feral rush of being alive. They tasted like all the things that didn't belong in heavens, grit between my molars and on the back of my throat.

And when the sky got close enough to touch me, I bit it.

ELEVEN

I snapped awake with a start as my teeth clacked together, jarring enough to knock me out of it.

What happened? I squinted around, dazed, and my first half-coherent thought was that I'd ended up in Emma's room and it'd gotten somehow smaller. I could feel thin mattress cushions underneath me and see the hazy glow of string lights—like the ones she hung over her bedposts, next to posters of stern-eyed anime boys—but they hung too low, too far away. The walls looked wrinkled and dark, edged with white PVC pipes and smelling faintly like exhaust.

I sat up, my head swimming and my stomach aching at the motion, the stale taste of oil in my mouth. My head just about brushed that ceiling, and I realized with a start that it was a tarp, stretched overhead.

The pickup truck. Right. Monica had mentioned grabbing some pipe to hang up the tarp. Which meant—

To my right, I saw Monica, sitting cross-legged in one corner with a pile of plastic wrappers and bottles in her lap. The entire floor of the pickup bed had been lined with mattress foam, I noticed, turning it into a cozy little sitting space scattered with backpacks and cans. She'd changed clothes, ditching the daytime horse shirt and jeans for a black T-shirt and baggy purple sweatpants, her hair wrapped in a satiny cap that smelled like coconut.

As I caught her eye, she jumped, startled, then gave a tired smile.

She wasn't wearing her mask in here, so I saw a wink of teeth and the smudged dark lines where the straps had worn against her skin.

"Ian," she sighed. "You're awake." Then, less certainly: "How're you... feeling?"

An unspoken question sat in the middle of that: *Are you still you?*

I thought it over, pressing a hand to the back of my head, then to my bandaged stomach. They tingled, somehow both numb and sore, and I shook my head. In a way, it felt like any other seizure—same aches, same disorientation, same stretch of time, suddenly gone. Almost like normal.

"Gross. But still here, at least?"

And she smiled back for real this time, all the way up to her eyes. "Good. Sometimes that's the best we can ask for." She brushed crumbs off her lap, dusting them neatly into a plastic bag with an empty can and a handful of wrappers.

Another glance around, and this time I saw the truck bed for what it was. How she'd jammed pipes along the bed's sides, propping up the tarp like a tent overhead, one with battery-powered lights hung along its edges by lines of dangling thumbtacks. The lights cast everything in a soft glow. Made it feel outright cozy in a Pinteresty way.

But still... I looked back and forth, frowning.

"Where's Angel?" The closest I could see was her backpack, leaning against the truck cab, and a pair of dusty boots.

"She's on the roof. She . . ." Monica trailed off. "She helped drag you out of that place, and set all this up, but afterward... I think she needed space." A small smile. "I don't blame her."

"I don't blame *you*, either. Do you mind if I check on her?"

"Mm-mm. Take this with you?" Monica held out a plastic vacuum-sealed baggie, labeled CHILI MAC in blocky military font. "Sometimes I think she forgets she needs to eat, too."

"Sure. Dehydrated macaroni?" I took it and nearly dropped it;

it felt not just warm but *hot*, enough to waft steam and the scent of processed cheese. I peeked under the seal flap and saw a medley of dew-coated plastic bags with stark black labels: MACARONI & CHILI SAUCE, SALTINE CRACKER, FRUIT JERKY, COOKIE.

"It's an MRE, apparently. Military rations. Angel found them." Pause. "I don't know where."

I couldn't think of anywhere Angel might've found them around here; all I could picture was a mail-order box, picked up from her home—wherever it was—and crammed into her school locker.

Monica must've noticed me looking at the bag, because she pushed on.

"Angel told me about you. About the... *diet* she's been suggesting, to keep you alive longer."

I dropped the MRE. It rustled against the truck bed, metal and plastic. "I-I'm sorry, I haven't been—I wouldn't hurt anyone, I *haven't*, other than the dollar store guy and there wasn't any way to save him left, s-so—"

"It's okay. I get it, Ian." She smiled, but there was something heavier than it behind her eyes. "It would happen on the farm, sometimes. If one of the chickens got killed or hurt... or even if a chicken got its own injury... we'd have to take them away from the others. Otherwise they'd peck and peck at the wounds, trying to eat it. I used to yell at them for it, but... in the end, it's just them being what they are.

"Even if something's messed up or creepy... I want it to live. I want *us* to live. I think... I think I'd even eat people, too, if I had to. I'd be gross and hungry and everything. So... I get it."

I watched her for a while, with no idea what to say, what to do, other than pick up the MRE and hold it close as the ugly truth settled between us.

It was cozy, in a messed-up way.

"I like getting to know the gross side of us," I said at last. And I pushed my way out, lifting a tarp edge and slipping underneath into the world.

Outside, without those glowing string lights or tarp shelter, the shock of nightfall hit me hard. It'd been so summer-warm this morning, but with the sun gone and the sky cloudy-dark overhead, the air tasted cold and wet.

It looked like it might rain soon. I couldn't decide if that meant good or bad: if it'd kill off the smoke and embers from the hospital, or if it'd just send them swirling into the river and lakes, to mix with whatever runoff had already trailed from the mountains.

Mountains. I closed my eyes and could just about see rocky peaks and a writhing sky overhead, a dozen dead people looking up at heaven. But not well, not clearly; it already seemed dreamy, the details and edges blurring away, and I let them go.

Monica and Angel had moved the truck, I noticed. Pulled it farther down the parking lot and away from the smoldering remains, but I could still smell smoke and feel wafts of toasty air when the wind shifted. I traced those smoke clouds up, along the truck's rusted sides and to the roof of the cab... where I saw Angel.

She sat hunched forward, burrowed in her oversized coat like a sleepy bird—but as soon as I stepped closer, my shoes crunching over rocks, her head whipped toward me, alert, and I held up my hands, MRE dangling from my fingers like a white flag.

"Hey, Angel," I called. "Can I come up?"

Once she saw me—once she *heard* me, still speaking words and having thoughts like a living person—she relaxed, focusing back on the horizon. I took that as permission.

Hmm. I glanced at the truck's dented bumper, its arched wheel wells. There wasn't, exactly, a clear path *up*.

I edged toward the front instead, to the slope of the engine cover. It took a few tries—the MRE gripped between my teeth, fingers clinging to metal—but I managed to pull myself up, then scramble over the windshield and onto the cab roof.

We sat for a while in silence, taking in the view.

Up here, the hospital didn't seem so tall and professional—it stood level with lines of trees, dwarfed by hills and mountains above, its burnt chunk nothing more than a smudge in the middle of miles of sprawling greenery. I even spotted a red-tinged paper soda cup, buried in Angel's lap under the coat, like she'd brought movie theater snacks to watch it burn. Like it could be entertaining and harmless from here.

"Hey, uh . . ." I fumbled, unsure how to start. "Thanks for helping me out of there. And... I'm sorry."

"For what?" she asked.

I shrugged. For fainting. Yelling at her. The end of the world. All of it.

"I don't know." Below us, the hospital smoldered on. "So, me and Monica found a lot of interesting notes. Apparently this hospital was, like, *the* place to send mostly dead people? All the intake forms were for dead guys. Glad the fire didn't spread to those, at least."

"It wouldn't have. Too damp. Bodies are at least seventy percent water. Even decaying, they don't make good kindling for long."

"Decaying and full of oil instead of blood, though?"

"Even then." She hummed under her breath. "Would make a hell of an incident to report, though, I suppose."

"Yeah." I frowned as the mental image settled in. "You think... is that what triggered the evacuation? A bunch of firefighters show up, see a way-too-crowded hospital full of people who all just sorta... spontaneously combusted and burned all their blood off? I know if I was a firefighter seeing that, I'd be *freaked*."

Angel nodded, and I swore a flicker of pride danced across her neutral face. "Most likely. Especially if a number of victims were outsiders. Their families would have wanted answers. No one would accept that Kittakoop is just like this. Gathering people up for emergency testing is the next logical step."

"Before somewhere else explodes."

"Mmhmm."

It sounded so simple, coming from her monotone voice. I could even imagine the headlines: ***200 PEOPLE FATALLY COMBUST IN A SMALL TOWN HOSPITAL, MYSTERY BLOOD ILLNESS TERRIFIES COMMUNITY, IS YOUR FAMILY NEXT?!***

I shuddered. Angel reached out, squeezing part of my jacket. I lifted my arm and she pulled closer, pressing against my side. I wasn't sure how much of it was her clumsy attempt at a hug and how much was her trying to smother herself in as much jacket texture as possible. Maybe both. Didn't matter.

"I'm sorry you had to see all those bodies," I muttered.

"You saw them, too."

"And I fainted. Didn't work out too well."

"That part was inconvenient. You're heavy to drag."

"Sorry."

"Stop saying sorry."

"Sor—" I made a face, then clamped my mouth shut.

We sat there for a while again, not talking. Watching the hospital burn. Finally, Angel spoke up.

"It smells good, doesn't it?"

"What? *No.*" I grimaced... then reconsidered, taking a dainty little sniff. Up here, away from the worst of the burnt parts and the rubbery stench of melting things... it really did smell good, kind of. Like wood-smoke and ham, sweet and full. "It... yeah. It does. Is that... because of what I am?"

"No. A barbecue smells like a barbecue. Here." She grasped the cup, holding it out to me to juggle awkwardly in my lap with the cooling MRE.

"Where did you find soda in—"

"It's people."

I froze. The soda cup sat heavy and tepid-cool in my hands. Its cute little striped straw smelled like charcoal and blood.

"No, Angel."

"You need to eat to stay alive longer." Angel glared at the tree line, unblinking. "Monica said you at least wouldn't want to look at it. So I found a cup in the break room."

"I don't want—" I stopped. "Wait. You... went back in for me?"

"Obviously."

"But it terrified you."

"Yes."

I didn't have an argument for that. At least, not one that wouldn't seem—of all things—ungrateful. All I had was the MRE, and I grasped it as a distraction. "Okay, but... you gotta eat, too, Angel. Monica wanted you to have this." I handed it over, but she just looked at it with a raised eyebrow.

"That's mine."

"Er, yeah, it is."

"You're attempting to gift me my own item. Why?"

"Okay, when you say it like *that*, it sounds weird. You don't *have* to eat it, just—" I blushed, hard. "Know that she cares about you. Me, too. We don't want you to forget to eat. Or something?"

"You're very strange, Ian."

"Yeah, well. I'm dead, so I'm allowed to be." I gestured to the cup like it explained everything.

"And you mention being dead a lot."

"It's still weird for me! Kind of an important change. I'm thinking about it a lot." I tapped at the cup. "I appreciate you trying, but this *doesn't help*."

"I can take it back."

"No, no. I'm grateful for it... I guess. It's just... a lot to think about."

"Oh." She hesitated... then grasped the MRE, pulling it into her lap and smothering it somewhere beneath the massive folds of her coat. Absorbed it, maybe, in the way an alien might absorb nutrients.

No, not an alien. I watched her, and for the first time since we'd met I really tried to *see* her, as a person—her ruler-straight hair, her intense brown eyes, her small nose and hands. A kid like us, younger than us, even, with unbrushed hair and short, chewed nails and bad posture.

For all her military bravado and brutal truth facts, she was just a shaken little kid doing her best.

"Angel . . ." I breathed, in and out. "Will you do me a favor, and let me know how you're doing?"

"Fine," she started, automatically.

"Wait, let me finish? What I mean is... I can't always tell. I almost messed up really bad, back there, when I tried to touch you. You always seem like you're handling this so well—like you always know how to survive—but I think that sometimes that means I assume you can handle anything. And I don't want to assume that for you." I tried a smile. "So do me a favor? If you need anything or aren't doing well, let me know, and I'll try to help?"

She raised an eyebrow again, and I couldn't blame her; that ramble didn't make sense even to my own ears. But then she smiled back, and I let myself relax an inch.

"Very well. I'm doing fine right now, Ian." She tilted her head back, letting the breeze rustle her bangs. "I don't want to talk to Monica right now. She's... well-meaning. Pretty. Organized. Frustrated with me. Like a teacher. But otherwise it's quiet and slow, and I don't have to learn anything, and I like it."

"Yeah... it is, huh?" I tilted my own head back, watching the clouds roll by. "It's weird to think about, for me. Everything's been so rapid-fire chaos since I woke up. The end of the world happened *today.*" I closed my eyes. "But other times...I look outside and I see the cars still parked and the lights all off, and it still feels like this is the longest day in the world, but...in a slower, better way."

"Mmhmm." She kept her eyes closed. Her face, lit by faint moonlight between clouds, shone soft and round and pale as a coin. "I wasn't able to breathe before this. My lungs were too large. Like an ancient god, thousands of years old and buried underground, while everything grew and buzzed over top of it."

"An ancient god?"

"Yes. Everything overhead was noise and movement and progress and quick, rapid breaths of not enough air. But now I can pull it all into my lungs, and hold it for days, and let it out, and it won't be different."

"Huh. That makes sense. Weirdly. Not a lot of stimuli in an empty town." The wind picked up, rustling the tree line. "My parents wanted that for me. They wanted me and my sister to grow up in a town without any flashing lights or noises that could fry our brains. They uprooted everything they ever knew, their jobs and friends and everything, and I've felt like I owe them ever since. But...they're right, it's cozier out here."

"It's nice." She went quiet, then, softly: "I shouldn't tell her. It would be hurtful. But I wish my dad had died instead of Monica's mom. It... frustrates me that you're both so obsessed with not being abandoned. I don't understand it. Being abandoned like this is wonderful, I think."

I stared at her, trying to process that. My gut instinct was to defend myself, but I shoved that down, trying to see the world as she did. Trying to coax the real meaning out of her words, like a stray pup lured out by handfuls of food.

"Yeah? What was your dad like?"

"Rude." I waited, giving her space, and she went on. "Discontent with most things. Pollution, climate, greed. Obsessed with the end of days. He was arrested several times. Labeled antisocial. Given an option of a hospital or a prison. He chose the hospital. It seemed safer."

"Was it?"

She considered. "In some ways. It gave him quiet. But it lasted so long. Years. When he got out… everything was different. Louder. Everyone had cell phones and internet, computers. Even Mom. And he distrusted all of it. Too new, too different, too constant. Took me away from Mom, to the countryside. Raised me to be vigilant. To stay alive without any of those. To prepare for the end, when the towers would go down and everyone on their cell phones would die."

"Jesus."

"Yes. There was a lot of talk of Jesus." She hunched forward harder. "And now it's the end, and he's gone, but the other survivors have phones and talk like the kids at school." A pause. "But at least it's quieter."

"It is. And… even if I'm just a school kid with a phone, I'm glad you're here instead of him." I didn't know what else to say to help—but maybe I didn't need to. Maybe Angel didn't need talking and noise and social graces. She liked the quiet, so maybe it was enough to sit here with her, covered in nice textures, and watch the sky.

So we did.

With only God knew how many hours left to be alive, with so much left unsaid and undone and Eric somewhere out there, I chose to take a while and sit with Angel in the quiet. I drank a warm slurry of charcoal and other more coppery tastes I refused to think about, and once again it tasted like *being alive*, like an electric warmth in my stomach keeping everything going a little while longer. Angel chewed at her MRE, plastic silverware scuffing against the bag and artificial cheese scent wafting around her. And overhead the clouds gathered and started to sprinkle a thin, fine rain, washing out the smoke and leaving the air clean around us.

TWELVE

At some point the rain picked up and we climbed back down from the roof, skidding along slick metal and onto the damp-speckled asphalt. Angel hesitated in front of the tarped pickup back, Monica's string lights glowing within, but I offered her a jacket sleeve again.

"Only if you're ready," I muttered. "We can camp in the cab, too, or back in the waiting room. Your choice."

Neither of those seemed like the best option—the cab too cramped and the hospital waiting room thick with smoke and trauma—so I bit back a sigh of relief when Angel shook her head and took the first step toward the tarp.

Inside, Monica looked already half asleep, wrapped in a tangled cotton blanket, but she perked up to see us, and Angel managed a nod back.

"Thank you for the food," Angel said with that slight emotional lilt to her voice that I recognized as being from a recited line, maybe from some textbook somewhere. *1001 Common Socializing Phrases.*

Monica shifted to give us more space. "Of course. Make yourself comfy."

She dug around our supplies, passing us twin pairs of pajamas in plastic grocery baggies. Deeper in the bags, I saw, were toothbrushes, mouthwash bottles, deodorant... whole kits of nighttime hygiene for the traveler without a real bathroom to use.

Monica really was the most organized of all of us.

We all took turns outside, peeing behind trees and wiping the smoke off our skin with packs of acidic wet wipes. The hospital probably had showers—real ones, with shampoo bars and hot city water pumped in—but we never brought up going back. It felt cleaner to stand in the rain. Safer.

I could still taste sickly sweet oil and dust in the back of my throat, mixed with charcoal and blood. I tried mouthwash, and a half bottle of water that settled dizzily in my battered stomach but tasted better than dead people.

When I came back in, I was both surprised and not to find Angel wearing my jacket, her usual army one shoved into our growing corner pile of dirty clothes. She waved at me, the sleeve dangling off her hand, and I laughed back.

"Nice look."

"It's yours," she said.

"I figured that part. You can keep it, if you want. It suits you." I handed my bag back to Monica. "Thanks for these. Brushing my teeth helped a lot more than I thought, actually."

"You're welcome." She'd scrubbed at her face, I noticed, that careful makeup worn away for the night, her hair tucked back in a scrunchy satin cap. "I told you, looking good is vital for mental health."

"You weren't wrong! Guess I'll have to try the eyeliner next time."

"I'll hold you to that."

We kept chatting, huddled together against the dark. At some point we fell asleep, all piled over one another in a mess of limbs and backpacks and that shared cotton blanket, the string lights still glowing overhead.

Or... Monica and Angel fell asleep, anyway. I drifted through a dozen half-awake, fitful dreams instead, snapping in and out of awareness.

In one, I fell into the fountain water and sank, farther and farther, loose change glittering past and synth music warbling overhead, layered over a voice crackling **"THIS IS A TEST OF THE EMERGENCY BROADCAST SYSTEM."** I drifted through deep blue and winking metal until they turned into sky and starlight, until I felt something around me, grasping close and whispering, *come home, love.*

In another, I was at the dollar store with Eric, digging through the freezers past mounds of icy fish to pick out something for dinner. But all the fish were wrong, with black eyes and tumor growths and rotting fins, and when I tried to ask the clerk what was up, I choked on gunk in my mouth and found pieces of rebar sticking out of my stomach, all the blood and bits of me draining out of the holes, and no matter how hard I tried, I couldn't gather it all back in. He laughed at me in Mr. Owens's waterlogged voice, cackling, *Gonna need a bigger filter than the one in your sink for what's pouring down the mountains these days, boy!*

In another, I was back in that pediatric office with all the other dead people, settled in a beautiful picnic, but when I turned back to the door I found it locked behind me, Angel and Monica staring through the glass window as I yanked at it, as I screamed for them to let me out, as behind me all those bodies rustled and began to move. . . .

I finally snapped awake for good, shuddering in dry, heaving breaths and sitting up from the little blanket nest between Monica's side and Angel's back. The dreams faded, blurring into half-memories, but their seasick dizziness remained, and I burped up sour bile with it.

I couldn't stay here. The truck bed felt *cozy* earlier tonight and *claustrophobic* now, with stale kerosene air. I couldn't shake that twitchy restlessness in my legs, either—telling me to keep moving, to search for help somewhere else, *hurry,* reminding me that I was now a couple minutes closer to gone-for-real, and hey, what was I doing wasting time *sleeping*, anyway?

So I pressed down against the mattress pad, sliding out into the world.

Outside, the sky still seemed cloudy and grayish—tinged with all the smoke we didn't see in the dark—but underneath that it'd gone pinkish and thin with morning light. I squinted up at it, at the silhouettes of trees against that gray-pink glow, and listened to warblers chirp until my vision adjusted.

A new day. Despite everything, I had at least one more day left to exist.

The asphalt pressed cold and rough against my socks. I reached back, fishing out my sneakers from beneath a pile of clothes. Angel didn't stir, curled up in a ball in maybe the first safe-feeling place she'd ever had, but Monica shifted, hand stretching over the space I'd left, and I promised myself to come back soon.

And I started walking. I tucked my hands deep into the pockets of those hand-me-down sweatpants, a size too big and gathered in folds at my ankles, and I hunched against the cold.

The hospital was uphill a ways from Main Street, separated by a winding entryway and lines of brick, but with us parked so far from the building, it didn't take long for me to shortcut across swaths of damp wildgrass and down straight to the road.

Technically, this part of town wasn't Kittakoop anymore—this far out probably crossed into Deepwell or Snow Hill—but I still considered it home enough to be eerie when I saw it empty now. I still recognized most of the parts: a long office building with a dozen beige pillars, a wood-paneled liquor store with lottery numbers across the front door, a colonial brick square with Civil War figurines and wrinkled flags across the windowsill.

But they refused to fit together. Not with the streets empty, the lights out, the insides dark. Buildings, but not a street. A place, but not a town. Pieces, but not a puzzle.

I stared at each one as I passed, engraving them into my memory down to the brick. Down to each dull metal figurine and liquor brand, and if I couldn't recite them when I looked away, I tried again and again.

I didn't want to forget anything. I wanted to gather up everything I knew and pour it into a box, locked up tight. How the town looked when it was full. How the weather felt, thin mountain air and cold dew. The faces of my mom and dad and sister and crush. The whole world, seen and recorded and wrapped up in a tiny box where none of it could leak out when I wasn't looking.

But that wasn't possible, was it? It leaked out faster than I could shove it back, and I missed so many little bits. I remembered the brands in the liquor store window, but when I asked myself *what color, though? What shape? What size?* I couldn't say for sure.

What if it caught on fire like the hospital did, and the owner came back and I was the only one who could tell him what it'd looked like, help him put it back like it was, but I couldn't answer because I'd forgotten?

What did my little sister's face look like?

What did my dad's voice sound like?

What else had leaked out when I wasn't thinking about it?

I couldn't hold everything at once, and it scared me to think about how much might not come back when I called, sprinting off to freedom like wild dogs.

Just past the colonial building, lined up in rows in parking spaces, I passed several cars, mostly beat-'em-up trucks with cigarette boxes and hunter camouflage on the seats. Two stood out: twin white pickups, a little dusty but still better made than any of the rest. One with stacks of wiring against the front window, and one with a rounded tank and ladder hooked onto the back. Both smelled like river water and chlorine.

A patrol truck and a water truck, taken from up by the Quiet Zone and left to rest here. I couldn't see anyone inside, no one up gathering water samples in the middle of the night, but I glared at them, anyway.

"Still running tests, huh?" I asked. "Bet it's great data, getting to find out how everyone in Nowhere Town reacts to the newest mutation in being dead. Especially the weirdos with epilepsy or autism or chronic pain. Gotta know *that* before bringing it up to real people."

No answer. If there was some secret recording software in either truck, it didn't sound an alarm at me calling it out. No anti-tampering guns slid out of their side panels, and no agent crackled over the speakers to compliment me on figuring it out. I glared, anyway.

"I went to the hospital, you know," I said. "I did everything right. As soon as I noticed I died, I went just like everyone else, so I could get checked in and examined like usual, and it would make sense. And you know what? There was *no one there.* Some guy lit a cigarette in a room full of gasoline, and now it's empty and the whole town's been evacuated. So what am I supposed to do *now*?" My voice cracked. "I did everything right! *What am I supposed to do now?*"

No answer.

Both sat there, stupid and bland and dead in a town full of stupid, bland, dead things, and I sighed, settling down beside them.

"Or maybe you don't know," I muttered.

Maybe they weren't listening. Maybe that was the dark truth of it. It was easy to believe in a conspiracy of hyper-smart listening devices experimenting on humans for a big master plan. Fun, even.

Harder to swallow that those devices were run by a bunch of

normal people who didn't know what to do with the piles of data they spat out.

Kittakoop was real small, for a town. I'd met the mayor a time or two before, usually at the same Food Lion that Dad and I went to on weekends. I'd once seen him drop a whole bag of grapes after trying to grab it from the bottom, and Dad laughed so hard he'd called him Grape Man during the next election.

So maybe that's what happened with the evacuation, and with the Quiet Zone, and with the dead people. Maybe some guy or girl in a naval base wrote a zero instead of an *O* and maybe their supply person bought a different sealant because their usual brand ran out, and maybe a sample that was supposed to go in recycling went down the sink instead and into the river.

Maybe everyone involved thought they were doing their best, but someone grabbed a bag on the wrong end, and the next person didn't know the bag was upside down, and the next person thought it was supposed to be upside down to begin with, and everybody dropped it at the same time, and it cracked open like an egg. And maybe even the thing that hatched from it just wanted to go home and eat, somewhere up the river and on the mountain top.

Maybe none of it was supposed to be so hurtful and lonely and fatal.

Who was I supposed to blame *then*?

What was I supposed to do with myself *then*?

I closed my eyes, letting the thin warmth of sunrise settle into me and the sun bloom red across my eyelids. I listened to the sound of birds twittering at each other, whooping and singing, and the heavy silence of an empty town underneath. . . .

. . . Or, mostly silent. If I turned my head to the side, I swore I could hear something else. Music?

Yeah, definitely music. Swishy, elegant ballroom music, full of orchestral strings and grand piano. It rolled over the hills behind me, echoing in the thin air.

Who'd be listening to music out here? Couldn't be Angel and Monica, still asleep back in the truck. And Eric wasn't a fan of classical, least not enough to blare it for the world to hear.

So, someone else.

Maybe someone who could help?

I blinked and found myself standing up again, walking toward the source. Across the empty street, between buildings, sneakers rustling over weeds and dandelion fluff, drawn like a duck on a string to the sound.

Up a hill, down again, through a copse of trees, and now I could see lights glowing in the distance, all kinds: portable work lights glaring through grated mesh screens, flashlights scattered in the grass, fairy lights—like the kind Monica and Angel hung up—woven through the tree branches. A festival of lights, glittering pretty in the sunrise glow like stars.

And between them I swore I could see flickers of *people*, moving, talking, dancing together. A dozen silhouettes, their muffled voices bleeding beneath the music in a steady rumble.

I pressed a hand to my mouth.

People. Other people.

And then I was running, head pounding and lungs rasping, feet skidding against the dirt, a graceless stumble-rush downhill toward *people*, toward the sound of laughter and chatter and everything I hadn't realized I'd missed so much until I heard it again—I staggered into the circle of lights and swung my arms to catch myself, brushing against someone's flannel shirt sleeve, someone *real*, someone *safe*, and he turned and smiled at me, all burly arms and scruffy beard—

And shiny black eyes.

A dead man.

As I caught myself, I saw maybe seven other people in the circle, all dead: a blond woman with a bobbed can-I-speak-to-your-manager haircut, a little boy in a monster truck T-shirt, a middle-aged politician in a starched blue suit, others bobbing and weaving in the back. All of them strangers, all of them dead.

All of them dancing and laughing and talking together like living people, anyway.

"So I said to Jim, I said, who does he think he is, anyway—"

"I wanna watch *Paw Patrol*, can we watch *Paw Patrol*, I wanna—"

"We have a special on designer jeans today—"

"What? No way. You're kidding—"

I couldn't tell if they were talking *with* one another or *at* one another. It all blended together in a mess of laughing noise, party babble echoing between bars of music.

None of these people looked like they'd come back from an evacuation, ready to set everything right again and fix me.

But at the same time, I didn't feel disappointed for it. The music and the conversation blended together into a steady hum, and that hum whispered, *we're here, child. You've been so afraid of dying in an empty town. Of not knowing what to do, what to expect, what comes after. You've been holding that weight for so long, haven't you? Let us carry it with you for a bit. We're all dead, here, and it's not so bad.*

So, desperate to be included, I did. I stepped forward, slower now, and they accepted me into their group, making room for me to stand on the grass and sway along. A woman laughed, trailing the edges of her skirt in a twirl, and I laughed along with, and I wondered if this was how every dead person in that hospital had felt before the fire—if they'd all gone to the same place not to look for something, but just for the relief of not being alone while our bodies and minds fell apart. Of not being the only dead person in the room.

Sure, Monica and Angel were caring and supportive, and I loved them. But around all the other dead people, it didn't feel so bad to die. To forget. Everything in me would fade, but it would blend into that pleasant noise, and the music would continue long after I was gone.

One of them spoke to me and I nodded, speaking back, though I couldn't remember what I said, even as I felt it still buzzing in my throat. The music drowned it all out. She grasped my hand with her swollen one and a finger fell off, oozing oil from the wound that smeared across our fingers and bound us together. We traced a circle around the group, and as my eyes adjusted I picked out every individual dancer—the little boy, the burly man, the old lady. And someone else in a faded red jacket, hood up and hunched in on themself, like . . .

Everything slowed down as I drifted to a stop. Red fabric seared across my eyes, and the music shifted—from classical to something poppier, more distorted, something that echoed through fountain water as I drowned.

". . . Eric?"

He didn't turn, but I saw his shoulders twitch, his head lift. I stepped closer, away from my dance partner, excited and afraid and wary all at once.

"Eric, there you are! What happened? Are you... okay?" I didn't want to say *dead.* Say *one of us.* In part because it terrified me... and in part because, deep down, a part of me *wanted* it.

A part of me wanted him to be dead, so he'd understand what I felt and I wouldn't be alone anymore.

I shook the thought away before it could take root, but it lingered anyway, stale cigarette stench bled into a couch cushion.

Closer, and he seemed *wrong*, standing with a tilt to one side instead of his usual military straightness, his shoulders too short and his jacket hanging loose in all the wrong ways—

And when he turned to me, I saw washed-out blue-green hair and a bumped nose, intense blue eyes in a rectangular face.

"Try again," Zoey said.

I didn't think, least not in sentences; more in words, like *rebar!* and *stabbed!* and *danger!* I swung a fist at her face and got a second of seeing her genuinely startled, before it hit with a thud that rattled up my fingers and across my wrist. I let out a wild laugh as she staggered, hand pressed to her swelling cheek.

Her own punch hit a lot harder.

I saw her jerk an arm back, and then I saw flares of white and I blinked to find myself faceup on the ground, head spinning and mouth full of drool and rattled teeth.

She pressed her foot against my chest before I could get back up, battered sneaker digging in as if I hadn't gotten the message to stay down. I swallowed and the tip of it brushed my throat, too far away to choke and way too close to be comfortable.

Shit.

"How 'bout we try another question," Zoey hummed, looming over me. "Like: What's a dead kid like you want with a guy like Eric?"

She shifted for balance, the edges of Eric's jacket—*his* jacket, his favorite one, the one he wore until it frayed at the sleeves and smelled like musk—bunching up against her wrists like she *owned* the goddamn thing, and I scowled back.

"Get bent. What did you do to him? If you hurt him, I *swear* I'll eat you."

That, at least, got her to look surprised, until she laughed. "Oh, hey, you got some salt in ya. That's neat."

"I *said*, 'what did you do to him—' "

"Easy. I didn't touch him. He's my . . ." She thought it over. "Friend? Friend, sure. Ally in figuring out what the hell happened in town, anyway."

I raised an eyebrow. "I've never met you before. Eric doesn't have a lot of friends."

"Yeah, yeah, this evacuation is making strange bedfellows all up and down the place. But y'know, I kinda got a whole *thing* about defending what's mine—roller girl and all—so when the guy I'm allied with starts gettin' stalked by a little zombie that gives him a PTSD meltdown in a Dollar Tree, I feel the need to *mediate* a bit."

The lights flickered overhead, less like pretty stars and more like cheap Walmart fairy lights tied half-assedly around trees. From down here, too, I could see a pink, clunky 2000s-era CD player propped against a set of tree roots and crumpled Monster cans, its plastic speakers humming music and its battery case duct-taped closed.

"So you tried to lure me out with—" I glanced at the CD player. "Flashy lights and Beethoven music? I'm, er, really more of a rock fan. Why did you think that would work?"

"Okay, first off, it's Chopin. Read a Goddamn book. Second off, it *did* work, so."

Touché. I winced as Zoey kept on.

"I didn't expect you to stay sentient this long, actually. I heard somewhere that no matter how gone a person gets, some parts don't fade. Instinctual stuff. How to grasp at things, shout in pain, go 'Ooh' at pretty lights and 'Ahh' at pretty music." She shrugged. "So I figured even if you were all but real-dead, you'd eventually wander toward the brightest, noisiest thing in town."

One of the other dead drifted by, laughing to herself, and Zoey grimaced at her. "I'll admit I also wasn't expecting there to be *this many* other zombie people in Kittakoop. I thought there'd be like, three, max."

"You should see the hospital," I muttered. "There were at least a dozen in there."

"No shit? What were they all doin', jackin' off?"

"I don't—" *Mountains looking at mountains going home being together becoming whole.* My head pounded, and I sharply inhaled. "I don't know. It—it doesn't matter. They were all burned up by the time we got there. It looked like an accident."

"Well, *that's* a great sign that everything is goin' *well.*" Sarcasm dripped off her words as thick as her Appalachian drawl. "You sure it was an accident, and not our National Guard friends wantin' to keep things quiet?"

"I don't know. I think even if it was an accident, it got us a lot of attention." If it weren't for the foot at my neck, the conversation would've been outright casual. Two mutual refugees, catching up on the mess. I tried a different approach. "I, look, um. You're... Zoey, right?"

"Mmhmm." Her eyes narrowed.

"I'm Ian. And I know you don't like me. But... I'm Eric's friend, too. I *promise* I'm not trying to stalk him or hurt him. I didn't even know he'd *be* at that dollar store." I put my hands against the dirt, to shift myself more upright and away from her foot, but she kept it ground tight against my chest.

"Uh-huh. And that big, moving speech you gave him about runnin' away together? All improv?"

"I just—" My voice caught. I tried again. "I... wanted to let him know that... that I love him. That I always will, no matter what happens. I didn't get a chance to say that... before I died."

And there it was, out in the open at last. The confession I'd died trying to make. I stared at the CD player instead of at Zoey, for something to focus on that wasn't my burning face or the taste of the words I couldn't un-speak.

For a long minute, Zoey didn't say anything at all. Then she sighed, shifting her foot at last off my chest and onto the grass beside it, giving me room to breathe.

"Okay. I *think* I get what's happening here, now. Good news, I don't think you're evil."

"Thank you—"

"I *do* think you're a selfish dumbass, though."

My heart lurched. "What?"

"Didya' ever think about how that would go down from *his* perspective?" Zoey shook her head, her braid bouncing on her shoulder. "I get the feeling you're a bit new to bein' out of the closet, so I'll give this bluntlike: you're dead, kid. And you made it your goal in dying to tell him that you love him. He already blames himself, how do you think he'd feel about *that*?" She spread her arms wide. "What if he didn't like you back? He'd have the guilt of rejecting a dying kid on him for *the rest of his life.* For God's sake, that's like proposing a marriage in a crowd—you're literally making him *unable to say no to you* without lookin' like the world's biggest asshole."

Oh.

I opened my mouth. Closed it. The words stuttered in the back of my throat, battering against the sinking ache in my gut and the weight of a possibility I hadn't even thought about. "I—I didn't mean it like that. He—he can still say no, he *likes* being an asshole sometimes, so it's okay—"

"*Is* it? The options are: He doesn't like you, and he has to break your heart on your deathbed. Or he *does,* and it means now you've committed him to maybe a day of a relationship before he has to put you out of your rotting misery at the end. Ain't that a romantic date idea?"

"I—no. It's not. But—I don't need him to do that for me. I'll—I'll find someone else to do the putting-out part. I just—I wanted him to feel like he deserves to be loved and he shouldn't hate himself, so I really don't mind if he doesn't love me back or answer at all—" The lie tasted sour, babbled out too fast to take back.

"Of *course* he loves you back, you dumbass!" Zoey scrubbed at her face, dragging down her eyelids and grimacing at the heavens. "You think we'd still be meandering around this dump if he didn't love you and want to put things right?"

"I—I'm sorry, I didn't mean to make things wrong, I really didn't—" Something clicked, even through my backpedaling panic. "Wait. He does?"

"Oh for *God's sake*." It took a second for Zoey to pull herself together; to take a breath, hold it, and let it out. "*Yes*, he loves you, Ian. He never *shuts up* about you. He loves your cheery dumbass face and he loves your terrible dumbass choices, and he hates himself for panicking and running away after he pulled you out of the fountain and saw your baby-black eyes."

I stared back at her, trying to pick sense out of everything she'd thrown at me, and only really able to grasp one part of it, over and over and over: *He loves me. He loves me! He loves me?!*

"I—I need to talk to him." I shifted to get up again, and again Zoey put her foot back against my throat and nudged me to the dirt.

"You *need* to leave him the hell *alone* and *move on* so he can *get over this*."

"What do you know? You met him *yesterday*!"

For a split second, something else flickered behind her scowl, something more pained. "Look, I know what it's like to deal with dead people you care about, okay? *Trust me*, it's not worth what you'll do to him if you pop back into his life like this."

"I can't just leave him *alone*, either! I'm supposed to look after him!"

"He's got company! Are you *actually* trying to look after him, or are you just trying to *be* the person that looks after him?"

"What the hell's the difference?"

"The *difference* is that one does the hard thing even when it's not what you want and doesn't make you look good, and the other is jumping up on the first *selfish impulse* you get and jury-riggin' up a bunch of reasons later on why it's actually noble—"

"So let me be selfish!"

Zoey hadn't expected me to shout. She froze, eyes wide and eyebrows shot up damn near to her hairline, as I huffed for breath.

"I've *always*, always tried to do the hard thing that I don't want. To look after other people first. And maybe that's on me—maybe I want to be seen as a good, noble person more than I want to actually be a good person. But... you said it yourself. I'm dying. And I want to take up space and be selfish before I do, just one time." I caught her eye, holding it with my own wide, dead ones. "Please, Zoey. Let me talk to him. Then I'll leave him alone. I promise."

And we stayed there, frozen and silent and stalemated, while Chopin played on and the dead danced circles beside us.

I didn't know what Zoey was thinking. I didn't know *her*, least not anything other than her faded Huntington T-shirt, her allyship with Eric, and her weird taste in classical music. I probably wouldn't get a chance to know her—not as a friend, not really, not with this little time left, and it hurt to think about all the things I'd miss out on. All the things I was expected to patiently, gracefully leave behind.

Just one time, I want to be selfish.

Finally, she sighed, hard enough to slump her shoulders and flutter her bangs.

"You're doin' that thing I just said. The thing where you put the other person in a spot where they can't say no without lookin' like an asshole."

"I know."

"You're okay with that?"

"Mmhmm."

"One time."

"Yeah."

"And then you'll never come back."

"I won't let him see me rot. I promise."

"And you won't say a *goddamn word* at first. Got that? You're gonna stand there like a li'l porcelain doll and let me do all the talking when we first get there, right up until I give the say-so for you to speak up. If you peep up *one thing* before that, I'm stabbing you myself."

A part of me wanted to argue that—when did *she* become the professional on *my* childhood friend's feelings?—but I bit it down. "I will."

Another long silence. Another sigh.

Then, finally, she offered me a hand.

"Must be outta my damn mind."

"Welcome to the club." I grinned, and we shook.

THIRTEEN

Zoey had a car: a bluish sedan with a dented passenger door and a *Jesus Saves* bumper decal, that I low-key doubted she actually owned. She wrenched open the driver's side door in a plume of dried mud and wintergreen air freshener. Then, when she saw me tugging at the rusted passenger side handle, she wrenched it open, too, with a low crack and several jerking, squealing movements of the hinge.

God, she was strong.

I skittered inside, nestling against the cupholders in a seat too low and too reclined, that I didn't dare move enough to adjust.

Were Monica and Angel awake yet, I wondered? Had they noticed I wasn't with them anymore? I almost asked Zoey to detour back to the hospital, let me explain the situation a little... but one look at the hard set in her scowl and I knew better than to push for yet another favor.

Just had to make this quick, then. Get back before they woke up and started to worry too much.

We started moving and I twisted, trying to see where we might be going, but all I could see from my angle were rolling blue skies and the occasional treetop outside. My only clue—and I held on to it like a prayer—was what she'd said outright: *You think we'd still be meandering around this dump if he didn't love you?*

Meaning that, wherever Eric was now, it was somewhere in Kittakoop. Not too far to turn back for the others.

(And meaning that he loved me.)

I couldn't decide if I should be excited or terrified. I settled on both, swallowing them down in rapid breaths through my nose.

Sure, I'd been all confidence and speeches back in the woods, but to say I had no idea what I was doing would be the worst sort of understatement. I couldn't even *think* about what I was doing. If I focused too long on anything, I wouldn't *stop* focusing on it, stressing over it until it broke. Everything bounced around my head like popcorn kernels, skittering around a steady microwave hum of white noise.

What am I gonna say to him? Zoey's right, I shouldn't force him into anything. I don't want him pulled into watching me die.

But I do, I do! I don't wanna die alone. I want to be with him and I want support, I want someone who always knows how to solve problems, even if it hurts him—

That's a horrible thing to do to him!

I DON'T CARE.

That's not loving him, though, is it? That's just loving what he can do for me. Even if I'm trying to be more selfish, I gotta draw a line somewhere, right? I can't drag the people I love into suffering.

Wait, is my phone still charged? I still need to call Mom and Dad and Emma, if I'm gonna be pulling the people I love into this.

I should've given Monica and Angel my phone number, too. Then I wouldn't have to worry that they don't know what's happening—

Never mind that, where are we GOING?

What am I gonna DO?

As it turned out, the car ride lasted maybe ten minutes. Not nearly long enough to get my head in order. I couldn't guess what time it was, but when we pulled to a stop, that murky sunrise overhead had resolved itself into a day clear and sunny enough to make my eyes water. Zoey, too. She squinted through the windshield and tugged the visor down before cutting the engine, leaving us both in a rattled silence.

"A'ight, come on," she grunted, the only three words she'd said the entire trip.

I didn't argue. Just pushed open my creaky side door and jumped out to stand beside her as she popped her back and groaned under her breath. I couldn't figure out what to do with my hands without jacket pockets to shove them into, so I hooked my thumbs on the waistband of Monica's loaner sweatpants, leaning into it like a douchey clothes model, all fake casual.

At first I didn't recognize anything around us. Only clumps of battered trees and faded asphalt road to either side. But then I spotted a line of chain-link fence ahead, a stretch of dirt piles and tin-roof buildings and blackberry bushes, and it clicked: the park. The one behind the strip mall, where I'd had my big grand idea to confess to Eric.

She'd taken us all the way back to where I'd started.

Behind us, sure enough, sat a square of flat gray cinder blocks that I recognized as the back of the strip mall, where all the fire exits and employee entrances lined up in rectangle rows. Zoey led the way forward and I trotted behind, up the concrete steps and through the first door we could reach, into that cool off-white darkness within.

Our shoes squeaked against the tiles. Overhead, the skylights shone with pearly blue sky and fluffy clouds. A warm summer day with nothing wrong in the world.

We passed the Dairy Queen kiosk, and soon enough the Dairy Queen herself, still sitting on the bench where I'd left her. Her head was rolled back against the support, but I caught a glimpse of her eyes, half closed in a peaceful stare and bright white. She seemed happy, and a part of me relaxed at that. At seeing someone I didn't completely mess up trying to help.

Zoey, on the other hand, muttered "Ugh" under her breath, swatting at gnat flurries. She pushed on, past rows of empty storefronts and toward the clothing store at the very end, the last store in this place still lit up and alive and leaking Muzak through its broken display window.

"All right, then," she muttered. Then, cupping her hands to her mouth: "Hey, Eric, I found you someone! No hard feelings, okay?"

No response, but I twitched anyway, rubbing at the goose bumps along my arms. They felt cool to the touch, tiny dots along skin gone gray and dry and a little numb at the edges. Creepy dead person skin, with gasoline underneath.

Zoey gave it a few seconds more, then rolled her eyes. She gestured to me, hands out and flat: *stay here.* I nodded, and she strode into the clothing store, far enough to be out of sight, but close enough for me to still hear muttering voices somewhere near the jeans section.

"Come on, get up. You can't stay here moping for the rest of your life."

"I'm not moping. I'm sorting all the shit we stole."

"You've been 'sorting' the same three cans of beans since I left. Come on, at least see what I got."

"Fine. Why not."

Eric's voice, low and rough. I lifted my head, shoulders straight, fingers digging trenches into my arms, and did my best to not say anything, even as he walked back to the entrance and I got to see him again.

First thing I noticed was his new jacket, a black hooded one I recognized off a mannequin from the front display. Had he slept here? No, he hadn't slept last night. I could tell that much from the bags under his eyes, from the twitchy way he moved, from the way his thumb kept flicking across the top of his pocket, toying with his dad's lighter.

Even twitchy, though, he stood tall and broad, with a square, handsome face lined in scruff and a worker's tan. Same long nose, same ruffles of dark hair—surprisingly soft, grown back like baby duckling fluff every time his dad shaved it away—same strong arms—spotted with faint freckles all along the back like stars—and calloused hands tucked deep in his pockets.

I hated him for it, a little. He made it so hard to focus when all I wanted to do was hug him.

He stared back, and I watched his eyes widen. This time, though, he at least seemed to expect me—or he just didn't care anymore, because that shocked look faded back into sad real quick as he glanced over at Zoey.

"I didn't ask you to help. Stop cutting in."

"Call it a favor." Zoey shrugged. "Do me a favor back, and remind me again of what this kid is to you? A boyfriend, right?"

Eric reached out between us, hand half raised...then seemed to think better of it and put his hand down again.

"Not your business."

"Uh-huh. Kinda *is* my business when I need your help and you're having breakdowns in the Dollar Tree. Spill."

"Shit." Eric drew in a breath, shuddering it out. "Just an...old friend. Okay? The only one hopeless enough to keep reaching out to me after I scared everyone else away." He laughed at that, dry and humorless.

"So all this moping around is 'cause you feel like you owe him for that?" Zoey put a hand on my back like we were best buddies, and I fought back the urge to jerk away from it and closer to Eric.

"No. Sorta? I feel like I should've *protected* him. He was always so...I don't know. Nice, and selfless, and *good*, and . . ." Another low breath. "And I let him die, okay? I was too distracted to even notice him falling, and by the time I pulled him up, he was... he was already gone." His voice caught, his hands tight fists against the straining fabric of his jacket pockets. "I don't know if he can even hear me like this anymore. Is he in pain? Does he even realize what *happened* to him?"

I twitched and opened my mouth, then felt Zoey's hand on my back dig in just a little harder, her friendly, sympathetic smile get just a little more strained, and I shut up.

Goddamn it. I glared daggers at Zoey, hoping she'd get the hint: *I'm dead, not comatose. You know that. Let me talk to him. Let me do SOMETHING.*

She didn't. Both of them looked past me, past every nervous motion I made and look I gave them as the mindless actions of the dead. She stepped closer to Eric, instead, lowering her voice to a soft therapist's tone.

"Hard to say. But you wanna know what I think? I think if he was half as good and selfless as you say, he'd want you to forgive yourself."

Another of those dry, awful laughs. "God...'course he would. Little punk wouldn't even hold a grudge."

I'd hold a little bit of a grudge, actually, I thought. *Like right now? Big grudge. I hate this.*

"And I think if you have anything *specific* you wanna say to him, this is your best chance to do it, *Eric,*" Zoey added.

Eric hesitated. For the first time since this conversation started, he looked at me—and I stared back, hugging my chest as my heart hammered like a woodpecker against my ribs. As everything I wanted to say and couldn't put on him weighed heavy in the back of my throat.

He crouched down a couple inches, closer to my height, farther from the military-rigid posture he usually took. He looked like a tired adult and he looked like a scared child—both at once, stuck in the middle and carrying the hurt of both.

He cleared his throat. Cleared it again.

"Um... hey, Ian." He tried a smile, strained and awkward on his dirt-stained face, not quite reaching his warm brown eyes. "It's me. Do you still remember me?"

I glanced at Zoey, but she seemed busy staring at the wall opposite us, so I chanced a tiny, tiny nod. Eric's smile turned a little more genuine.

"Hey! That's... great. I'm glad. *God*, you must've been scared, huh? Bet you never wanted to be like this."

I considered, then gave another nod.

"I can imagine. Look, Ian, I . . ." He trailed off.

Paused.

And then he pulled me into a tight hug, and I smelled dust and sweat and his dad's stale beer and his own cheap wintergreen shampoo, and it felt so familiar it hurt. He smelled like *home*, like everything that'd gone right and simple before this mess, and I hugged back, blinking away tears.

"I'm sorry," Eric muttered. "I'm sorry I wasn't the person you deserved to have around. And I'm sorry I left you behind." He squeezed. "Shit, Ian, I love you so much. And I know you deserve better than messed-up trailer trash who don't know love except the abusive, broken flavor, but it's true. I love you."

I shook my head, trying to form the words in pats against his back like some intimate Morse code—he'd always been enough, would always *be* enough, and I was the one who should be sorry, and Goddamn it, I'd *missed* him.

"Shh, hey, it's okay. I'm here now. I'm gonna make this right, okay?" he muttered, and I leaned into that gentle comfort. Eric always knew what to do; even, it turned out, when it came to holding dead kids.

"You must be so tired," he hummed. "Get some rest. We can talk all about it when you wake up. Or... or pick blackberries again, or see a movie. Whatever you wanna do, fluffy."

Something about that threw me off, and I froze, hand still raised to pat his back. It sounded like the voice he'd used with Mr. Owens, all soft and warm and *he didn't even feel it.* I noticed his arm around my back, gripping in a firm hug, but the other arm . . .?

Out of the corner of my eye, I spotted the rounded edge of a pocketknife in his fist. One of those cheap gas station ones he carried around sometimes next to the lighter, for cleaning his nails or jabbing his initials into trees, but still sharp enough to hurt. Still pointed at my head.

And I realized too late how Eric dealt with dead people.

"*No*!" I yelped and shoved at his chest, startling him enough for me to knock his grip loose and stumble back. I swayed for balance, arms outstretched—and Zoey shouted behind me.

"Eric!"

He grunted. "I'm okay! Get the exit!"

What? I turned toward the store doorway as he said it, but Zoey moved faster, stepping wide and crouching low to block the way out.

My heart lurched, hammering the same as it had been but now for all sorts of new reasons, churning around whatever dregs of blood I hadn't spilled out of myself already. I glanced around at everything and nothing—at *clothes* and *hangers* and *shelves* and *THREAT* and *FRIEND???* and everything but another exit, all flashing by in panicked glimpses.

And in front of them all, I saw Eric, his hands outstretched, one open like a peace offering, the other closed around that pocketknife.

Okay, to hell with Zoey's threat. I cleared my throat and glared at him, trying to make him see *me* underneath all the dead parts.

"Eric, don't *do* this," I hissed. "It's me. I'm here. I'm still me in here."

That had to work, right? Him hearing my voice?

Instead, his grip tightened on the knife. It shook in his fingers, rattling against skin seared white from the pressure... but, weirdly enough, he kept up that peaceful, serene look.

"Ian... Ian, it's gonna be okay. I promise. Take it easy—" he started.

"I'm not gonna *take it easy* until you *put the knife away*."

"He's getting upset," Zoey noted. "Don't drag this out."

"Don't you gaslight me, either!" I glared at her, then back at him, darting between the two.

"Ian, listen. You're *not* yourself anymore," Eric said. "I know it *feels* like it, but... you've done things the person you were when alive would never let himself do. You've *eaten* people."

That one hit hard, so soft and soothing and *rational*, but I shoved it down with everything else to process later. "I—yeah, maybe that's true. I wanted to stay alive longer. But I still didn't ask you to—to mercy-kill me from myself! That's not what we agreed on, Zoey!"

For a second, Eric's focus shifted. "Wait, agreed on what?"

And Zoey—asshole that she was—shrugged, and my heart sank somehow farther. "No idea what he's on about."

"You... you *liar*!" Even when I finally let myself speak, I couldn't pick out words vicious enough from the pile of unsaid ones jammed up in me. "You *know* what I'm talking about! You agreed to let me see him! Just see him! Not—not get *stabbed* by him!"

"Did I?" She crossed her arms, raising an eyebrow at me. "How long ago was that?"

"What? That's easy, it was . . ." I started to speak... then trailed off. The answer, which had been *right there*, vanished as soon as I got to it, replaced with a steady hum of white noise. "Earlier... today? Yesterday?"

"What kinda car did I drive?"

"It was a—" More static hum. So much of my memory, trying to look back now, seemed unreal. Confusing. Wrong. I swallowed hard. "I—I don't remember. A truck, I think." No, that was Monica and Angel's car. Wasn't it? "I don't know."

No, no, no. I could almost *feel* the air shifting, this entire situation spiraling out of my control.

"Ian . . . ," Eric murmured.

"This is what the dead are like, Eric," Zoey said. "They're cold, empty, and terrified of being alone. So they latch on to the last memories they have. Go after the people they love. Anything to feel warm again. And the people they love will cling back until both of you start to rot. But this *ain't him anymore*, Eric. You gotta let him go."

I opened my mouth, but all that came out was a dry croak. I swallowed. Tried again. "I *am* myself. She's lying. Please believe me."

I stared at him and he stared back *through* me, and he didn't say anything at all.

And suddenly I was back at the front entrance with Angel, next to the Dairy Queen, and she had a knife at my neck, too. And she was asking me if I wanted to die, calling it the noble option, calling it selfless and moral and everything I'd ever wanted to be as a sickly, living martyr. I'd said no, at the time, because even a martyr like me wanted to live.

Was that true? Or even then, was I something *other* than the "real" Ian?

The real Ian is a good person. A model son and community member. He'd never eat people. He'd die before he hurt his loved ones. And whenever he got sick, he did it so beautifully, and he never stopped smiling through it. An inspiration and a model to us all.

"No, I'm still . . . I . . ."

I backed up a step. Another. I didn't want to get closer to Eric or to Zoey opposite him, so I edged sideways, toward the display window.

Toward that glint of broken glass, sparkling in the light, where I'd thrown the bucket at it days and years ago.

Zoey saw where I was going, and her eyes widened. She lunged forward, but too slow, too late.

I darted for the window and I leaped through the hole, tumbling to the tile outside in a mess of glass shards and dozens of new cuts, searing hot across my skin. Didn't matter; I shook it off, staggering to my feet, and then—with Eric and Zoey both shouting behind me—I took off running.

It hurt to run. My shoes pounded against the tile in thuds that echoed up the walls, leaving thin smears of mismatched red footprints behind. I'd cut my foot, I guessed, and the back of my hand and a dozen other spots I couldn't slow down long enough to pinpoint. My breath heaved in and out, and the world wouldn't stop pulsing out of sickly focus.

Need to get out of here—or hide somewhere, lose them, then head back to Monica and Angel—

There's the fountain, still there, I hate that thing—

Is Zoey's car still outside? Can I steal her car?

I'm still myself, I'm still me, please let me still be me—

I wanna go home, I miss home, I wanna go home—

The main exit sat only a couple yards away, glittering silvery glass and metallic edging. I reached out for the handle, toward fields of grass and trees and clear air beyond—

And something grabbed the back of my collar, yanking me away. My legs gave out and I fell onto my back, yelling and skidding hard across dusty linoleum.

I blinked, and I saw Eric standing over me, face so red it was half purple, looking winded and as panicked as I felt. He crouched over me, grasping the front of my shirt and staring with those wild wide eyes.

"Stop *fighting*, Ian!" he shouted, as if I somehow couldn't hear him from two feet away. "Goddamn it, I'm trying to *help* you!"

"I don't wanna *die*, Eric!" I cried back, twisting against him. *"Please, stop!"*

"I *know*, I know! You *already* died, just—" He shifted his grip, and in his other hand shone that pocketknife, chipped and small and deadly. *"Let me fix this*!"

I couldn't get free. Not with him holding so tight his hand shook, not with my limbs shaking and the world spinning, so I watched him lift the knife high and I squeezed my eyes shut and I screamed as it came down, as I heard the cracking of tile and the screech of metal next to my ear and I waited for the pain to hit . . .

. . . But nothing happened. Not even the cold non-pain of when Zoey had stabbed me before, all adrenaline and dizzy confusion.

So I cracked open an eye to see Eric's arm inches from my head, his knife buried, quivering, in cracked ceramic flooring.

Above me, Eric started crying. Something cracked in him, too, and it came out damp and exhausted, in twin water trails along his face and in dark droplets hitting his outstretched arm like rain.

"P-please . . . just let me fix this . . . It's my fault, just . . ." He might've said something else, a strained noise I couldn't make out as words.

"Eric . . .?"

He shook his head. "I can't. I *can't*. I'm sorry. I just . . ." Swallowed, hard. Tried again. "I . . . can't . . . hurt you anymore."

His shoulders shook, those tears working their way up into full-blown sobs as he let go of my shirt at last, of the knife at last. He leaned back, pulling away from me, and I took the opportunity to catch my breath, huffing around the ear-pounding ache of my heartbeat and the dizzy rush of adrenaline.

I can't hurt you.

I blinked hard, but my eyes watered, anyway.

This time, it was my turn to sit up and pull Eric into a hug. This time, he was the one who hugged back, clinging to me tight, and—still shaking, still winded—I rubbed at his back, breathing in dust and Goodwill laundry soap.

"I'm so *fucking pathetic*," he muttered. He kept repeating *fuck*, in all its different ways, hissing it and spitting it and whimpering it, until I finally, gently shushed him.

"You're not," I murmured back. Considered. "Kind of scary, maybe. But... same, I guess."

That got a tiny laugh, or at least a huff of air. Encouraged, I kept going.

"Did... do you think what happened at the mall was your fault?"

"I just—" His breath shuddered in and out against my shoulder. "Shit, Ian. I don't want you to *suffer*. I promised your folks that I'd always watch out for you. I *practiced* it. But when things actually went bad, I was the one who told you to *shut up* and *look at the flashy lights*. I did that, and then I *left you*. I got you killed."

I didn't say anything to that, not for a bit. I thought it over instead, picking out my words all careful.

"You didn't, though. No one can tell how they're gonna actually react in an emergency before it happens—if they're gonna freeze up or run away or just... die. You were trying to figure out what was going on, and that's not a bad thing." I squeezed. "I'm the one who expected you to always fix it when things go wrong, even things you didn't see happening. And that wasn't fair, and you don't have to blame yourself for it."

The more I talked, the more I felt each word of it hitting home for him, striking some internal string that made his whole body twitch and his shoulders hunch up. He scrubbed at his face, scrunching it like he couldn't decide if he wanted to laugh or cry. Maybe both.

I decided, then, to add something else.

"You don't have to keep hating yourself, either. I love you."

He pulled back at that. Enough for me to see his bloodshot eyes with my own dead ones, and this time, when he looked, he *saw* me, and I saw him.

Then we were hugging again, him damn near tight enough to pull me off my feet, and I didn't mind the weight off and I didn't mind that little crook of space between his neck and collarbone to hide my face in and cry into.

He kept saying, "I'm sorry, I'm sorry, I'm so sorry," and I kept saying, "It's okay, you're okay, it's okay," back, and then I said, "I'm sorry, I'm sorry," for a while and he said, "It's okay, you're safe, it's okay," back, and both of us clung tight like we could keep ourselves from falling apart if only we gripped hard enough.

He apologized for everything he'd done and then some, and I apologized back because here I was clinging to him and both of us knew deep down what that meant—that I was everything Zoey said, cold and empty and terrified of being alone, but that I was asking him to stay and rot with me, anyway, and he'd do it, too. He clung back because he loved me more than he hated himself and maybe that's what love meant.

Once I had a hand free, I reached up to scrub at my damp eyes, smearing tears across the backs of my hands.

Except, when I glanced at them, they weren't tears.

It was oil, viscous and black against my gray skin. Dark oil leaked down my face, gathering at the corners of my lips and the back of my tongue.

Now, too, I could see every cut I'd gotten from the glass was oozing black instead of red, long and angry stripes that soaked my T-shirt and sweats. My heartbeat lurched, spluttering in my chest like an old engine.

As soon as I spotted it—as soon as we both spotted it, staring in shared unease—I heard someone laughing, a congested and bitter noise. I turned and saw Zoey standing in the clothing store entryway, her braid fully undone and her eyes so baggy and tired, her arms crossed against her chest.

"So he couldn't do it, huh? Don't matter. Looks like your time's almost up, anyway, dead kid," she noted.

Eric glared daggers at Zoey, but I couldn't stop staring at the black smudges. The world swam and my ears rang, loud and sharp as an alarm. I sank against Eric for balance, retreating into the comfort of a familiar scent and feel and sound, like Mr. Owens and the Dairy Queen and everyone at the hospital must've done right before they never came home again.

FOURTEEN

I didn't want to let go, but it worked out fine: I leaned against Eric, half walked and half dragged into the clothing store. He'd made a little nest, in the maternity section next to the bathrooms: two fitting room benches pushed together, layered with billowy muumuus and puffs of tulle until it passed for a bed. Next to it sat a shoe rack, cleaned off and refilled with rows of dollar store cans and paper plates and jugs of water.

Someone had put out a grocery basket with a plastic bag lining, full of empty cans and dirty paper plates. Someone had scattered their chip bags and empty seltzer water cans across the floor. Someone had set up candles and matches on the top shelf, sorted and stacked. Someone had crammed the bottom shelf full of bags and toppled cans. A constant, low-key tension between order and mess.

Weird how all of us made our own little homes out here. I looked at the shelves with a pang of homesickness for the truck, full of survival rations and string lights and gasoline grit.

In a bit, I'd ask—no, *demand*—to go back. I'd make sure Monica and Angel knew I was okay, and I'd trade phone numbers so this wouldn't happen again. I'd be responsible and more.

For now, though... for now I drifted through uneasy half-dreams, head spinning and mouth dry, while Eric patched up what he could of all my glass cuts. He wiped at each angry line with a damp washcloth, water pulled up from a bowl jammed in the water fountain, while I watched the ceiling spin overhead.

Zoey came by at some point, but she didn't look at us or make small talk. She trudged to the bathroom across the store, and when she came back out, she'd wiped her face and pulled her hair back up. Eric didn't look twice, but I found myself watching until she settled just outside the front entrance, her back to the shattered window. Another low-key tension, another uneasy truce.

At a later point Eric gave me a smoothie of some kind, one of those nutrient slurries for diets that tasted like salty pancake mix and went down like sand. I guess I must've drank it, though, because when I settled down on the tulle pile my stomach had stopped twisting on itself like a rubber band, and all the hurt spots went from tingling numb to regular sore.

Should probably still see a doctor about that, haha. If only the hospital hadn't burned down. If only there hadn't been dozens of dead people in it, all full of oil and factory chemicals instead of blood, waiting for a random spark to cause an explosion so big and so creepy that the entire town got evacuated over it.

I dreamed of the mountains again. Of course I did; they felt like home, like Zoey's field of lights and dead dancers felt like home, like the truck bed full of mattress pads felt like home. I was sick with desperate attachment for places I'd barely been.

The white overhead resolved into snowy peaks and cloudy skies, blending in and out of each other in wisps of icy wind. I stood on top of it all, drifted like a dandelion seed to the highest point and left to hover there, breathless and cold, with a trail of all the oily pieces of myself I'd dripped away behind me, gathered in piles where everyone before me and after me had climbed up to rest.

I couldn't go any higher than this. There weren't any taller mountains, any more towering skyscrapers. This was the most ancient place, and only here, away from noise or lights or buzzing things, could I listen to its slow lungs and know peace.

It had to be up here. Away from the noise. Close to the sky. Closer than I could ever get, reaching out with the oil and pieces of everyone underneath my shoes. To my right stood a radio telescope, to my left stood a naval base, and around our discarded bodies stood a dozen towns and cities, connected to one another in a fine web, and all the lines and spirals of the web drew back to us.

Here, in the last quiet place on earth, there was only this breathless moment of me reaching up, stretching that final inch higher, listening that final breath longer, for the sky to whisper back. Until I could hear again the sky singing to me in her quiet words, ones I'd stay awake forever to listen to, long after my body rotted around me.

I'm here. I've climbed as high as I can. I've thrown away everything I can. There is nothing left of me but you. I'm ready, now.

I stared into that wisping white, deeper... until I saw beyond it, and I saw something infinite, as dark as space, a single held note. I saw everything, and with that everything came a certain numb sort of peace; there was nothing left to wonder in the face of the wonderful, nothing terrible in the face of the terrific, no awful in awe.

Except, for a moment—for a flicker, as my fingers stretched toward it, a mass of infinites unfurled toward me, and in one of them I saw teeth.

In one of them I saw a hundred teeth grinding together, and I realized there was something horrible about dissolving yourself into a symbol, wasn't there?

Ian Chandler, beautiful living boy, wouldn't be afraid of it. It'd been his dream all his life to become something infinite, sweetly senseless, filled with divine purpose and peace. Ian Chandler was an angel, too pure to rot.

But I wasn't him anymore. I'd done things he'd never do. I was something made of Ian's leftover teeth and meat, so I screamed and jerked back, my foot slipping behind me, and I tumbled off the mountain and into the dark.

"Ian? *Ian*!"

Someone grasped my shoulders, shaking hard. I spluttered awake, twisting out of their grip and into a mess of tulle and puffy sleeves. I flailed, gasping for breath and disoriented, until I managed to tear a handful away from my face—

And I saw Eric looming overhead, his face somehow both relieved and disappointed, a thin-lipped sour-lemon smile. Like he'd wanted me to open my eyes and forgotten for a second what they looked like beneath the lids.

I blinked, pulling my bearings together—the clothing store, right. No mountains, no angels, no infinite teeth. Only this simple comfort, puffy fabric and humming lights, paler than eternal glories but still kinda soft to touch.

Jeez, my head hurt. In the dream-logic things like *infinity* and *glory* made sense, but trying to imagine eternity here, in the middle of the maternity clothes section, made my brain spin and my eyes go cross. I shook my head, scattering eternity like dandruff, and focused on Eric instead. He stared back.

"You were twitching in your sleep," he said. "I got, y'know, worried."

"'M okay," I mumbled back. "Still here. Wasn't a seizure or anything, just a weird dream."

"Mmm. Good."

He trailed off, and we sat there in awkward silence for a while, the lights humming overhead and the rest of the world otherwise quiet. (*But not quiet enough*, a part of my mind whispered. *Not quiet enough to hear the whisper of something so beautiful you'd come back from the dead to hear them once more.*)

There'd been so much I'd wanted to say before meeting up again—the big gay confession, obviously, mixed with long-winded rants about how much he sucked, mixed with worried questions about where he'd been and how he'd taken the evacuation news. A dozen rambling conversations.

But here, with him sitting on a dented cardboard box with his knees spread and his arms dangling between them, I couldn't think of anything.

At least he seemed to have the same problem. He scratched at his cheek, picked at a Band-Aid on his palm, did anything but pick the conversation up.

I coughed. "So."

"Yeah."

"Um. I guess we... have a lot of catching up to do, huh?"

"Guess so. You wanna start?"

"Nope!" I huffed a laugh, looking around. I couldn't see Zoey anywhere near her old spot by the window, so I focused on the shelves of canned goods instead. "This place is nice."

"It ain't bad." Eric shrugged. "To be honest, Zoey did most of the work. I pretty much just crawled back here to die. But I guess she's used to being a caretaker."

"Oh." What was I supposed to say to *that*? I fiddled with my hands, running a sliver of tulle between them. "I'm... glad she did. I'm glad you're not dead."

"Likewi—" he started, and cut off. "Goddamn it. I'm sorry."

I laughed. "It's okay, that was funny—"

"It's not *okay*, damn it, this whole thing is *wrong*—"

"But it's *okay* to not be *okay*!"

He stopped. I watched him, then pushed on.

"Everything sucks, and I'm really, *really* scared about it. But...I think it's okay to be scared, and hurt, and angry, and not know what to do. I think it's okay to be selfish or to rely on other people for help." I twisted the tulle around itself, over and over, forming a tight little spiral of fabric. "And...I think it's okay to hope for something to surprise you, still, even when you're scared and angry. To hope that... that maybe things will still somehow turn out okay."

Eric didn't look like he knew how to respond to that. He kept looking at his hands, clenching his fingers, picking at the Band-Aid, until I got sick of them moving like that and I grabbed at one.

I held it up between us, and I pressed our palms against each other, lacing our fingers together.

And we held hands. Like a real couple of boyfriends.

I looked over at him and saw he'd buried his face in his other hand, but through either side I could see his beet-red ears and blotchy cheeks. It made him look so much younger—like for once he hadn't been forced to grow up quick, like all this could be new and moving again. I laughed at it and he laughed back, winded, oh-my-god-we're-doing-this chuckles.

"Okay, okay, I'm trying. This is me trying," he said. "God, this feels ridiculous."

"*Surprise*," I said, drawing the word out in a little singsong: *Surpriiiise.*

He laughed again, shaking his head—but he kept holding on, and even held a little harder, savoring it. We sat there for a while, holding hands in the most unnatural, awkward way possible, both of us red-faced and avoiding each other's eyes, until he sighed, lowering our hands to be less upright and more level with the top of his sitting-box.

"Thanks, Ian. This place was too quiet without you," he muttered.

He still didn't make eye-contact, admitting that affection to a plastic cup on the shelf, still with the dregs of pinkish smoothie grit around its edges and an empty can of vanilla SlimFast next to it.

"Yeah, because you're always too quiet and moody. Someone had to fill in the gap."

"I like hearing myself think."

"Sounds boring. Have you tried not thinking?"

"Maybe I should, at this rate. Thinking's only brought trouble." He laughed, winded, and softened. "I'm gonna miss you, you know."

"What?" I said, like a genius, and then it clicked. Right. Dying. I sobered up and turned to—at last—meet his eyes. "Eric, I'm not gonna die any time soon." I didn't realize the words were out until I'd said them, but they didn't feel wrong, either. He stared at me with obvious doubt—stared right into those pitch-black dead-person eyes—and I glared back. "I mean it. I don't care if I already did and it hasn't caught up. I'm gonna outrun it as long as I can, and I'm gonna wring out a full lifetime before I slow down."

Eric grit his teeth, making that face he always made whenever he was about to deliver some bad news. Sure enough: "That ain't realistic."

"I don't care about realism, though. I *like* being too selfish and thoughtless to know better. Giving up and sacrificing myself is easy and noble. Zoey was right about that." I breathed. "But I don't *want* to."

For a moment, Eric didn't say anything back. He stared deep and hard into that plastic cup, hunting for an answer in every direction but at me, that blush slowly fading from his face and turning it old and haunted again.

He scratched at the Band-Aid on his palm again, and I wondered how he hadn't picked the damn thing off by now, until I saw how fresh it was. It sat clean and new, over skin still red and irritated-looking.

"How did . . .?" I started, then glanced back at the smoothie.

Cream-white vanilla mix. But pink residue on the cup. And it'd tasted like salt.

Oh.

Eric went quiet, lost in some distant thought. He seemed so much older, now. I hesitated, wanting to call him out, but the words wouldn't come, so I tried other ones.

"Eric... what happened to you? While I was... when I first died, I mean."

He breathed. "Not a lot. Couldn't've been more than a couple seconds that you were in the water, but you cracked your head *hard*. When I pulled you out, you were already pale and had those big dark eyes, even in the middle of seizing up.

"As soon as I saw it... I dropped you and ran away. Nowhere in particular. Just wanted to get out of town before you woke up and realized it. I took off for the park and then past it, into the trees and the foothills for a while, until I couldn't run any more. I just... it's immature as hell, but I kept thinking of my dad, screaming at me for ruining something good again. Like he always did whenever I broke a dish or didn't do chores. Like I'd dropped you in the sink or something."

He laughed. I didn't.

"I didn't come back until dark, and by then you were gone. Everyone was gone, like me messing up had ruined the entire town with it. So I just curled up and waited to either get raptured or die, too." He swallowed. "Zoey found me while looking for stragglers. She was so happy to not be alone anymore. Wouldn't let me die easy, not if it meant leaving her alone again."

"Good." I squeezed his hand again, tethering him to here and now. "I'm glad you're alive. Even—even if I'm still angry with her for lying—and for stabbing me at the dollar store—I *am* happy she was there to help you, in... in her own way."

"All her '*help*' did was *piss me off*."

"Yeah, but that means you *felt something*. It's more than waiting to die, so I'll take it."

"I guess." He shrugged, and I didn't push it. I knew when I'd hit as far as he could go without him shutting down more, and soon enough he changed the subject: "What happened to you?"

"Me? It... it's kinda funny. When I first woke up and realized what'd happened, I spent a while at the mall moping, too." I laughed, a little, like that was something normal people did. Something we had in common. "And I was found by other stragglers. Two of them. We helped each other."

"Yeah?"

"Mm. Their names are..." I floundered for a moment, trying to remember. "Monica and Angel. You'd like them, I think. Monica is so organized, smart, pretty—she has a protective streak, too, and I swear she doesn't get shaken up by *any* of the gross things we've dealt with. And Angel is quiet and pretty blunt, but she's an expert at survival. She hot-wired a car and everything...." I sighed.

"Where are they now?"

"By now? I don't know. Back at the hospital, probably. We were there to look for Monica's mom, to... to find people who might help us." Overhead, clouds drifted past the skylight, lazy and fat like dandelion fluff. "They're probably real worried by now."

Eric considered. Then he pushed himself up and off the box, popping his neck as he moved.

"We need to get you back," he said.

"I mean... yeah. Yeah, you do." I took his hand again, this time to pull myself off the benches and onto my feet. My legs tingled and ached, but held. "You know where the hospital is?"

"Nah. Haven't been. Can you show me?" I couldn't remember the last time he'd asked me so bluntly for help. Something stubborn in him had gotten broken out here, a hard old scab flaked off with raw tissue underneath.

I nodded back. "Sure. It's about ten miles out, to the south, near Deepwell. So we should probably take the car." His face soured at that, and I tilted my head. "Something wrong?"

"Little bit," he said. "Zoey has the key."

FIFTEEN

We found Zoey outside the mall and in the parking lot, sitting in the sedan—*her* sedan—with the passenger door propped open. Radio sounds rumbled out of the speakers, a steady hum of some narrator's voice. She sat in the driver's seat, leaned back, a hand towel pressed to her face and her eyes closed, bottles of ibuprofen and multivitamins scattered across the dashboard. A headache from me punching her, or a hangover from staying up all night.

Eric started forward, but I held up a hand and took the lead, instead. He grimaced, but hung back cautiously by the entrance doors, arms crossed like a bouncer at some exclusive club. Another weird role reversal for us.

The sun hung high overhead, ringed by the drifting remnants of last night's rain clouds. Cold puddles sat drying between parked cars, droplets trickling off dark windows. Every so often a damp wind would pick up, and I shivered, crossing my arms over my hand-me-down sweats and wishing for my jacket back.

Zoey didn't open her eyes or move at all when I got close, but before I could call out, she spoke up, like she'd expected me the whole time.

"Listen to that, will ya?"

I listened. This close I could make out the radio's words, edged with static and muffled bass.

"—Warren Buffett's absolute mastery with investing, to be sure, but his down-to-earth wisdom can still have a profound effect on the lives of everyone. Even you and me. Take, for example, his formula about going to bed smarter every day. According to Buffett, knowledge builds up like compound interest. . . ."

I glanced at the radio speaker, then up at her as she laughed, short and breathy.

"Someone out there tryin' to start a business. Wild, huh? Our whole town gets uprooted and quarantined for bein' fulla dead people, but the stock market is still goin' and the news station is still givin' traffic updates like nothin' happened." She squinted open a bloodshot eye. "Passenger side's open if you wanna sit."

"How'd you know it was me?" I hesitated, not trusting being alone in a car with her for a second—not when she could still drive away and throw me off a cliff somewhere and call it *closure*. But the engine wasn't on and the passenger door was open, so I settled for perching on the edge of the seat like a bird, ready to bolt at any second.

"Footsteps. Eric always walks like he's marching to war, but you drag your feet." She closed her eye again, leaning her head against the headrest. "You're gonna die twice as fast that way."

I flinched, watching my sneakers. Did I really drag my feet...? No, focus. "Eric isn't gonna mercy-kill me. And he'll stop you if you try. So... I want you to take me back to the hospital."

"Done catchin' up? Learn anything new?" She smirked, and I glared back.

"There're other people worried about me. People who *aren't* trying to kill me." I wasn't sure why, but I added: "We're leaving Kittakoop. And once we're out, we're gonna tell everyone everything. About the hospital fire, about the water contamination, about what it feels like to be dead. Everyone will know."

"The whole world, huh?"

"Ain't you mad at them for not noticing until it got too bad to ignore? For doing this—this—doing *stocks*, instead?" I flapped my hands at the radio, like that could make my stammering make sense.

She shrugged, shifting her hand towel to press the other side to her eye. It was only a flicker of movement, but underneath I could see swollen purple eye bags. "Eh. I don't blame them. It ain't possible to care about everything at once. You'll burn out that way. And it's kind of a comfort, when everything goes bad and catches fire, to know that somewhere out there, people got their own lives. Gives perspective."

I didn't know what to say to that. It seemed like a dismissive version of Angel and Monica's argument at the hospital: *they don't care about us, they left us behind, we'll die out here if we wait for their approval.* Back then it'd felt so brutal, so final.

It still did. I pulled my legs up, settling my feet on the edge of the seat with the rest of me. They moved stiff, the joints swollen and sore.

"I don't see why it's so wrong to want people to care," I muttered.

"It ain't wrong to want *people* to care. It's wrong to want *the world* to care. Too big and too busy and too fulla' other people's thoughts to have a thought of its own," Zoey said. "So if you need validation, just focus on one person. Care about them and let them care about you. Surround yourself with people who care. Build your own world that way." She trailed off, then. Smiled grimly. "And hope they don't die, first."

We sat there. I watched my hands—they were grayer than they were this morning, washed out and lined with darker veins, and my palms smelled like sour vinegar. An unpleasant, rotting smell. By contrast, the glass cuts on my arms, even cleaned and taped closed, seemed the same as ever; before dying, they probably would've scabbed or gone inflamed by now, but instead they stood out like tattoos, too dead to heal.

"Zoey . . ." I trailed off. Tried again. "If it's okay to ask...you lost someone once, too, didn't you? Someone who...you know . . ."

"Went all undead, rotted, and died?" Zoey blinked at me. "You can say it. No point in hiding the truth after everything's ended."

But I couldn't. I nodded instead, rubbing my palms on the knees of my sweats, like that could make the gray smudge off.

Zoey leaned back, watching the sedan's matte beige roof while she thought it over. Overhead, a row of lights and air conditioner settings stared back, twin shiny insect eyes in a plastic shell.

Then: "Her name was Willow, first off. My older sister." She must've seen something in my face, then, because she grinned back. "That's right, I've always been the sweet li'l baby of the family. Can't you tell?"

I squinted. "Not really."

"Really? Huh. Anyway, Willow was the captain of our roller girl team. Real shinin' star. Rail-thin, weasel-faced, but tall as a reed and too stubborn to knock over. I looked up to her, literally. Every weekend it'd be me, her, and all our un-blood sisters, pasting rainbow stickers over bruises."

She sighed, letting her eye settle closed again, lost in some old memory. One that probably smelled like floor polish and sweat and sounded like girls laughing.

"I always worried that she'd wreck herself somehow, with how much she threw herself into blocking like she had nothin' to lose. But it was a car accident that ended her. Ain't that a little funny? Five years of trying to kill herself for the sport, and she skidded out on a highway on her way there instead. Got a call from the hospital and walked in to her with big black eyes in a clinic bed, bitching about the *delay*."

Another chuckle, breathy and thin.

"I dunno. Maybe she would've lasted longer after if she'd been careful and delicate. We talked about it a lot; what she wanted to do, bucket list, and so on. But then she wouldn't have been *Willow*. She always hated the thought of being treated like a doll or told to smile more. She was stubborn and angry and bitter about it, and refused to act like there was anything wrong. Not when we had games to win.

"So we kept playing games each day, even as she got slower and dazed and bruised all over. Felt god-awful, but we did it. We let her take the star and hobble her way around laps and... and cheer like she *did it*. We won. Yay." Her voice shifted, stumbling over the words.

"Half the girls quit. Couldn't take it anymore. Can't blame 'em. Once Willow died, the team died with it, and anything after was some straggling afterlife. They left, and the other half started making excuses to not show up, went home early... Until one day it was just me and her. Me holding her hand and guiding her around the track, her staring ahead at nothing, legs bowed out like a kid learning to skate for the first time all over, stickers all up and down her arms. She didn't even notice everyone else was gone—by that point she'd gotten lost in a memory, smiling at our old team and chatting like they were still there. Guess in her head, they were.

"We went in circles for hours. Long after the rink closed and everyone went home. No music, no lights. I knew—*knew*—that as soon as I went home, she wouldn't be able to come back anymore. Too far gone. So I just kept going 'round with her all night."

She stopped. Sighed.

"I know a lotta people like to take care of dead relatives themselves. Let them lie in bed and fade away naturally, or take them behind the woodshed and end it quick. There's even the ones who feed 'em blood and organs, living things, to drag it out as long as possible."

She paused there, laughing at my startled expression. "Yeah, yeah, I know about that trick. Believe you me, when Willow died, I was searching *every* possible trick I could find that might bring her back. But I couldn't make myself kill her and I knew she'd hate to delicately fade away, so our family took her to the hospital and did it formally. Said goodbyes and gave her the shot, and watched her close her eyes still dreamin' of victory with the girls. She seemed happy. I guess."

Zoey cut off there, to scrub at her face.

In the stale air of the car, still echoing with her story, I could almost see it: the empty rink, a stretch of wood boards covered in shiny, scuffed laminate. The smell of polish and rubber and dust. Wall decorations, all jagged patterns and neon lightning bolts, faintly glowing in the dark. And two sisters going around in slow circles, over and over and over again, their wheels clicking in unison.

"I'm sorry," I mumbled. "I didn't know."

"Anyway, that's what it's like, Ian. It ain't worth it and never will be. Not to me. If I ever come back dazed and rotting, I'm finishing the job, myself. Couldn't live like that."

I kept watching my hands, my lap, anywhere but her, anywhere but that haunted look in her eye. Dug my fingers into my knees. Breathed. Kept breathing. In and out. The only thing I knew how to do, the same thing I'd been doing.

"I... think... I'm a bad person," I said. "It's still worth it to me."

And Zoey sighed. She shifted, resting her hands against the wheel. I could see a fresh bandage over one, a wrinkled Band-Aid covering what looked like a handful of glass cuts. It matched the marks on her face, which matched in turn the scabs and scars across her knuckles and knees. Another blood donation to the cause of me trying to stay alive a few more hours.

"All right. Live, then," she said. Simple as that. "Nothin' wrong with bein' a bad person, as long as you know it and don't hide it behind delusions of selflessness. You said you wanna head back? Eric going with you?"

"Mmhmm. You can come with, too, if you want."

"Because it's my car?" She cracked a grin at me. "I'm *graciously allowed* to drive y'all back, how nice."

"You're *graciously allowed* a chance to still set things right after *trying to get me killed*," I glared back. "And I know how to hot-wire a car, just saying. I can get another one."

She laughed at that, hard enough to drop the towel from her face. Her eyes underneath stood out bloodshot and dark... but, at the same time, not as bad as I'd feared. Either I was getting used to seeing gross things, or she knew how to recover quick. Maybe both.

"Oh damn, *excuse* me." She leaned forward, fishing the towel out from a footwell mess of old receipts and roller skate laces. "So what made you reach out to *me* and *my keys*, then, O great hot-wirer of cars?"

Because I really don't want to electrocute myself trying, I thought, but didn't say. Instead: "Because—because I don't think you're a bad person. I'm still upset about what you did, but... I get you wanted to help people. And... maybe you *still* want to help people, despite everything."

"Even if we don't exactly get along? Somethin' tells me your friends back at the hospital won't welcome your 'kidnappers' with open arms."

"Especially then. You said to build a world of people who care about one another, but I don't want people who care just because they happen to agree all the time."

"*Would* get pretty boring. I like your idea of the world. So . . ." She stretched, sitting upright in her seat. "All right, Captain, you twisted my arm, I'll do it." She waved a hand, dismissive, as if she didn't care either way—but by this point I was starting to notice her habit of acting aloof, even when she built up a whole habit of caretaking. Maybe that made it easier to cope with loss, for her. "Speaking of people, where *is* Eric, anyway?"

I gestured toward the mall's exit doors, where Eric still kept a somber, steady watch. She caught his eye and gave him a friendly wave, and he scowled back, crossing the parking lot to us in long, marching strides.

He didn't wait for an invite or an update. As soon as he got close, he opened the back door and settled into the seat behind me, one hand on a backpack slung over his shoulder and one on his knife.

"As a heads up: if you hurt him, I'll kill you," he said, instead of a hello.

"And yet you're letting me drive you back. Bold of ya to just assume I'm not gonna say 'screw these guys' and drive us into the nearest pole."

"And take yourself with us? You're too vain for that and we both know it."

Zoey slapped the dashboard. "Driver's seat has the airbag. *I'll* be fine."

"I'm behind you. I'll slit your throat if you even try it."

"And my body'll still be slumped over on the gas, so, good luck, buddy."

"*Guys,*" I cut in, "can we please just go to the hospital? And maybe *not* die or kill anything along the way? Please?"

Zoey glanced at me, then back at Eric. "The captain *has* spoken."

"Fine," Eric said. Then, after a moment: "Sorry."

I blushed. "It's okay, I'm—not really a captain or anything—" Reconsidered. "But if it gets us there, then—then fine. I'm the captain. Let's, um, march. Or peel out. Or something."

Again, Zoey glanced at Eric, and this time I saw a little hint of an *oh-that's-adorable* smile before she focused. One of those stifled-laughter smiles. It seemed weird, for her and Eric to shift so quick from threatening to kill each other to sharing looks, but then again, maybe that was how they got along.

A dead captain. A roller girl with a habit of stabbing people. My depressed maybe-boyfriend. All three of us on our way to meet a farm girl and a survivalist.

If this was me making a world of my own, then what a weird, patchwork world this was gonna be.

I rubbed my wrists, trying to work some feeling into my joints, and sat up straighter in the passenger seat as we drove, like a captain should.

SIXTEEN

We reached the freeway in record time—unlike Monica, who drove slow and careful, Zoey didn't see the point of speed limits in an empty town, and she slammed through red lights and past stop signs with casual abandon. She kept turning to us to talk, too, shouting over the pounding bass and screaming vocals of her cranked-up radio while I dug my hands into the armrests and Eric looked green in the back seat.

"Check it out! There's the hill I crashed my skateboard on back when I was eleven, still got a wicked scar from that—oh, hey, check out that car there, dude really did just abandon it in the middle of the lane, *wild*—anyway, I'm turning here, right?"

"Right." I swallowed. Then: "No—wait, left, I mean *left*!"

"Left!" And Zoey twisted the wheel, skidding us around a wide turn that lurched the car and sent Eric and me both up against the windows. The cab shifted for one dizzy second, and I thought for sure we'd roll, but it caught itself and settled to the sound of Zoey's wild laughter.

"Can we take it *easy*?" I asked, the words coming out sharper than I wanted as I shouted them over the music. Trees and power lines flickered past, too fast to get my bearings for where we were.

"You washed out every toxin except for POSITIVITY! And you never swallow pride 'cause you HATE EATING CALORIES!

Found the secret to life in a MARKETING SCHEME! Selling only GOOD VIBES and BAD SELF-ESTEEM!"

Zoey sang along, screeching out the words, before shaking her head. "No way! If I can't go *Fast and Furious* at the end of the world, when else *can* I?"

"Spikes," Eric said, dully.

"What?" I said.

"What?" Zoey echoed. Then: "Oh *shit, spikes*!"

I saw it for a split second: across the empty road, lying in jagged rows like roadkill, sat several wooden boards, glaring pale against the dark asphalt. Some of them were smudged dark at their edges, like they'd been pulled out of someone's firepit, but they all glittered with nails.

And then she *stomped* on the brakes, hard enough to send us all sprawling forward. I hit the dash at an angle, my seat belt yanking one shoulder back as the other thudded against the glove box. The brakes squealed, filling the air with a hot stink of rubber.

We slowed, but not soon enough. A heavy *thud* rattled through the undercarriage as we ran over the boards, and the sedan gave an ugly lurch to the right, swaying on drunken wheels as Zoey screamed curses and tried to coax it back into a line. Another thud, and the steering wheel jerked out of Zoey's grip and to the side, sending us tumbling the other way.

Then, slowly, lazily, it drifted back, curving along a wide half circle across all four freeway lanes before crawling to a spluttering stop. The sedan twitched, once, rocking us to an uneasy stop, and went still.

It all happened over maybe a second or two, but it took us all several seconds more to get our bearings over *what just happened.*

The radio, meanwhile, kept blasting indie rock. Zoey reached over with a shaking hand and clicked it off. We sat there in silence, breathing in rubber fumes and staring at the road sprawled sideways outside the windshield.

My arm felt stiff. I looked down and saw Eric gripping it tight, just above the elbow, his other arm wrapped around his backpack and pressing it to his chest. He caught my eye, and I reached up to press my hand over his.

"It's okay. We're okay."

He let go, just in time for Zoey to thud her head against the wheel.

"Son of a *bitch*, my *tires*!" she spat. "Bitch, bitch, *bitch*—"

Still *bitch*ing, she shoved open the driver's side door, spilling out onto the road in a staggering side-step. I pushed out afterward, gulping fresh air, while Eric went last, hunched and watchful.

To either side of the freeway I could see grassy hills and broad ditches, curving up to the occasional flat-roofed business standing alone between stretches of empty fields. One in particular stood out, its dark windows plastered with faded beer ads, and I realized we'd just about hit the same spot of road I'd walked down last night. All the buildings looked brighter in the daytime, their overgrown lawns buzzing with gnats and crickets, but they lined up the same as they did in the dark, bar to salon to civil war tourist shop.

Except, in the parking lot of the bar, I spotted a truck I hadn't seen there last night. A dented 90s beat-'em-up truck, with a tarp in the back.

And at the same time I realized that was *our* truck, I heard footsteps crunching over the road. Eric shifted closer, enough for me to hear the rabbit hitch of his breath against my back, and feel the tensed muscles in his arm as he grasped his knife.

I peered around the car, and just barely made out Zoey standing by her door—and, beyond her, a figure rising out of the ditch, knife drawn and jacket coated in sprigs of dead weeds.

Angel. Angel stepped forward, all four-foot-nothing of her, still wearing my old purple jacket and her thick-laced army boots. I couldn't even see the handle of her knife, with a sleeve dangling over her hand and bunching up at the edges, but I could make out its tip, serrated and gleaming.

Behind Eric, in the other ditch, came another rustling. Monica pushed her way out, one hand brushing stubborn thistles and dandelions off her skirt, the other pointing her own cane at us. She'd hammered a few extra nails into it, I saw, turning it into some sort of wicked spear.

Terrifying Valkyries, bent on revenge.

Monica glanced at me and I saw her glare flicker into a mix of concern and relief before settling back on anger. Angel didn't even flinch, too focused on trying to kill Zoey with her stare alone. Zoey glared back, arms spread, while Eric's death grip on his knife tightened a notch.

"Who—?" he started.

"*Great.* Couplea' wannabe raiders popped my *tires*," Zoey spat. "You assholes know how *hard* it is to find a mechanic in an *evacuation*?"

"We're the assholes?" Monica spat back. "You *kidnapped* our friend. You do *not* get to turn this on *us*, you absolute *double bitch*—"

"Okay, first of all, he *asked* to come with us. And second of all, we were bringing him *back*, until you *popped my tires*—"

"Bull*shit*, you were on the highway to who-knows-where. But if you don't let him go right now—"

"Bitch, *what?* You're, like, *twelve*. Do you want to *go*? Because I'll—" Zoey started, and I cut in.

"Monica, Angel!"

Everyone froze. I nudged Eric's arm away from me to get some space, and I ran toward Monica's ditch. She jumped, startled, her cane falling from her fingers to clatter into the grass, but I didn't slow down. I spread my arms wide and pulled her into a tight hug, one that was all elbows and limbs and graceless, dizzy, laughing movement.

Footsteps pounded across the asphalt, and then I felt something collide with my back, tiny arms digging into my sides and turning the hug into a group hug. I wriggled my arm free and back, pulling Angel into the fold in a waft of Home Depot scent and purple cotton fabric. Monica squeezed harder, her citrusy perfume blending into the mess, all of us clinging like our lives depended on it.

"*Ian!*" Angel cried.

And then we all started talking at once, babbling over one another.

"Oh man, I'm so glad to see you guys again—"

"Thought you were gone, thought you were gone—"

"Are you okay? How's your head? I got some more thread if we need—"

"I'm okay, Monica—oh no, I'm sorry, you go first—"

"Going to *kill* them."

"No, Angel, it's fine, Zoey's right—"

"Oh my God, Ian. We searched *everywhere* for you, I swear—"

"I could tell, I'm so sorry, a lot happened, but I'm okay now—"

"Who is he?" Angel asked.

I glanced back. She stared at Eric—not that hateful glare of earlier, but a blanker, opener look. Eric, in turn, seemed unsure what to do with his hands; they twitched at his knife, then at his backpack strap, then back to his sides. He watched me close, tensed for any hint of danger.

"Oh! That's—that's Eric, actually. He's . . ." I started to speak, but the words wouldn't come out. They itched at my throat, too surreal to say, and my face burned. I watched Eric staring back at me, standing alone and confused, and I tried again, for his sake. "That's Eric. He's... my... boyfriend. I think."

A pause.

And then both Angel and Monica shouted at once. In Angel's case it was less words than a steady *eeeee* noise, her hands pressed to her chin and eyes wide as plates, while in Monica's case it was more spluttering shock.

"*What*? What, he's—no, *no*, Ian, I know it can be hard to come out sometimes, but you need *better taste*, did you forget he's the one who *stabbed you*—?"

"Um, technically that was Zoey—" I mumbled back.

"It's a long story, but we're kosher now," Zoey added. "Except for now we *don't have a car*—"

"We're... boyfriends?" Eric said, dazed, his face blooming a brilliant red from the revelation.

"I-I mean, not if you don't want to be!" I corrected. "I didn't mean to assume, sorry, just—with the confession and everything, maybe—"

"Wait, is *that* what you were trying to confess at the mall?" Eric said. "Holy shit, this whole time?"

"Yes! Yes, Eric, I've always liked you—"

"Ian, I'm happy for you and all, but he tried to *kill you*—" Monica added.

"I know, but he wanted to *help*—"

"Also, hang on," Zoey cut in. "You *weren't* boyfriends before all this? Goddamn it, Eric, you talked about your love for him, like, *five times*—"

"Of course I did, I thought I'd *killed him*—"

"It wasn't your *fault*, Eric, you didn't—um, hang on." Something tugged on my sleeve. I glanced down to see Angel pressed against my side, her expression twisted in a grimace and mouthing out words. Specifically, the words *shut up, shut up, shut up*.

I grimaced back, then up at the others, with all our loud voices and commotions. We stood around in a rough semicircle, the wrecked sedan and piles of boards behind us, none of us looking quite like we knew what to do now.

So I cleared my throat and, like a captain should, I stood up straighter and took the lead.

"Guys," I said, cutting off any other rambling trails of conversation. "I think we need to take a break. All of us."

And so we found ourselves sitting in the tarped back of the truck, all of us settled together with a pile of mattress pads and storage boxes. Eric and Monica passed out granola bars and dried fruit snacks from their packs, trading them around in a tense sort of peace treaty.

With just the three of us, it'd been small, but cozy. With five people, one of us actively rotting, it felt cramped and awkward and stank of old garlic. I sat hunched between Eric and Monica, my knees digging into a box and my elbows pressed against their sides.

But still, it felt like a hideout, a place for everyone to shush and take polite turns catching one another up. So we did, going around in a circle like we were in school and having a show-and-tell session.

I went first, describing whatever I could. Whenever I'd stumble over a word or trail off at a faded memory, I'd glance at Zoey or Eric to see if they had anything to add, but Eric seemed quiet as usual and Zoey shrugged it off, even as I recalled our argument and Monica and Angel gave her twin murderous glares. *Shame* and *regret*, I was beginning to realize, weren't easy words in Zoey's vocabulary.

(Yet she'd still driven us back, I reminded myself. Once again, she'd gone out of her way to help set things right.)

Once I'd gotten through it all, I sat back and fished out a bottle of water from our stock—one of Angel's vending machine hauls, I guessed—and drank while Monica and Angel took over.

Their story, at least, was a shorter one. They'd noticed I was gone as soon as they woke up, sometime around eight a.m. ("Maybe nine... or ten-ish," Monica admitted. "But we definitely wouldn't sleep in later than that.") They thought I might've wandered off, disoriented and forgetful, so they searched the hospital, then the woods around it, working their way in growing circles deeper into town.

"And that's when we saw that radio in the middle of nowhere, surrounded by stomped grass and fairy lights," Monica said, "and we realized something bad might've happened."

"Oh yeah. Didya' take that radio back with ya?" Zoey asked.

"What? No. We left it there."

"Seemed too much like a trap," Angel added.

"Damn it." Zoey shook her head. "That was a nice radio. Remind me to go back and get it."

After finding the radio, Monica and Angel decided to prep for an attack—mostly by going back to the hospital's burned-out pediatric ward and gathering debris to scatter across the road to stop anyone getting in or out.

"By that point, we really thought someone might've killed you for good," she said—mumbling it into her chest, arms crossed in a self-hug. "And I knew if they had, I'd kill them back. I'd make it *hurt*. Focusing on that all day was easier than worrying."

If the boards hadn't worked out, they'd planned to take the truck and do slow sweeps around town, hunting for any other signs of life. But they'd heard Zoey's engine first—with no other sounds around other than faint animal noises, it echoed well in advance, and they ducked into the ditches to ambush us.

"We promised to look out for one another," Angel muttered.

I didn't know what to say to that. I scrubbed at my eye and squeezed at my water bottle until it crinkled.

It seemed unfair: all this effort to get me back because they cared for a dead guy. I'd tried so hard to come to terms with dying, to find people to fix it for me, and all I'd gotten were more people to love and leave behind.

Zoey really was right. Being a caretaker was heartbreaking. I glanced at her now, but she'd shifted focus to those string lights along the tarp edges. They looked just like the ones she'd placed around the clearing, I realized—maybe they'd even been taken from the same Walmart or Sheetz, pulled off the same looted shelf next to the knick-knacks and fake plants. Another weird connection between strangers, drawn together by the end of the world.

Monica leaned close, and I leaned back against her, resting my head against hers. Angel reached out a hand, that same one-fingered not-hand-holding she'd wanted back at the dollar store, and I tapped a finger back on hers. And Eric, still sober and quiet, reached out to squeeze my arm, a little too tight, a little too protective.

All of us with our own ways of reaching out to one another, connecting to one another.

Then Zoey spoke up, slow and thoughtful in a way I'd never heard her be before.

". . . Wait. What happened to the other dead people?" she asked.

"Hmm?" Monica peeked over, her hair rustling and tickling against my face.

"You said the radio was surrounded by footprints and lights. But nothin' about the *dozen dead people* that shoulda' also been there. Just realized that."

Monica shivered. "I didn't see anyone. Just . . . pieces. Like . . . a stray finger. A tooth. Bits of that black gunk. Things they'd... I don't know... *shed.*"

"But no actual dead people?"

"No. Why?"

No dead people. But I remembered the party of swaying forest bodies, embracing the pure joy of being together in death. The ease of letting ourselves fall into a hum of nothingness together, like hypnosis or sleep. I remembered the taste of black gunk on my tongue, coughed up from me or eaten from someone else, in that same casual way ingredients in a mixing bowl slipped into one another on their way to become something combined.

Where had they gone, after Zoey and I left and her CD player finally played itself out?

Where would the group at the hospital have gone, if they weren't set on fire?

What were all the dead people doing, gathering in the same town they'd first appeared in?

Zoey looked at me, then, and this time, for once, we had the same understanding between us: a wary sort of confusion. She cracked her neck, turning toward the back of the truck.

"You got keys for this thing? Because I think it's time I get my radio back."

SEVENTEEN

Monica insisted on driving, and Zoey insisted on at least sitting in the cab to point the way, with Angel squished in the middle seat between them like a human barrier to keep them from ripping out each other's throats in the process. God knew both of them looked ready to, trading dry looks as they settled in, and Angel kept her expression flat and her old bowie knife pointed up in her lap like a tiny flag of warning.

Which left me and Eric in the back of the truck, pulling down PVC pipe and rolling up the tarp to shove between storage boxes. Without the tarp overhead, the back seemed less cozily intimate, but it gave enough space to stand up and to breathe fresh air. Angel had even given me my jacket back for it, but the sun overhead beat down hot and the breeze felt nice, so I kept it tied around my waist, its iron-on patches scraping against one another.

I settled onto a plastic tub bulging with spare clothes and fabric, while Eric sat on the edge of the truck bed, one shoe resting on the floor and one against the wheel well. As Monica drove, the wind rustled his hair into swept tufts, the sunlight catching new angles of his beard scruff and bare, tanned arms.

Goddamn it. Of course the end of the world would only make him prettier.

I caught him glancing back as if he was thinking the same thing, which seemed like a nice joke—the only thing the end of the world got me looking like was closer to spoiled milk. But he still reached out a hand, and I still reached out my own back, and we held hands across the truck bed.

Should we do more than hold hands? I didn't know, and the thought of it made my throat run dry. Holding hands already felt so wild, so unbelievable, so *gay*, that I couldn't even figure where to go next. Did he want to cuddle? Kiss? How far *could* we even go before my dead body caught up, anyway? How much could we wring out of this?

I'd spent so much of my afterlife trying to figure out my own wants and feelings, to learn how to be selfish and go for them, that now that I had one here, fulfilled, I didn't know what to do next.

His grip tightened on mine, and I glanced up to find him watching me with a concerned, soft expression. Another of those expressions I hadn't hardly seen him wear before all this.

"Hey. You doin' okay?" he asked.

I shrugged. "Kinda. Just... still a little in shock, I guess. I thought all this time that you'd hate me."

"Nah. Not you. Never you."

I smiled back, but it didn't feel sincere. Not entirely. I wanted to say something stubborn and brave, like nothing was wrong and would ever be wrong, but... it was funny. I'd never heard her voice before, but somehow all the words I could think of sounded like Willow's. Like the words of a roller girl doing laps around her dying memories with her exhausted sister.

How could I learn to be selfish without hurting him in the process?

"Hey, Eric . . . ," I tried, "you'll be okay after this, won't you? I need you to promise me that. Got it?"

"To be okay?" He raised an eyebrow back.

"I *mean* that you won't let anything that happens drag you back to the clothing store to die again." I gripped his hand tight. "Dying in a mall ain't fun, and... I want you to be selfish and to feel things and to have fun, too. I want you to make it out of this whole."

His face twisted. It wasn't that raw, broken pain he'd had back at the dollar store, but it wasn't comforting, either. He tried a smile, more like pulling back his lips to expose his teeth. "Thought you weren't gonna die any time soon, nerd."

"I ain't!"

"So stop talkin' like it."

"Only if you do!" I breathed, in and out. "Only if you promise me to never die, too."

"You know I can't guarantee that."

"I don't care. Try."

"You're ridiculous." He sighed. "But fine. I promise to never die."

"Me, too," I mumbled. "And I promise to be selfish the whole way, too. To grab everything I want and devour things and take up too much space."

He laughed. "That ain't like you at all, you know. Sure you don't want me to take over that part?"

"I'm sure. But I *also* promise to talk about everything I'm feeling, to not push people away, and to never run from my problems, if you wanna take over *that*."

Eric winced. "Bastard."

"Promise it."

"God, *fine*. I promise all that and more. We'll be a couple of selfish, emotional, blunt bastards."

"Deal."

We shook on it—already holding hands, it was really more like a bob up and down, then a settle, but I took it with a real smile this time, albeit a sad one. And he smiled back, soft and smooth, and before I knew what I was doing for sure I leaned forward to rest my head against his shoulder, and he leaned sideways to rest us both against the back window of the cab, and we rode the whole way like that, arms wrapped around each other for balance and hot summer wind rustling us ragged.

The truck slowed to a stop a minute later, grass brushing its underside and branches scraping the cab roof, and we pulled away to look around.

We'd made it to the same clearing as before, pulled up as close as the truck could get without hitting a tree. Same open space, same fairy lights wound around tree trunks—their LEDs glowing thin and dull in the sunshine—and, a ways ahead, same duct-taped CD player crammed between gnarled roots. It played nothing but a faint static now, its CD long since played out.

No dead people, though. As I straightened up, pushing myself off my box and onto the metal framing underneath, I couldn't spot so much as a body. In their place stood nothing but grass stomped flat by dozens of footsteps, speckled with the occasional scrap of fabric or splatter of black like sickly mushrooms sprouted from the damp ground.

Eric hopped down easily from the siding, then turned to offer me a hand, and I couldn't resist a laugh. Now that he wasn't trying to mercy-kill me, he'd swapped pretty quick into acting like everything else might kill me first. It'd be sweet if it wasn't a little embarrassing.

(On the other hand, who knew? I was rotting. Maybe a jump really would snap an ankle or break a toe.)

I decided to risk it, leaving the hand in favor of a hop over the side—then grimaced as a rock crunched under my sneaker. I reached to fish it out of the treads... and saw it wasn't a rock.

Under my sole, buried halfway in rubber, sat a tooth.

That laugh I'd had dried up.

With the other dead around, the music playing so slow, I'd have eaten it without a second thought. Waste not, want not, and we were all part of a collective whole, here. I'd have eaten it like the dollar store clerk's eyes, desperate and hungry for some sense of belonging, of warmth, of any life left in its marrow.

Some things didn't fade as the body rotted: the hum of music, habits so engrained they became thoughtless, and that desperate want to not die alone and hungry.

Come home, love. I'm here.

I shivered, hard, and unknotted my jacket, pulling it on. It wasn't cold out here, but I felt cold, anyway, watching all the other living people wander around this emptied space. Contaminating it, almost, with their warm breath and thudding hearts.

The dead weren't here anymore.

So where did they *go*?

Zoey trotted over to her CD player, rambling something about batteries and tape, while Monica rolled her eyes and Angel ran protective hands over the tie-downs around our stockpile, checking for anything lost. Eric picked through the pieces of dead left behind, nudging fabric and gunk with his shoe. And me . . . ?

I wandered farther back, toward the edge of the clearing. Toward where the trees and scrubgrass clumped together, melting into rocks and grassy foothills.

Upward.

Beyond the foothills, I saw, were larger hills, then sheer-faced cliffs, speckled with spidery-thin trees and stubborn weeds. This far out in the countryside was all elevation, hills spilling up into mountain paths and boulders.

And there, high up between the trees and the rocks and the thistle growths, I spotted a flicker of red.

A piece of flannel, torn off someone's jacket and left to sway in the breeze. A piece of someone dead.

I swayed, too.

Come home, love. It's time. No more wandering.

"They went up," I mumbled.

Eric turned to me. Monica followed suit, trotting over in slow cane steps, and Zoey glanced up from her radio.

"What?" Eric said.

I swallowed. The air here suddenly felt too thin, too cold—sharp mountain air. "They went up to the mountain." Swallow. "Something's calling us up there. Whatever—whatever we came from, it wants us to come back and become whole together. To—to fall apart up there, so our oil can go in the water again."

Come here, come here, come here.

I hunched forward and retched, coughing up sickly bile composed of black fluid. Eric and Monica cried out, running to grab either of my sides and hold me steady, but I didn't look up from the mess at my feet.

In the middle of the gunk, sitting bright and pale and small, was one of my own teeth.

They stared at me with concerned eyes, living eyes, and I found myself ranting back at them, an agitated spiel that didn't want to work itself into real words.

"No—no-no-no, I don't want to fall apart, leave me alone, please, no, don't let me forget—go away go away stop whispering at me stop calling me stop it I don't want to *go*—"

"Ian! *Focus.*" Eric grasped my shoulders, turning me to face him, but I couldn't look at him, not with my throat itching and my head pounding. I looked everywhere else, instead, blown-wide black pupils trying to see everything at once before I lost myself.

"I don't want to go . . . ," I mumbled, glancing up and away at Eric's confused stare.

Monica cut in, her voice soft, soothing, leaning around Eric toward me. "Okay, Ian. You're still here. You don't have to go anywhere. Okay? Let's get you back to the truck."

Right. Okay. Breathe, in and out. Focus on right now.

My name is Ian Chandler. It's a warm summer afternoon. At some point very soon, I'm gonna die. But not right now. Right now I'm still breathing. Right now I'm here. Right now I'm me.

Focus on being me.

I blinked and I found myself sitting in the truck bed, back pressed against a plastic tub, but I couldn't remember climbing in. Eric and Monica sat to either side of me, twin bodyguards. Eric hunched forward on the plastic tub, his hands clasped between his knees, while Monica sat cross-legged, brushing shaky hands through her hair.

Ahead of us, Angel wandered the clearing, gathering up pieces of the dead, while Zoey stood beside the truck, leaning against its hitch with her arms crossed on top of it. Her face looked flat, unimpressed, lined with flyaway hairs and speckles of stress acne.

I shuddered out a breath, massaging my eyes with the palms of my hands. They ached, and I pressed harder, until spots and colors flashed in the dark.

"... Lemme get this straight," Zoey said, "It's like a cycle, right? The dead have this itch in them to climb up the mountain and fall apart at the top, oil gets into the water, we drink the runoff, and when we die we fill up with oil until we wanna climb up there, too."

"I think so, yeah," Monica noted. "It's like what they warned us about when we were kids, with the sink filters."

"That's gross. Hate that."

"I'm... trying really, really hard not to think about it."

"But you said this shit's flammable?"

"Mm. So if we get up there first... I don't know. Maybe we can set it on fire. Stop the cycle before Ian reaches it, and... keep him."

"You know I'm down for setting things on fire. But we don't got climbing gear or anyone to spot us if we fall. We don't even know what we'll find up there. And . . ." She shifted, from airy flippantness to, for once, something softer. "You know if we pull that off, it won't save him, right? Just maybe buy you an extra day or two."

"There's a lot you can do with an extra day."

I dropped my hands, then, away from my pounding head and the echoes of whispers in my brain. Toward here, and now, and that tempting, destructive word: *fire*.

"I want to try it," I mumbled. The words came out raw, scraped with vomit and dry breaths.

Zoey tilted her head, toward me. "Yeah?"

"I keep hearing this...voice, in my head, trying to call me home. She feels infinite, and unstoppable, and full of teeth." Even at the mention of it, my throat itched again. I swallowed it back down, squeezed my fingers into fists. "I want to set her on fire. I want to tell her *no*."

"Oh good, there you have it. She's an infinite voice in his head fulla teeth. Now *everything* makes sense. Don't know why I was ever confused in the *first place*—"

"Shut up, Zoey," Eric interrupted. Then, after a pause: "Please."

She shut up. I grimaced back, trying to focus, to put every jumping, skittering thought into words that made sense.

"I don't know what she really is. I'm just saying what my body wants right now. And...that there's a part of *me* that refuses to give in." I couldn't stop shivering.

Eric didn't say anything, but I saw his hands tighten their grip on each other, knuckles searing white. On my other side, Monica flinched, then shook her head.

"Don't worry, we won't let her take you," she said.

"Please don't." I hated the whine in my voice, but I couldn't stop it.

"Probably should leave him behind, then, right?" Zoey asked. "Mountain monster lady wants to eat dead people... bringing her a dead kid... seems a little self-fulfilling, doesn't it?"

"Agreed," Eric muttered.

But Monica hummed under her breath. "Can we *find* her without Ian?"

"Sure. How hard can it be to find a giant clump of corpses on a mountain?"

"In West Virginia? Pretty hard. Do you know how many mountains we have, Zoey?"

I nodded back, more to cut off an argument than anything. "It's okay. I *want* to go with. If we're setting this thing on fire... I want to help."

"Yeah, you *look* like you're ready to climb a mountain all day, kiddo." Zoey's usual sarcasm bled into her words, but underneath, smothered as far as she could, I caught an edge of concern. An edge of that begrudging caretaker. I cracked open an eye to look at her and give her a soft smile, but she glared pointedly away before she could notice it.

A rustle. Behind Zoey, carrying a plastic take-out baggie full of pieces, Angel trotted up. She wasn't tall enough to rest her arms on the hitch like Zoey, so she hefted the baggie over the side, letting it tap and rustle against the metal interior.

She stared at us with her usual blank expression, with those same dark eyebrows and hollowed-out eyes and tiny, thin mouth. Even without my jacket anymore, she hadn't yet gone back to wearing her oversized army jacket, and in just a plain shirt—green, long-sleeved, the sleeve edges gripped in her hands and so worn they'd gone spotted with holes—she seemed smaller. Plainer. Almost normal, if you ignored the bag of body parts.

"Just go to a ski lodge," she said. "Lock him in here."

"What?" Zoey asked.

"There's several ski lodges near here. Closest is Trollhagen Park.

Eleven miles away by access road. View of every mountain in the area." A pause. "And ski lifts. Could cover a lot of ground that way. Beats rock climbing. Drive Ian to the lodge and have him point the way, then lock him safely in there while we take the lift to the top and set it on fire."

We stared at each other, all of us. I vaguely remembered the ski lodge—it'd been one of a dozen vacation spots my parents dragged Emma and me to while still adjusting to West Virginia, muttering about *culture* and *good learning opportunities.* I could still recall wood-paneled walls and crackling fireplaces and the plastic pinch of ski-boot buckles.

Would that work? Would that be high enough, quiet enough, close enough to point the way to her, without getting pulled in and falling apart, too?

I didn't know... but somewhere, in that growing hum and in the itching rot in my bones, it seemed right enough. It seemed like *up*, like *closer*, like *home.*

Like dying.

And for a wild second, I wanted to abandon the whole suicidal idea. Let the rest of the dead die—they would, anyway, and I didn't have to be their caretaker. Let Eric and Monica and Angel and Zoey waste one of their infinite living days scouring up and down mountains with torches held high, delivering my revenge secondhand.

How far could the truck take me? If I started driving now—I didn't know how to drive, but it didn't seem too hard—I could make it to Maryland before dark. And from there it was only a short ways to the Chesapeake Bay, then out toward the ocean.

I'd always wanted to see the ocean. I'd never gotten a chance, and suddenly I wanted to, more than anything. Forget mountains—I'd go somewhere flat and low, somewhere so close to sea level that I could reach out and touch the water. I could find a pretty beach and sleep on it, drink in hand and towel laid out, and any voices calling me home from the mountaintops could sing themselves hoarse.

I wanted to outrun dying. Like a plane flying toward the sun, chasing it around and around the world so it never had to get dark. I wanted to take my last days left and turn them into the longest days in history.

So why did I nod at Angel? Why did I hear myself say, "It'll work"? Why did I sit up straighter, watching the mountains on the horizon, and let everyone else settle around me, preparing to head *up*?

Maybe I was never very good at being selfish, after all. Not really. Every lesson I'd taken to be more than a martyr figure—survival with Angel, family with Monica, caretaking with Zoey, confessions with Eric...they all still involved helping other people. I hadn't stopped wanting to die for a cause; all I'd done was change the cause, from what was expected of me, to what I wanted for myself.

Was that what being a martyr meant? Not all that posing myself as the perfect candidate for a sacrifice I'd been groomed for, but finding my own reasons to sacrifice myself? Being terrified of dying, but risking it anyway, for the sake of what I wanted?

Beside the truck, Zoey straightened up, popping her back. "You know how to drive, shortstop?"

Angel shook her head.

"All right, just give me the directions, then."

"Really? You're driving our truck?" Monica asked.

"Don't want to. But what the hell. You've got everything covered back here, so I can't *not* do something useful. You know how it is." She glanced at me then, finally, and I stared back, and she almost, almost smiled. "Caretaking really is a Goddamn nightmare."

I nodded.

And pleased, she moved to the driver's seat, Angel tagging along behind, while my twin bodyguards stayed behind with me—their living-people eyes bright and alert, watching either side for any sign of the dead.

Or any sign of teeth.

EIGHTEEN

We rode in thoughtful, tired silence, off the clearing's dirt and back onto smooth highway road. Zoey didn't even race, this time—if she still held a grudge from her tires popping or if she just wanted to be considerate of the passengers rattling around in the back, I didn't know, but she coaxed our truck along at an almost normal speed.

Eric sat closer than ever, enough to feel the brush of his jeans against my side and the radiating warmth of his skin, but I couldn't even think about pushing things between us. Not when it was hard enough trying not to think about things with *teeth.* My thoughts skittered around, full of distorted lizard-brain instincts, half-conscious urges like *climb* and *fear* and *eat* and *die.*

Breathe in.

My name is Ian Chandler. I live in West Virginia. It's a sunny afternoon in July, I don't remember what day. I don't remember a lot of things. I'm dying, but before I go, I want to break the cycle that started all this. I'm on my way to set its source on fire. I'm breathing. I'm here. I'm still me.

Breathe out.

We turned onto a side road, the tilt of it sliding me against Monica's side, against T-shirt cotton and the scent of citrus body spray. She patted my back absently, but didn't look up from the hitch, from the highway unrolling behind us, its divider lines unfurling in steady Morse-code patterns. Dash, dash, dash.

The road wound upward, curving higher, higher. Metal shifted underneath us, shifting us gently farther back to tap against the hitch, along with every other plastic tub and grocery baggie and rolled-up bundle of mattress pads. String lights, wound in tight wire circles, tapped against my foot.

Higher, and something in my ears shifted and popped. The wind picked up, colder now, speckled with a thin mist of rain. Those steady Morse-code road lines darkened, bleeding into the asphalt.

Monica stretched, uncrossing and recrossing her legs. She rubbed her bare arms, but when I looked up at her, I found her forcing a smile back at me.

"Hey," she said, all soft and gentle. "It's going to be okay. Got it?" The same voice she'd used back at the mall, when she'd trotted around with a notebook and a backpack full of supplies and a plan on exactly where to go from here. *It's okay. I have this under control. I'm ready.*

I didn't believe it this time, either, but I suspected I didn't need to. It was enough for both of us to pretend. So I smiled back.

"Yeah. Get in, start a fire, get out. Easy."

Higher. The road grew bumpier, speckled with potholes and scraggly tar patches. To either side rose sheer hills, lined with patchy forest clumps. The air tasted piney and damp, and my fingers left streaks of condensation as I ran them idly down the metal flooring.

Higher. Eric pushed himself off the plastic tub and Monica dug around inside, pulling out spare coats and a fluffy blanket from beneath piles of crisp jeans and crinkling packages of socks. One was Angel's army jacket, I noticed, rumpled, and five sizes too big, and she passed it off to Eric with barely a word. It fit him fine, and that seemed wrong somehow—this was a coat meant to hide your hands and face in.

Her own choice—a peacoat with a fuzzy collar, fashionable and sleek—seemed wrong in its own way. A middle finger at the grunge and ruin the end of the world wanted to dress us in. But so did my jacket, still smudged with dried blood and covered in cheery patchwork iron ons.

None of us felt right.

My name is Ian Chandler. I'm breathing. I'm me. I'm—

(Come home love come home love you're so close can't you feel me calling up here you wouldn't hurt me would you)

—still me. I'm in a truck with my friends. Once we stop this thing, we'll go home, and everything will be okay.

Higher. We huddled together under the blanket, pressed against one another's sides, sliding along through each winding turn and bump. The truck drifted right, and as I tapped to a stop—this time against Eric's side, pressed up against a bundle of army green fabric—I looked up, and I saw the ski resort ahead.

I saw the mountains first, a line of jagged peaks against a horizon half hidden in rolls of fog. The afternoon sun cut between them, casting everything in a faded blue glow like a bleached-out shirt. Lines of dead ski lifts arched from their peaks toward squat little maintenance buildings, metal benches creaking in the wind. The slopes below them, well out of season, looked bare and sad, all dead brown grass and dry birch trees with stubborn dregs of snow clinging to all the shadowy parts.

To the right stood a massive cabin, its walls stained dark as logs and its porch lined with glistening picture windows. Half of it sat on the slope and the other half stretched outward, balanced on dizzying wood pillars and walls of speckled cobblestone. Its curtains were drawn, its walkway overgrown with spidery brush. Across its front entryway and leading back toward the slopes were lines of orange rope and rebar poles, wrapped with neon plastic ribbons.

SKI RESORT CLOSED, read a sign dangling from the rope, over a crossed-out picture of a skiing stick figure. **NO HIKING, SKIING, RIDING**.

Another sign, in a cheerier font: **We're sorry—TROLLHAGEN RESORT is CLOSED for the season! See you all next winter!**

We parked, anyway, pulling up along the walkway—twigs scratching at the truck's underside—next to a faded wooden cutout of a cartoon bunny in vibrant ski gear. He stared at us with big, chipped eyes and a dopey grin as we stood up, stretching our legs and working blood back into our joints.

Despite all the holes in my brain, I recognized that bunny. He pointed the way to the kiddie slopes farther ahead, next to the shop full of rental gear and changing stations. My dad still had a picture of us there: him standing tall despite holding at least a half dozen overstuffed bags of gear; toddler Emma already facing away from the camera and trying to wander everywhere; and a tiny version of me, dressed up too warm and choking back tears at the idea of skiing down hill.

I'd been scared of everything back then—skiing, heights, even Emma herself, the tough to my fluff. But Dad never lost patience, guiding us back and coaxing us through with constant, gentle reassurance.

My heart hurt. I pressed a hand to it, hesitating as Eric and Monica hoisted themselves out of the bed.

"Hey?" I asked. They both glanced back, and I rubbed my arm. "Can I hang back for a sec? You all can go on ahead, I just...need a minute to adjust."

Eric looked skeptical, and I couldn't even blame him—not when I was already losing my mind a little more by the hour, not when we'd headed out here in the first place on my rambling request. Not when everything up here wanted to call me *home*.

"I can stay with you," he said.

But Monica bit her lip, more sympathetic. "Unless you want a bit of time alone?"

I nodded. "I think I should call my parents before we do this. If that's okay."

Eric raised an eyebrow—he'd never had a good parent in his life. To him, being without his dad probably felt like a weight off his shoulders. Why would I waste time caring about them now?

But Monica, who'd sent us all on a quest for her mom and understood that lonely sort of affection, nodded and reached for Eric's arm. "It's fine. We can watch from the windows or something. Give you a bit of privacy."

Eric still had that doubtful look, that protective itch. But by that point Angel and Zoey had climbed out of the cab, and Monica tugged him naturally into their little group and onward toward the cabin. She flowed so quick into leadership, gathering them up and keeping them talking, moving.

They'll be okay without me, I realized. It'll hurt them, I think—Eric maybe the worst, but everyone else, too. Even Zoey. But they'll have each other, and they'll be okay.

So I can be okay, too.

I glanced at my phone, pushing it to life. Its screen popped up with a **LOW BATTERY** warning, but underneath that were dozens of new missed calls and texts. They'd shifted past anger and desperation, now, into a quiet acceptance that somehow stung worse.

New message: DAD:

Were settled in for the night at the quarantine site.. Emma has already made a couple new friends..! If you get this message at any point, know we're waiting for you and hope to see you soon......!!!!

New message: EMMA:

omfgggg ian nvm im so glad yur not here bc theyre serving cheezburger cassarol & it is GROSSSSSS lmao <3 <3 <3

New message: MOM:

It's 10am, Ian.

Reminder to get up if you haven't already.

Change your clothes, brush & floss your teeth, & take your medication.

Text back when you can.

Love, Mom

Dad's long chains of periods. Emma's bad grammar. Mom's stiff, informative sentences. How had I forgotten those little details? All their own ways of saying *I love you*?

I hopped down, crossing toward the passenger's side door, and wrenched it open in a squeal of old hinges and rust flakes. I didn't see anything in the cab at first besides seats and crumpled wrappers—but there, crammed between the passenger seat and the wall, I found the notebook I'd been using. My survivor's To-Do List.

And there, a couple pages in, in scribbled handwriting and scratched-out notes, I found the letter I'd started planning out to them. Words I'd already forgotten writing stood out in scratchy, desperate letters against yellow paper.

I reread it as I hit DIAL, trying to memorize as much of it as I could between blaring phone rings. My fingers tapped nervous patterns against the paper, smearing sweat and ink, and I could hear my own breath rustling through the speakers.

Okay—I love all of you—won't be showing up—donate clothes, games to Eric—Does he still want the games? I should ask him myself—Take care of Emma, and—

The line clicked. My heart dropped into my shoes.

No more time to prepare.

Dad's voice came through—crackling with static, muffled, quiet, but still *him*. "Jack Chandler speaking." All formal, like he didn't recognize my own number. Or like he was bracing to hear someone else on the other end, a professional stranger ready to give him terrible news.

I tried to speak, but my throat swelled up and the words wouldn't come. They built up in a hard little ball in my throat that tasted like salt. I swallowed, tried again. And again. "Dad? It's me."

A pause.

Then I heard heavy rustling, scrambling, crackles in and out as he adjusted the phone. When he spoke up again, his voice came through clearer, closer.

"Ian?" he said, somehow forcing hope and disbelief and joy and relief all into those two staticky syllables. "My God, Ian, where have you *been*? Are you okay? We're all worried about you—Is Eric looking after you? He knows he's always welcome here—ah, hang on—"

More rustling, muffled voices in the background. Pieces of sentences: *Just called... Hey!... will in just a second... settle down... I know, I'll do that... yeah, it is...* Mom and Emma in the background, Emma shouting for attention as usual, Mom curt and straightforward and trying to shove as many useful things as she could fit into a single sentence. All of them excited.

I waited until they'd trailed off, until I heard the rustle of Dad getting back on the line. "Okay, okay. Sorry about that. Are you okay, fluff? Do you need anything?"

Fluff. He hadn't used that nickname in a long time. Not since I'd turned thirteen and the baby chick fluff of my hair started settling down into something normal.

I hadn't realized I'd miss it so much.

"I . . ." I considered. "I'm still kickin'." It wasn't technically a lie. I kicked at a truck tire, gently, just to make sure. "Eric's here, too. He's keeping an eye out for any trouble. And we found a couple friends to stick with. We missed the evacuation, but we're holding out and we're staying safe together—"

"Wait, you're still in Kittakoop?" he cut in.

"Well, I *think* we're almost in Deepwell by now. We took Angel's truck up to the ski lodge to the north."

"Oh, thank Christ. Wait, who's—?" He sighed, hard. "Never mind. Ian, listen. The volunteers keep saying it's not safe in Kittakoop right now. There's something *toxic* in the mountain runoff. They did a whole emergency investigation after the hospital fire, found that almost everyone there was up to their gills in contamination, and it caused some chemical reaction. They don't know if it's contagious or how far it's spread, so they're trying to contain and test as many people as they can as soon as possible. You make sure that no matter what, you're stickin' to bottled water and filters, got it?"

"I will, Dad. We've got a whole truckload of bottles we've been drinking from." *Except the part right before all this, where I drowned in a mall fountain. Drank a whole bunch of unfiltered water, then. Came back all dead-eyed and weird for it, and now the mountain's calling me back home.*

"Good job, fluff. Oh, and one more thing: *pick up your damn phone*, will ya? We've been calling for over a day now and worried sick."

I winced. "I know, I'm *sorry.* I just . . ." Another hesitation. Should I lie? Make something up? "There was so much going on. I...got... distracted. And I needed to...find a charger."

Dad sighed again, a flicker of static over the line. "Damn it, fluff. You'd lose your own head if it weren't screwed on."

Already have, Dad.

"Guess so, huh?" I laughed. "My bad."

"It's fine. I'm glad to hear from you, fluff. Oh! Hang on, Emma-mama's trying to rip this thing clean outta my hands. Be back in a sec, I love you. Here you *go, sheesh*!"

Emma's voice came on, way too loud. I jerked the phone away from my ear, holding it an arm's length away as the speakers crackled with her voice. "*Ian*! Oh my *god*! I thought you straight-up died!"

"Well—"

"Didya' see all those military trucks? That was *insane.* I texted my best friend, Robin, about it, and they said that it was like some freak *occupation* thing. They said that even their sister Marissa hadn't seen anything like it, and she's been to, like, *fifty* protests and gotten *pepper sprayed* and everything—"

"I saw them. They were pretty insane, all right—"

"Oh my god, wait, does this mean you're still in town?"

"I mean—I was for a little while, yeah—"

She squealed. "Did you see any looters or anything? I saw a TikTok a while back of streets after a hurricane and people were just, like, smashing windows everywhere as soon as everyone left."

"I mean...we did *kinda* steal some stuff? Like, food and water and all that."

"Oh my *god*! Mom! Mom, Ian *stole* stuff!"

"Hey, wait—don't tell Mom, that's not—" Before I could continue, I heard more rustling, then a third voice, clipped and strong. Mom's voice.

"*Ian Chandler.* You didn't pick up the phone for a day and a half because you've been *stealing*?"

"No! Kinda? I just—Dad said to get bottled water!" I scrambled through my notebook, flipping across pages for a good line. That goodbye note I'd worked on didn't have anything about this.

"We have bottled water *at the house.* And did it really take you a *day and a half* to get *water*?"

"We—we got other stuff, too! Like—canned food, and...clothes. Blankets."

"Again, all of which we have *at the house.* An emergency drill isn't an excuse for you to abandon your phone and go ham at the Sheetz, Ian. You *know* better!" Her voice cracked.

Something about that sounded off, and I pulled the phone closer. "Mom?"

A hitched noise, a rasp of breath. I realized after a second that Mom was crying. "I am just...*so* mad at you right now. Please, don't *ever* do that again, Ian."

"I . . ." I gripped tighter, fingers digging into the plastic edges of my phone case. I blinked, hard, but my eyes still felt so dry. "I won't, Mom."

That clipped voice came back, only slightly congested. "You're grounded for a year. And don't *think* about staying any longer at Kittakoop. You tell Eric to get you both onto the interstate and head straight out. They have signs all over the place for the evacuation camp up here. Get yourself registered and vaccinated. No more distractions. No more stealing. Straight to Sutton—"

Emma's voice. "We're in Charleston, Mom. We went north."

"Goddamn it, I am far too upset for *geography.* Emma's right. Get to Charleston, Ian!"

Her voice squawked over the words, and I couldn't help it; I laughed. I couldn't stop laughing. Once I started, they all tumbled out of me, giggling and hiccupping and tearful. I laughed until Mom at last trailed off on her instructions, until it was only me on the phone.

"Ian? Can you still hear us?" Mom asked.

"Yeah. Yeah, I can. Sorry, I just . . ." I sniffled. "I was thinking that I love you. That's all. And I almost forgot how much I miss talking to you."

It went quiet. Something shifted over there. Something all the way in Charleston, in a bigger town, where Mom and Dad and Emma were having "cheezburger cassarol" at a quarantine camp and everything was settling back to normal.

Mom cleared her throat. "I miss you, too, Ian. All the time."

Why can't you say that, then? Why do you have to blend it into scolding and instructions, like the only way you can care about me is through orders?

And then: Maybe for the same reason Emma has to say it by throwing me under the bus or Dad has to say it in the middle of rambling stories about life. Maybe it's too hard to say our feelings directly. Love burns hot. Maybe all of us have to wrap it up in ourselves a bit first before it gets safe to touch.

Maybe that's what makes being selfish so important—we gotta have enough ego built up that we can afford to keep loving each other and giving it away.

Emma's voice, blunt as always: "Are you coming here with us, Ian?"

"I . . ." The words wouldn't come. They sat there on a wrinkled piece of notebook paper, smudged with sweat and dripped tears until they barely seemed like words at all.

I'm not going there. I'm not going to be with you ever again.

I'd never been good at being selfish. Disabled kids don't get to have a *self*, not really. They couldn't afford to get in trouble when their whole existence caused trouble to begin with, when they spent so much time trying to compensate for themselves. They became martyrs instead, endlessly patient and helpful to all.

Every part of me wanted to help this, too. I wanted to tell Emma and Mom and Dad everything they wanted to hear and then some. *Yes, I'm on my way. I'll be there soon. It'll be okay. There's no need to worry. I can make this work. I'm taking my meds and I drank filtered water and I stayed on the good side of town.*

I'm not dead, because I did everything right.

I squeezed my eyes shut. Dug my fingers against the phone case.

"I can't," I mumbled. "I won't be coming back."

Silence. Then Emma's voice, crackling through. Emma, who'd always been prone to wander, to make new friends, who'd always been empathetic and curious and observant, tough instead of fluff. Emma, who'd had a sick older brother for years and knew, in some instinctual sibling way, what it always meant.

"Hey, Ian... are you still alive?" she asked.

My breath hitched. That hard ball in my throat swelled up another notch, choking tight, and I pressed a hand to my mouth to hold back a sob.

"No," I mumbled. "I didn't make it. I'm sorry. Take care of Mom and Dad for me, okay?"

And I hung up. I hung up and I threw the phone, scattering it across the dead brown grass and wild brush overgrowth. And I pressed my hands to my face and sobbed, big toddler wails, like I'd never actually left that day at Trollhagen Park, like everything after was an anxious fantasy, like I was still five years old and fluffy-haired and staring terrified of the slopes below, with Dad squeezing my hand and telling me it'll be all right, take it slow, little fluffy boy, it's not so bad, and we have all the time in the world to try.

NINETEEN

Someone came and got me a few minutes later, after those wild sobs had dried out into heavy breaths and low keening noises like an upset dog. I heard their footsteps crunching over dead twigs and I looked up, scrubbing at my blotched cheeks and damp eyes.

I couldn't remember her name at first, but I recognized her face. The beautiful coily tufts of her hair, the round jaw line, the long nose and soft brown eyes like a baby deer. Mary? Maureen?

No, breathe. You can remember this. Your childhood rival, the only other disabled kid in town. Picnics on hospital lawns with a mom that's no longer around for either of us—Mom, Mom, Mom-mom-mon-mon—Monica.

She's Monica. Monica, Monica, Monica.

I clung to the memory and held on tight.

Monica crouched by me—when had I sat down?—and reached out a hand to grasp my arm.

"Hey, Ian," she said, soft and soothing, an older sister's voice, or a farmer girl soothing frightened horses. Responsible. "I think that was very brave of you. Sounds like it was hard to do, too."

I shuddered out a breath. "Add it to the list, I guess."

"Heh. For sure. Hey, listen. We don't have to do this mountain thing right now. Want to take a break? Get some rest, first?"

"I'm okay," I lied. "We should get this done quick."

She pursed her lips in a little *o*, but didn't argue back. We both knew we were out of time for that. She held my hand and I gripped hers back, warm and close—and then we heard a voice calling from the porch. A blunt, drawling voice.

Zoey stood along the cabin's side, leaned against the rain gutter, braid half undone and faded blue hairs wisping around her jaw.

"Hey, guys. We found one of those touristy binocular things around the back." She jerked a thumb behind her, around the cabin's side. "Wanna give it a try? Might help us spot some dead."

"Sounds good," I muttered.

Monica stood up, and I followed behind her, keeping a slow pace up the porch steps and around the cabin's side.

Along the back, the porch opened up, going from an entrance and walkway to a wide outdoor lounge. Thin wooden roof slats arched over tasteful arrays of wicker chairs and glass-topped tables, all ringed around a brickwork firepit. Against the cabin wall I spotted a long metallic countertop, spaced out with a sink, a drying rack, potted plants—even a grill and trash cans, with an elegant **PLEASE recycle!** sign over them.

Once upon a time, it'd been grand.

Out of season, though, all the plants looked dry and brown, curled up on themselves in faded pots. The chairs had plastic sheets over them speckled with dirt and fragments of leaves, and the firepit was swept out and barren. A lone dish sat in the dryer, smudged with dust where it leaned against the rack.

Up ahead, toward the porch's railing, I saw the other two: Eric and Angel. I mouthed their names to myself, over and over, as we crossed to them.

Monica, Zoey, Eric, Angel. Mom, Dad, Emma. Remember them. Keep remembering them. Hold on to them.

Sure enough, once we got close, I spotted a touristy binocular thing—one of those big metal viewer ones bolted to the ground. Next to it, nailed to the porch railing, was an embossed plate.

Enjoy a spectacular view of the Allegheny Mountains! Can you spot the Black Diamond course from here?

I glanced up. The view ahead stretched onward, all rolling hills of dead grass and rocky, jagged mountain faces lined with leafless trees. They loomed overhead, rough and massive and silent aside from the whistling breeze, and I craned my head up higher, to their peaks.

As soon as I saw the peaks, my head lurched with déjà vu, the kind that dried my throat and glazed my eyes over and threatened to scatter every memory I had.

I'd seen those peaks in my dreams. They traced crooked lines in my brain like a cracked eggshell, letting all the insides spill out. I'd stared at them and been pulled to them, and they'd crunched under my feet with a sound as nostalgic as home.

The wind died down, and in its quiet—in air so thin my ears rang, between patches of drying midsummer snow—I swore I heard something else whispering. It hummed in my bones, itching beneath the skin, a hundred-hundred wasp eggs begging to be born.

You're so close, little one. I can feel you breathing. Isn't it tiring, breathing in and out constantly? Isn't that body heavy? Come here, shed it off. You'll fly, light and free. You'll—

A hand on my shoulder. I jerked back with a strangled noise and saw Eric staring down at me, brows knitted in concern. I blinked, hard, and focused back on him. On Monica, leaning around his shoulder and sharing his expression. On hold on to here and now.

"It's—" Swallow. Try again. "She's up there. Right there. That peak." I didn't want to look back at it, but I pointed where it was—the tallest one, arching overhead in the middle of all those other dusty hills. The one that stabbed hardest at the sky, slicing it open, and in that bleeding wound strange things leaked out, humming like insects and lullabies, tenderly close and burrowing closer.

Eric followed my point, while Monica grasped at the viewer, tilting it up until it creaked against its bolted stand. She grimaced and gave it a hard shove, enough for the hinges to crack and whine, enough to wrench it up an extra forbidden inch.

Behind us, Zoey whistled, and I swore I heard her mutter, "Damn, girl." Angel leaned against the creaking wood railing. Footsteps shuffled. A dozen other human noises, drowning out her whispers and grounding me here.

A few tense seconds later, Monica cried out, loud enough for all of us to flinch and startle back.

"I see something!" she cried. "About halfway up, there's something moving. A few things. I can't tell what they are, but... they've gotta be people, right?" She glanced toward us, eyes wide, and I nodded back. Zoey and Eric followed suit—shipmates following my lead.

"A'ight. Let's go get 'em, then," Zoey said, arms crossed.

"Yeah? How are we gonna do that? The truck can only get us so high," Eric said.

"That's the Black Diamond course. There's ski lift cables going right to the top." Monica turned the binoculars, hunched in front of them with her hands cupped to either side, squinting into the lenses. "But it doesn't look like there are lifts actually on the cables, let alone running...."

Angel cut in, then. "They got detached. It's summer. Maintenance killed the engine and put them away."

We all glanced at her, and she shrugged and looked pointedly away, her hands shoved in my jacket's pockets as she hunched away from the eye contact.

"Hmm, so . . . ," Zoey said, "Angel, is there a way we can get them reconnected *without* getting our hands cut off in the process?"

"Obviously," Angel said. "It's meant for a skeleton crew. Basic three-person bench lifts. Cheap as possible. Main engine might be hard to run, but backup is probably just diesel. Easy for any seasonal trainee to start and run." She motioned with her hands, in a vague circular pattern. "Connect the bench, start the engine, let the belts loop around. Easy."

I stared at Monica, who stared blankly back. Zoey seemed to get it, at least, but looked skeptical—I guessed she still didn't have faith in the idea of pulling this off without losing a hand.

Eric, though, was the one who stepped forward, nodding at Angel. Whether that was because he trusted her or because he was more ready to risk dismemberment than Zoey, though, I didn't know. One of his dozens of random fix-it skills he'd gathered.

"Seems fine," he said. "Not the first time I've had to put broken shit back together. You want a hand lifting things?"

Angel nodded, then—the issue apparently solved—turned to go. Eric followed behind, so the rest of us trailed along like lost toddlers, unsure about the idea but less sure still about being alone.

The maintenance shed seemed tiny from far away, tinier than the cabin, but as we got closer, I realized that "tinier than the cabin" still meant "pretty damn big." It stretched across a lawn of hard dirt, looking like a bland wooden shack and smelling like diesel fuel.

Eric and Angel shoved the doors open, creaking along old hinges and scratching semicircle marks in the dirt, exposing an inside that looked like an exploded truck engine. A pair of massive machines in red and blue took up most of the floor, lined with metal fans and vents and dizzying coils of wires. The walls and ceiling inside were all metal sheet board, cut through with massive open windows for the actual ski lift bale. Bolts the size of my fist wound up one wall toward a section of fan belts and thick fuse boxes, with electrical outlets leading past them toward a set of metal chairlifts wrapped in chain and hooks. All of it was marked here and there with silver marker scrawl measurements, numbers and letters.

It all seemed way, way out of my depth, and I gripped my hands against my chest like that could make it safer.

Angel, for whatever reason, nodded like this all made sense. Maybe to her, it did. She moved toward the blue machine with barely more than a glance, tapping her foot, then nodded at Eric.

"Still has fuel. Good. We'll hook up the lifts."

Zoey raised a hand. "Here to help if you need it. What the hell, maybe I'll learn somethin'."

Angel nodded, and Zoey headed on over. I watched Monica start to raise her hand, hesitate, then lower it down and hobble back against the wall instead. I couldn't blame her. I moved to stand beside her, and both of us tried our best to stay out of the way while the others worked.

I still couldn't exactly figure it out, but as Angel guided Eric and Zoey along, it did make a basic sort of sense. Unchain the lifts, raise one up to the rope overhead. Loosen a bolt on top, clamp it on, tighten it back up. Zoey dug around the back of the shed and came back with a long wrench, whacking the bolt into place with a kind of manic glee.

At one point, while Eric and Zoey were adjusting the grip, I strode over to the machine to offer Angel a bottle of water or something, at least, to help. She glanced up at me from where she sat, hunched over her glowing phone.

On the screen, for a second, I could see the search bar, along with the words ***HOW DO I ATTACH A SKI LIFT CHAIR?***

"Um, Angel?" I asked.

"Not now. Busy working."

"Right. Yeah. Never—never mind." I headed back, water bottle in hand, while Monica raised an eyebrow back at me.

"Is she doing okay?" she asked, her voice a low whisper. "Angel knows what she's doing with this, right?"

"Um." I forced a smile. "Sure!" And I chugged the water, fast, before Monica could ask any more questions about it.

After the chair was settled in place—with a pile of rocks and tools stacked on its seat to test if it would collapse under the weight of a person—Angel kick-started the engine. We all cried out as it roared to life, filling the shed with rumbling, rattling noise. The fans stuttered to life, spinning their belts around, and with a teeth-aching lurch, the rope started moving, tugging our sad single chairlift along.

Behind the machine, Angel cheered. Zoey looked dumbfounded. Eric sighed in relief. Monica didn't seem like she knew *how* to feel, and I didn't, either. We watched our chair trundle out through the window, swaying along a rickety path toward the mountain. Each of us held our breath, waiting for it to collapse on itself or drop its load... but it kept on, creaking upward and out of sight.

I made a note that, if I got through today still alive enough to remember, I'd never doubt Angel again.

We trooped back outside, where the machines were less deafening and we could watch the lift keep going a little farther—just in case it got halfway there and our slapdash job decided to fail. Just in case it wanted to drop one of us several hundred feet to a slab of dry grass and cold earth. Just in case we all died horribly, aiming to help already-dead people.

(God, I must be out of my mind.)

It was Monica who spoke up first, clearing her throat and nodding uneasily at the lift.

"Okay, right, um. Good work, first of all. Good work!" She clapped, awkwardly, then settled her shaky hands back down. "How's this for a plan: we'll let that do a few loops around, to make sure it's...y'know, functional...then whoever wants to go can go one at a time. That way we don't overload it, and everyone else can watch in case—in case it stops, or it's having issues, or whatever."

"It shouldn't have issues," Angel said flatly.

"Exactly! It'll be fine. It'll be *fine*." She stopped, there, then took a deep breath, held it, and let it out. "Zoey, do you still have that duct tape?"

"In my truck, yeah. Want me to go get it?"

"If—yeah, please do. And rope, and anything else we can get." She paused, there, debating with herself. "Focus on cutting off the dead people on their way up. Any way you can—tie them up, shove them, drag them, just keep them back from the peak. If you can lead them down the ski trail, Ian can get them back to the cabin, and keep them inside and away from that thing while we burn it. Got it?"

"Okay, sure, but then what, exactly?" Zoey asked. "We just gonna leave them to starve and rot in there? Or are we babysitting them until they fall apart, too?" She'd been flippant so far, but at the end I heard an edge to her voice, a crack in that devil-may-care armor.

"We don't have to do anything more," I interrupted. "They can die normally. Just...not as a part of...that thing."

Eric twitched. He'd been crossing his arms since we left the shed, but now he crossed them tighter, fingers digging into his sleeves. "Why drag them back at all, then? It's probably easier to kill them up there. Stab them or shove them over on their way up."

Zoey shrugged back, a casual eh-works-for-me gesture—like Eric was talking about going to get lunch or take a drive, some human pastime—and I fidgeted.

"That's—definitely an option, yeah," I said. "If everyone's comfortable with that? I don't wanna force you into anything—"

"I'll be fine," Angel said.

"Eh, been there, done that," Zoey added. "It's whatever."

But Monica frowned, watching my face close. She spoke up real soft, the softest person in the group. "Ian... are *you* okay with that?"

And they all trailed off, looking at me. The only dead person here. I stared back, and I again felt that ache of loneliness, of being together with people and still feeling alone in some crucial way.

It didn't matter if they killed off the other dead people from the clearing. It didn't really even matter if the corpses got eaten by some vague nightmare, then burned afterward. The dead were gone. I cared about them in that sympathetic way, in that sense of belonging I'd had. I cared like Willow did, refusing to let go, wanting to believe I could still find a happy future, and it wasn't realistic.

But . . .

I want them to be happy. I loved Eric when he killed Mr. Owens, because he took that choice away from me so I didn't have to think about if we were doing the right thing. He fixed the problem.

But now I have to choose for myself.

I thought of the Dairy Queen, on break and resting in peace. Still dead, but dead in her own way, in her own time. Living the life she'd enjoyed enough to linger around doing long after her shift should've ended.

Allowed to die, not mercy-killed.

I sighed, and I shook my head. "No. I'm not okay with that. Please don't. Let's try to keep them alive."

A flicker of movement. Zoey straightened up, her hands tucked deep in her pockets, her face set in a thin-lipped scowl.

"This is a stupid idea," she said.

"I know," I said.

"It's reckless and will probably get us all hurt, at the very least. You're asking a hell of a lot."

"Yeah."

"But you want us to do it, anyway."

"Please."

She sighed, hard. She crossed over to where I stood, shoes crunching over dead grass, and crouched to my level. I flinched, but I met her eyes, intense brown meeting wide black.

"And we'll do it anyway," she said, "because we care about you."

I nodded back. She stared a second longer, then gave a small smile, raising a fist up to her shoulder as if she wanted to fight, but held it there. I flinched, and then it clicked—and I fist-bumped her.

"All right, Captain," Zoey breathed. "Let's make it happen."

I smiled, then jumped as Monica and Angel both moved forward, pulling me and Zoey into a tight group hug. Angel squeezed too hard, my own iron-on patches digging into my sides, but I didn't mind at all. I liked it. I squeezed back, clinging to them for all they were worth, burying myself in body spray and sawdust.

Which just left Eric. I pulled away from the group and stared up at him.

He'd grown a little since that day at the park. Not in inches, no, but in the growing-out fluff of his hair, in the relaxed edges of his shoulders, in that more obvious softness in his eyes. He'd been hurt a hundred times before, each of them making him harder and colder, but now, away from people, he was letting himself get vulnerable again.

I wanted to see more of it. I wanted to see all of it.

He cleared his throat, glancing past me and toward the cabin.

"Hey. Um. You...should stay here, Ian," he said. I started to object, and he cut in, "I'm not just saying that. We don't know what's gonna happen, once we set that thing on fire. To all the other dead people, and...and to you." His voice shook, but he pushed on. "Even if it's fine, someone needs to make sure every dead person we bring down stays here. It makes sense for it to be you."

He had a point. I nodded. "Okay. Does anyone else want to stay here?"

Monica hesitated, then raised a hand, the other resting on her cane. "I like the idea, but...I'm not exactly fit for climbing mountains. I'm sorry. Is it okay if I stay?"

Angel rolled her eyes. "As if you need permission."

"Ah—right. What I mean is: I'm staying. Got it?" She scowled, defensively.

Zoey snorted a laugh. "Fine by me, Grandma. Probably gonna need at least a couple people back here runnin' interception, anyway. I'm down."

"Thank you, Monica, Zoey." I didn't say as much, but inside me something uncoiled with relief at Monica's volunteering. The thought of being alone in a cabin with that thing out there wasn't a good one to linger on.

"Then that means Angel, Zoey, and I will go." Eric hesitated there. He opened his mouth to speak, but it took a second for the words to come out, and they did slow and unsure. "Does that work for you, Ian?"

I nodded, smiling back. "It does. Thank you."

He blinked, a small blush rising on his face before he focused ahead again with a self-important throat-clearing. "*Right.* Okay. Be safe back there, both of you. We'll call if there's any trouble." He squeezed my shoulder. "I'll see you when we get back, and we'll laugh about all this. Okay?"

I couldn't help myself; the look on his face and the awkward shoulder-squeeze motion, Eric's first clumsy attempt in years at being sensitive, were too cute together. He'd always been *handsome*, but being *cute* was new, exciting territory.

So when he turned back, I let myself be selfish again. I let myself lean forward, reaching out, and before he could react, I kissed him.

It wasn't, by any means, a good kiss. Our teeth clicked together, our lips crammed awkwardly between them. He'd turned his face too far, so I met his lips at an off angle, more of a smooch at the corner of his mouth than a full-on thing. Both of our breaths smelled god-awful.

But it felt soft, and it felt amazing. This close I could feel the heat off his blushing face, the sandpaper brush of stubble. I could feel his chest against mine, close enough to catch the rabbity pace of his heart, and I could hear the startled little intake of breath he drew at it.

And I pulled back again, scrubbing a hand over my mouth. "For good luck, you know? Be safe out there."

Eric looked like he didn't know what to do with himself. His face bloomed too red, down to the tips of his ears, and his eyes were wide. For once I couldn't see any withdrawn hints or walls shoved up—what the apocalypse had worn away, pure surprise had torn down entirely.

Then he leaned forward and gave me a little peck of a kiss back. A polite one, on the top of the forehead, and he drew back too quick, but it left a little warm residue radiating under the skin.

"For luck. Yeah. Easy." He glanced around, like the others would judge him or stare at him—and to be fair, they *were* staring. But Zoey looked amused, Monica looked pleased, and Angel looked impatient to move on. "It's not like a big deal or anything."

I laughed back. He wasn't wrong, either; after dying and facing the empty town and a dozen other threats, being gay suddenly seemed like the least of our *deals*. But still, we could take it slow. That was fine. We could spend forever here, on this slow and lazy summer day, hanging out together and letting the world outside pass by.

That'd be fine by me.

Too soon, though, the ski lift came trundling back, swinging under its test weights of toolboxes and rocks. It rattled in a slow loop around the maintenance shed, and Monica and I pulled away from the others.

Angel went first, with a shrug and a gentle hop onto the seat.

"I made it. Makes sense to be first." She gave Monica a thumbs up, then shrugged my jacket up higher, huddling into a mass of purple fabric like a baby bird as the lift rode away. We watched her go, higher and higher, until she nearly disappeared up on the mountain, a tiny smudge of purple flopping off the lift.

A few seconds later, Monica's phone buzzed. She jumped, startled, then held it up as we all crowded around to see.

On her screen was a selfie of Angel, staring blankly up at her phone and flashing us the most deadpanned peace sign I'd ever seen. Underneath was a simple caption: Made it. Next.

"Oh my god." Monica buried her face in a hand, stifling a nervous twitter of laughter. "Well, guess it works, then. Good to know?"

Zoey went next, hopping on and sprawling out on the seat with her legs kicked over one armrest and her hands linked on the other. I gave her a wave, while Eric crossed his arms.

"Don't die," he said.

"Don't worry, I won't give you the satisfaction." She winked and rode away, up and out of sight.

Another text from Angel. Another selfie, this time of them both. Zoey matched Angel's peace sign with a similar hand gesture, but with her tongue jammed between the fingers.

"Ugh, *rude*," Monica muttered, deleting the picture. "Half wish she fell."

Last was Eric, and we stood there a moment as the lift made its crawl back. Neither of us exactly knew what to say, and there wasn't a lot of room for gentle whispers and sentiment with the engine roaring behind us.

So we settled for a hug, instead, holding each other tight and taking in the sound of each other's breathing. He pulled back, catching my eye, and then leaned forward to kiss me.

This time around, we got it right. No teeth, no bad angles. Just soft touch and the heat of our breath.

"For luck," he muttered as he pulled away.

"For luck," I echoed.

And then he was gone, on the lift and out. I followed it until it left the shed, then scurried outside and followed it farther, tracing its path higher and higher, into that whispering unknown.

Which left Monica and me, standing in the doorway and watching the ski ropes twitch empty overhead, twin black lines against a thin white sky.

I didn't breathe until Monica stepped up behind me, showing me her phone. Once I saw Eric standing with Angel and Zoey, all three in a weird little party, I let out a rush of air and sucked it back in.

"Thanks, Monica," I mumbled.

"They'll be okay. They'll look out for one another." She leaned closer with a small smile.

"I know. I believe it." I smiled back tiredly.

"All right," Monica said. She clapped her hands, a sharp noise echoing in the cold air, and I snapped to attention. "Let's make this place welcome."

TWENTY

We decided to leave the engine running for now—in part because it made sense to have it if we needed to get up the mountain, and in part because neither of us knew how to turn it off. We trotted away, letting that engine roar fade and that single lonely chair swivel in endless circles.

The cabin door was locked, obviously. But at this point breaking and entering was just one of a growing list of crimes for both of us, so we took turns kicking at the knob and jabbing at it with Monica's cane, until finally, with a creak of old wood and a bone-aching snap, it broke open. Both of us stumbled forward, arms aching and breath heavy, into a lobby full of dust and stale air.

Like the patio, the lobby was the sort of place that looked grand once and currently looked empty and sad. Plush leather couches and wicker tables sat in scattered half circles across a massive Persian rug, its detailed whorls and patterns faded in brown lines and permanent footprints. Across one wall stood a massive fireplace framed in cobblestone, its mantle lined with old books and paintings of soft landscapes, its interior swept clean and dry as a set piece. Opposite it stood what looked like a reception desk, a low bar with mailboxes and wood carvings lined up in the back. Glittery candelabras arched way overhead, casting flickering prisms across a winding second floor balcony and thick wooden rafters.

It smelled like dust, pine, and a little like raisins. I sneezed.

"So, um . . ." I tilted my head, taking it all in. "Do we have a plan to make this place more welcome? Maybe like, dust off the chairs or something…?"

Monica hummed, tapping her cane against the floorboards. Then, like a bolt of shock, she straightened up, eyes alight. "Oh! I have an idea."

"Yeah?"

"Wait here." A pause. "And—and close your eyes."

"Huh?" I blinked. "Um, sure, okay."

I didn't really get it, but she seemed too excited to say no to, so I wandered over to a couch and settled down, eyes closed. It felt dusty and stiff, the leather cracking under my weight, but still soft enough to relax into.

Ahead, I heard rustling. The door opened, then shut, and I sat in thoughtful quiet for a while. I swung my legs, leaned back, day-dreamed up plans. How many dead were in that clearing? Maybe a dozen. They'd liked the music Zoey left, so we should probably set up that CD player again, once they got close enough to hear it. And the doors would have to be shut to keep them wandering back out. Should we get them water? The dead didn't usually drink much, but that didn't mean they wouldn't be thirsty. Or—

The door creaked back open. I heard more rustling, the whisper of fabric, thuds, echoing all along the lobby with Monica's clicking cane-footsteps. A few plastic crinkles, metal clacks, and the scraping of furniture legs. Finally I heard her voice, bright and excited.

"Okay, it's ready! I think… Yeah, yeah, it's ready."

I opened my eyes… and stared.

Monica had cleared out a little space in the middle of the lobby, and in place of chairs and tables she'd laid out a knitted blanket. In one corner, holding it in place, sat a stack of aluminum cans and soda bottles, along with two of Angel's military rations in sagging brown bags. She'd laid out paper plates and plastic cups, two places' worth, and sat cross-legged in front of one, beaming up at me like she'd figured out all the secrets to the universe.

After a second, it clicked. "Wait, is this a picnic?"

"Got it in one." Monica laughed, shifting her legs to lean back more. "I never actually managed to invite you to one."

"Eating in the truck doesn't count?"

"That was more of a dinner."

"All right, fair." I pushed myself up, crossing over to the picnic. It felt totally silly, so I leaned into it, offering her a hand and a lopsided smile. "Howdy, stranger. My name's Ian. I just got out of an appointment. Can I sit here with you?"

Monica thought it over, then grinned, impishly. "No."

"Oh my god, *seriously?*"

She laughed, then scooted over, taking my hand. "All right, all right, you talked me into it. Yes, stranger, you can have a seat. I swear I've seen you around this place before."

"Really? Me, too." I let her pull me down to the other spot, flopping onto soft knit weave. "I swear we used to play together when we were little."

"Yeah! With the little bead toys? I remember." She reached over, grabbing a bottle of Sprite and pouring herself a cup. It burbled out, frothing at the cup rim and settling back down in a cloud of fizzy lemon-lime. "Wonder why we stopped."

"Got too big and self-conscious for the kids' section, I guess." I held out my own cup for a pour. "But I'm glad we were able to meet up again despite that."

"Same. Let's keep it, this time." She raised her cup. "To cozy reunions?"

I hesitated, thinking it over.

Was this cozy? It felt nice, but also a little sad, sitting here in an empty lodge with a friend I barely knew and the taste of bitter oil and blood in the back of my throat. Cozy in a desperate sort of way—like neither of us knew what the future would bring, and we were trying to cobble together mindfulness out of the pieces we had now. Like if we focused for long enough on the bubble of soda, we wouldn't have to look farther than the next sip.

But I didn't mind it that way, either. If the only certain thing we had was the next sip, then one sip was enough.

I tapped my cup against Monica's, letting soda froth over onto my fingers, cool and tingling.

"To cozy reunions."

Sip.

The soda tasted lukewarm and sour, but nice. It tickled on its way down, soothing away that residual oil aftertaste. I burped, and Monica made a face and patted at her chest, easing it down.

In terms of food to go with, I glanced over Monica's stockpile. She'd gathered a decent collection from our supply: canned green beans, a plastic tin of macaroni salad, canned soup, and . . .

I frowned. "Monica? Um . . . where's the can opener?"

She blinked, looked back. "Why do we need—" Then she went a shade paler, eyes wide. "Oh no . . ."

"Do we *have* one?"

"Oh my god, I'm so dumb." She buried her face in her hand. "I knew I forgot a ton of things, I'm sorry, I was so focused on *survival food* and not on basic stuff—"

"It's okay! It's okay. I'm sure there's one in the lodge somewhere. They gotta have a kitchen or a break room, right?" I stood up, holding my cup close to my chest to keep it from spilling over. "I kinda wanna take a look around this place, anyway, you know. Make sure we have space for people."

The relief on Monica's face spread like spilled ink. She pushed herself up. "Looking around sounds fun. Not often we get a whole lodge to ourselves."

"I feel it. Uh." I glanced around. The lobby stretched in every direction, and upward as well, its balconies looming, lined with doorways and halls—and most of them against inside walls, away from the doors and windows. Away from any sign of the others coming back.

Monica caught my expression and bit her lip, then gave a soft smile. "I'll stay here and keep watch on the door. You get us a can opener."

"Right. Got it. Call me as soon as you see anything?"

"I will. And same to you, okay?" A pause, then: "I love you, Ian."

I smiled. "Love you, too."

I trotted off down the hall with my cup held close, bubbling and popping and tasting like warm company and summer picnics out with a family I'd once known but let myself drift away from, too self-conscious and too grown for such things as these, until I'd grown so much I'd become selfish and small again, and could finally sit down and be home.

TWENTY-ONE

Halfway down the hall I heard faint, humming classical music, and I smiled to myself. Monica must've brought the radio after all. She gave herself so much flak for forgetting things, but she was the most detail-oriented of any of us.

Beyond the lodge and around a corner stood two lines of wood doors, all patterned with tiny gold numbers. Every so often a potted plant or a set of polished antlers would break up the row, but for the most part it looked identical right up to the broom closet at the end. Probably not here, then.

What wasn't here? I blinked. Right, I was searching for something. What was it, again? It'd been right on the edge of my brain, but when I looked for it, it fell away and dissolved like cotton candy in water. In its place was only a frustrated silence and the hum of classical music.

. . . Monica hadn't brought in the CD player. I realized that with a start, halfway down the hall. I'd looked over everything she'd dragged in, and it'd just been picnic supplies. Blanket, food, plates. No sign of that big, tacky pink CD player.

That hum droned on. Instead of getting quieter as I moved from the lobby, it pulsed louder, thrumming in my bones like something alive. Like a hundred-thousand somethings alive, itching under the skin.

You're so close, love. Did you think I'd let you ignore me? Did you think I'd let you sit idly back while the others worked for you, Captain?

I froze.

There was a window by one of the doors, a small one, barely more than a skylight, but enough for me to peer through and see the mountains outside. One of them, the tallest one, had a trickle of smoke blooming from its peak, and I smiled.

They'd actually done it. They'd reached the peak and set it on fire.

But... If I squinted, I could see our lone ski lift hanging in midair, frozen in the gap between peaks. Still, empty.

The engine had stopped. Did it run out of fuel? I couldn't hear it roaring away in the background, and in its wake was a new uneasy silence... and that constant humming. Not classical music, but a single note, held and held and held.

That wasn't good. How were the others supposed to get back if the ski lift was stopped? We needed to get out and start it again—

I told you to come home. You're a good boy, right? You always listen.

I stepped closer to the window, batting a finger against it like the dollar store employee, reaching toward the peak—then tore myself back, pressing hands to my scalp. Digging my fingers in.

No, no. Not now. Not yet. No *coming home, love.* No wandering off. I had to stay at the lodge, stay myself, until the others came back.

I'm here. I'm breathing. My name is . . .

What was my name, again?

I couldn't remember.

"Monica... ?" I tried to shout, but my voice came out as a low croak. "There's something wrong, Monica."

No answer. And who was Monica, anyway? I couldn't remember what her face looked like anymore. Was there anything beyond this little window and mountain view? Could I really be certain anything existed beyond this moment?

I could drown in a moment like this. Let myself go and dissolve into it completely, and be whole together with things that hummed and had teeth. No future necessary for dead kids, just a cozy and eternal present.

No. Focus. Breathe. I'm still breathing. I'm still here. *If I have a present right now, I have a future. Every breath I take is a couple more seconds of promised future. Focus on that, and keep moving.*

I turned a corner at the end of the hall, past the broom closet and the gray window, and around it I saw . . . another hallway. An identical hallway, with potted plants and faded beige walls. It even smelled the same, like spearmint candles and pine needles.

I crossed it at a jog, hunting for anything different. A staircase up, a bathroom, a break room. Instead, all I saw was another corner, and around it, another identical hallway.

Was there ever anything more than hallways? Looping around and around like two sisters at a roller rink?

You'll protect me, won't you, love? You won't let them hurt me?

No, no, *no*. I couldn't lose myself. Not yet, not now, not yet—

"Monica?!"

I passed a door, dark oak against pale wood, the words **EMERGENCY EXIT** in searing red overhead, and I shoved through it—

And I stumbled out onto the mountain.

The air hit me first, a shock of thin cold drawn in as I gasped for breath. Then the crunch of snow beneath my sneakers, crisp and *wet* and bright enough to sear my eyes, bright as an emergency alarm.

How did I get *here*? This was so much higher than the lodge was supposed to be. There were supposed a bunch of kiddie trails and rope, but I'd blinked and I'd gone past all those. And my hands hurt, stinging and raw, and I stared down at them to see them coated in dark scratches and broken pebbles, like I'd spent ages crawling up the rocks.

"No, no." I stumbled back, reaching blindly behind me for a door I couldn't find. (How had I wandered so far away from the *door*?) "No, I'm not supposed to be here, I'm supposed to be safe in the lodge. *Monica—*"

I took a step back, as if there was anywhere to run out here, and my shoe dug into something soft and damp. I slid, knocking against something else, and it grasped at my ankle, icy fingers digging in.

Below me, already half buried in ice, my reflection smiled, a scruffy-haired kid with wide black doll's eyes.

A body, buried in the snow and left to rot and seep back into the rivers below.

He smiled wider. Wider. He smiled until my own lips hurt, until it split up his face like wounds, until he opened his mouth and it looked as smudged and dark as his eyes, a violent crayon scribble of a grin. Like something I might've drawn years ago, frustrated and upset at the hospital but already too well-trained to look anything else but happy, happy, happy.

"I'm a good person," he whispered. "I always do what I'm told. I would never let anyone burn down the heaven I was promised. Not after I worked so hard for it."

The other me held up his hand. His fingernails were crusted with black oil, smudged across the knuckles. Like he'd been digging into his own skin, trying to pour the oil out.

He put that smudged, sharp hand into the back of his head, near the base of his skull, then he pressed in and his head rolled back like he'd severed all his puppet strings and turned boneless.

The stitches in the back of my head *throbbed*. I screamed and staggered back until the rocks under my shoes gave away—and my head cracked against *something*, ears ringing and the salt-copper taste of oily water in my nose, mouth.

Tile? I opened my eyes and I saw fluorescent lights, glittering over water. The water smeared red, blooming clouds of it mixed with chlorine blue. And overhead, the sound of ringing pop music over muffled speakers.

I pushed my hands back, palms chafing against piles of molding coins, and I hefted myself up, out of the water and upright.

Where . . . ?

Around me I saw the mall, open and empty. Same high ceiling and pillared walls, same tile floors and kiosks between lines of shuttered stores, same wavering pop music. Same empty chairs against fraying plastic ferns.

But when I stood up, coughing up mouthfuls of salty grit, I saw the fountain had leaked. And leaked. It kept pouring water from its spouts, but something had blocked the drains—*I'd* blocked the drains, pieces and clumps of me clotting up the holes, and now the water spilled over the plaster lip of it and across the floor, all across it, a mall-wide film of water across everything. Stray pennies drifted by, buffeted by the current, along with thin ribbons of red.

My head pounded and my lungs burned. Concussion. Drowning. Was it the concussion or the drowning that killed me? Both? People could be so weird that way. Stab a guy ten dozen times and he'll walk away, but fall wrong once and it's all over.

I'd never been real lucky.

I climbed out. I had to find—

Monica, need to let Monica know something's gone wrong, this isn't real, I'm losing focus, hallucinating, I need to get . . .

Eric, need to get him and go home to Mom and Dad and Emma, we were supposed to go together . . .

Need to find Her and hold Her close, the mountain's going to burn but as long as we're together we can rebuild, I can fall apart into something great for Her

—someone. Something. I stumbled down the hall, kicking up

sloshes of stale water, peering into rows and rows of shuttered stores. Lines of boxes and scattered cleaning tools sat behind metal grates, wrapped in shadow and motes of floating dust. And up ahead—

Up ahead, I spotted the kiosk for Dairy Queen. A squat, flat square of countertops, lined with ice-cream machines and faded advertisements. Menus glared overhead, lights flickering behind their signs.

And in the middle, of course, was the Dairy Queen herself. She sat on the counter, cross-legged, a small teen girl with sheets of dark hair and a pale, round face, her posture hunched into an oversized army jacket and fingers grasping at her sleeve hems. Angel.

She stared at me with wide black eyes and a wide black smile, and as I wandered closer, she grabbed an ice-cream cup and leaned toward the machine's spout. Her movements were twitching, jumpy, more like a spider than a person.

"Wherever you end up, we'll all miss you when you're gone," she said in her blunt, soft voice. That smile didn't move, plastered on her face like a mask. She pushed on the nozzle, and with a whirring, crunching noise, pieces of raw meat began drizzling out into the cup. "*Will* you miss us? Will you remember how to miss us?"

"I... I don't know." I squeezed my fingers against the counter. "I don't want to *forget* you. What's going on? I don't want this."

"No?" She tilted her head. The meat smelled sour, curdled. "You've been practicing your entire life to make room for others. Now you must make room for Her."

Around us, the walls groaned and shuddered, like old support beams creaking under the weight of a house. Something shuddered overhead, something massive and alien and *wrong*, trying to cram itself into a space far too small to fit.

Angel held out the cup to me. I took it—I don't know why—and squeezed it tight.

"I-I don't want Her. She'll kill me. Please. I changed my mind. I'm not ready to die. I just—I want more time—"

"You got an extra day. More than most people get."

"I want a *lifetime*, Angel."

"Didn't we give that to you?" She tilted her head the other way. Her neck joints cracked, popped. "A whole lifetime's worth of adventure."

"It wasn't *enough*!" I dropped the cup. Meat splattered against the water, bobbing in it, flecked with swarming gnats. I spread my arms, gripping the countertop edges until my fingers flared white. "You told me I should be selfish. I'm being selfish. I don't wanna go, Angel."

Her smile, that grotesque pitch-black wound of a smile, split further, dripping dark oil down her chin. She tilted her head farther, farther, until she sank against the counter. Until oil dribbled down her cheek and onto the counter.

"So loud . . ." She sank farther, her sleeves slipping up her hands and to her wrists, and the fingers underneath were covered in porcelain cracks and missing pieces. I yelped and grabbed her shoulders, hoisting her back upright.

"Angel! Angel, come on, keep yourself together! Please! I'm trying my best!" My voice cracked. I pushed on anyway. "I'm trying so hard, I promise."

"I'm *tired*," she moaned. "I'm tired of teaching you. Everything is too loud. You're all too loud. Digging into my brain. I want to be alone. It's not fair. Why do I always have to be the survivor type? Why did I have to run into a nervous burden like *you*?"

"Angel?" I tried to look her in the eyes, but she kept that morbid mask of a face turned away from me, letting it dribble oil down the counter in a growing pool.

"I changed my mind, too. It's fine to forget about me."

And as I squeezed her shoulders, they crumbled underneath me like rotting eggshells. She fell back behind the counter, collapsing into a mess of heavy green cotton and dripping oil.

The walls groaned again, and something cracked. Plaster dust sprinkled down from the ceiling, and the tile underneath the water chipped and splintered, falling apart. I cried out and ran to the wall, pressing my back against it as if I could hold it back by sheer willpower. As if by squinting my eyes shut and grinding my teeth together I could make this go away.

Keep it together. Focus. Don't let everything fall apart. Stay together. Stay—

Something crunched in my jaw. I probed my tongue back and tasted salt, and beneath that, smooth gums.

My molars had fallen out.

Before I could think long about them, I heard a voice call out from beyond one of those endless metal grates. She sounded bright, cheery, welcoming, and I drifted toward her like a starving moth.

"Hey, Ian!"

On the other side of a grate, instead of boxes and mops, I saw an open, dry lobby floor and a picnic blanket, stretched out and scattered with cafeteria trays and vending machine water bottles. It sat in the warm, golden glow of light bulbs overhead, shining like tiny suns. Like the light of an afternoon on a hillside near a parking lot.

And on the blanket sat the hospital girl, the one with the horse T-shirt and the coily dark hair pinned back, the one with stylish jeans and painted nails chipped from farmwork. The one with crisscrossed bandages on her inner elbow from a dozen blood draws, with dry cracks at the edges of the lips she'd glossed over, with callouses on her hand right where the handle of her cane fit, carrying it all with the sort of inspirational perfection I could never match.

I pulled up the grate with a heavy rattle of metal links, collapsing beside her.

"God, I'm so glad you're here," I muttered. "I don't know what to do. Everything's breaking down, and I can't stop it, and I'm scared."

"It's okay. Shh. I know the feeling." The hospital girl shook her head. "We've lost so much already. First everyone at the hospital burned. Then all the living people got evacuated. Now the bodies on the peak are burning. It's all falling away, piece by piece."

"Right? I feel it." I laughed. It felt so good to laugh. "At least... at least we can face it together, though, right?"

"Right." She handed me a can, and I took it with a nod of thanks, cracking the seal with a carbonated hiss. "At least you're still here."

"True! You can come to me anytime you need, promise." I sipped. It tasted warm and salty and thick, and I grimaced. "What *is* this?"

"You like it? I made it myself." The hospital girl smiled so bright, rubbing a hand over her bandaged arm.

"It's... definitely something." I tried a smile. It didn't quite work. That sour taste pooled in my mouth where my teeth weren't.

"Oh... you hate it, don't you?" Her voice sounded sad, but that smile didn't fade. "I knew it. You hate me. You always hated me, even when I tried so hard to impress you." She squeezed at that bandage, gripping until blood welled up between her fingers. "You're so petty and miserable inside, anxious and desperate to be liked, and you're always trying to drag me down with you. And now no one stayed behind for either of us."

She stared at a corner of the picnic blanket. At the spot where her mom had always sat before, tall and serene and gentle as a butterfly.

"I didn't mean to—"

"But they left anyway, didn't they? Mom's gone. The town's gone. We bled ourselves dry to impress other people and they *left anyway*." She pushed herself up to her feet, her face flushed. "Doesn't that make you so upset you could *burst*? What's the point of dying slowly and pretty if no one's even around anymore to *look*?"

"I—I don't know, but we don't need to do that—" I stood up, too, dropping that soda can. Letting it spill thick red fluid all along the picnic blanket. Her name clicked. "Monica, it's going to be okay. We still have each other, remember—?"

"It's not okay! We don't have each other! Not really. She's going to kill you and I'll be *alone*, with all the messes you left behind." She scrubbed at her eyes, smearing black oil tears. "At least you won the contest, Ian. You get to be a martyr."

"What? That—Monica, no, it's not like that, I don't feel like a winner at all—"

"But you *are*. Everyone will love what a good job of dying you did. You'll look so pretty and inspirational. I'll never be able to beat your record." She gripped her cane tight, strings of frayed pink duct tape curling around her fingers.

"I don't want to *win* anymore, Monica! Please, take it from me! Please!"

And she froze up. "Okay." She sounded so thoughtful. So hopeful. I held out a hand, hovering in the stale open air between us.

"Monica...?"

Her hands shifted on her cane. Looser, less like a cane grip and more like a baseball bat.

"If that's what you want, I'll help you, one last time. I always did want to help people. Unlike you, *I* can be selfless."

She lifted the cane high, its tip pointed toward those light bulbs like a spear.

Then, before I could process what was happening, she drove it back into her face. It hit with a hideous cracking noise, with a splattering of oil and echoes I could feel all the way up my shoes and into my lurching, racing heart.

"Monica, no, stop—!"

I wanted to grab it out of her hands. I wanted to run toward her, tackle her to the ground, *something, anything.* But I couldn't move. I couldn't even draw in enough breath to scream as she struck again, and again, and again. Each time the crunch of impact sounded more wet, each time the cane came away more smudged and dented. Each time she hurt more.

On the fourth time I finally managed to tear myself loose, lurching toward her and grabbing at the cane. She scrambled at it, her nails tearing at my hands, but I wrenched and twisted it free, knocking her off her feet and onto the blanket.

But she kept reaching out, grasping at my ankles and clawing at the air, her face in shadow and her mouth gaping like a wound—*SHE'S STILL ALIVE HOW IS SHE STILL ALIVE STOP STOP STOP*—until I swung at her, driving her back. Until she finally, mercifully went still. Until her dark black eyes rolled over and turned white.

I heaved in reedy breaths, in and out, arms shaking and too hot and smeared blackish-grayish-red all over.

I killed her.

(She helped me lose the contest.)

I didn't mean to.

(I was supposed to be the martyr.)

I dropped the cane and sank down, hunching forward into a little ball. I pressed my hands to my head like that could help it hold together, and when the walls shuddered again, a hundred-thousand wasp legs jabbing through the supports, I shuddered with them, clinging tighter. I couldn't scream, but I let out a panicked keening sound, hissing it through my leftover teeth.

This is a nightmare. This isn't happening. I'm going to wake up, and everything will be fixed. I'll get to go home, then. Everything will be—

Something clanged against the grating, metal on metal. I yelped, twisting around to see.

The roller derby girl and the boy I loved stood on the other side of the grate, glaring down at me. The girl grinned too sharp, her hands around a rebar pole, knocking it between the holes in the grate with a rattling hiss. Her hair hung wild in front of her crazed eyes, her mouth a rictus grin over a tattered jersey and faded jeans.

"There he is, Eric," she drawled. "Just look at 'im."

Eric stepped forward. I couldn't see his face, but I could see the tufts of his hair, his shoulders, his tanned arms and bitten nails. His shoes kicked up trails of fountain water, lapping up against the grating and the edge of our little picnic island.

"And you promise he won't feel anything?" he muttered.

"Guaranteed. He's long gone, and the rest is crumbling apart. You'd be doing him a mercy, y'know. Just like Mr. Owens." She tapped her bar against the grate, and I flinched back.

"That—that's not true." I glanced between her and Eric, eyes wide. "I'm still in here, Eric, look at me, I'm still real—"

"The dead ain't real anymore," she cut in. "They can't have a future. Because if they *did*, you know what that means, Ian?" The roller girl turned to me, face bright and scribbly and flat as a drawing. *"It means that we're murderers."*

My breath caught. She carried on.

"You drowned Mr. Owens. Eric pushed him into that lake for you, and you never told anyone. Either of you. So if you're stuck in here, that means Mr. Owens was stuck in *there*, begging to be kept alive, just... like... this." She slid the rebar across the grate. *Chik-chik-chik-chik.* "That means Willow was in her own head, too, back at the roller rink. And that person you ate and that Dairy Queen you and Angel let die. That means we're *all* murderers."

Chik-chik-chik. The sound of clanking metal dug into my skull, into my bones. I jammed my hands against my ears, trying to block it out.

"I was trying to help—I wanted to help . . . ," I heard myself mutter, over and over and over again. "I didn't want him to suffer anymore!"

"And now you're trying too late to make up for it by rescuing all these dead mountain people and breaking the cycle. By stealing all those bodies, and by cornering the god that made them on a mountain peak and letting Her burn. But we don't want you to *suffer*, either."

The water edged up through the grating, lapping at my shoes, at my back. I squeezed my eyes shut, hunched against it, until I felt something brush against my leg. Something heavy.

I cracked an eye open and I saw Mr. Owens's body, bobbing face down in the water. I could still make out the sunburned blisters under his thin hair, the waterlogged pajama shirt, the scratches and blackberry smears up and down his arms.

I gasped, kicking him back, pushing myself away, until my back pressed against the grating and my shoes slid in the water. Until I couldn't retreat anymore, and I pressed harder against my ears instead, blocking it out.

The walls shuddered. Plaster and dust rained down, and the grate behind me groaned, rust spilling across its links like old wounds. Monica's body lay curled on her side on the picnic blanket, her hair drifting in the water, mixing with swirls of oil.

And above it all, over the sound of crumbling walls and the roller girl's clattering pole and the trickle of water and my own racing, aching heart, that same hum carried on, risen up to a whine, a ringing in my ears like an emergency evacuation alarm. Through the cracks, I could see bright licks of fire, wisps of dark smoke, curling over shriveled bodies covered in oozing black oil.

EMERGENCY—EVACUATION—

LET ME IN, IAN, I'M BURNING. THEY'RE BURNING ME ALIVE. SAVE ME—

PLEASE EVACUATE FROM THE BUILDING—

LET ME IN, WE'LL JUMP INTO THE RIVER TOGETHER.

It hurt to look away. Behind me, past the grating, sat the tile floors and high ceilings of the mall, but also the scattered chairs and elegant rugs of the lodge lobby, on top of white hospital sheets and burnt walls piled with bodies, on top of the rusted hull and cracked seats of a stolen pickup truck we'd turned into a home. A dozen places all at once, flickering in and out of one another, cracking apart and bleeding together into white noise and screeching hums as smoke and fire bled through them.

A concrete fountain, its water flecked with mildewed change.

A river, trickling icy cold from the mountain rocks.

A fifteen-year-old boy on a mountain, the last dead person who hadn't been burned up or evacuated or dragged away, the only place left for a burning river god to escape to.

Everything I'd ever known, everything I'd ever been, falling and tearing apart to the hundred grasping arms of *something.*

And over it all, looming, spread across the ceiling and a dozen other flickering memories of ceilings . . .

I saw God.

It writhed, its edges burning.

Something ached in the front of my head, a stabbing jerk, and when I put a hand to my nose, it came away smeared with blood.

It felt like looking at the universe. Like a hole in a curtain, and underneath were edges swarming with bodies, arms and eyes and teeth, like everything and everyone at once, so much noise and light and sound that it became a single hum, a single voice whispering me home.

And for the first time, I knew why the dead's eyes were so wide.

Their pupils blown impossibly big, consuming the entire eye. I knew what they looked at before their eyes went white, before their bodies fell limp and never moved again. I knew what drew them to keep moving long after their bodies died.

I knew that, but at the same time, I didn't *know* it. I knew it in that distant, incomprehensible way, like the size of planets or like a global tragedy, an event so big it passed my ability to imagine it. I knew it enough to know this was *something*, that it was infinite enough to make everything in this room—everything in my life—seem smaller than a blip in the massive hum of it all.

It made sense now that I'd rot. That I'd bleed and itch and shatter, every muscle and vein too small to hold what I saw in my eyes. It made sense that humans—lonely and hurt and at war—would reach out to this, desperate to be a part of something bigger than skin and bones and blood. Something larger than the universe and small enough to drink in mountain water.

I stepped forward, drifting through the water, along the mall tile and the lobby rug and the truck bed metal, my eyes dripping black and my nose dripping and my mouth dripping, all those useless human things shriveling away at the sight of it, leaving nothing but what had been itching in my bones all along, leaving just this, blooming and infinite and perfect at last, a steady hum, a perfect light, infinite colors combined into glory, and—

And before I could get more than a step in, something tugged on my hand. Holding it back. My flesh slid under their grip, drying up and begging to slough off these weary bones, but the something held fast, tighter.

I turned, my wide eyes adjusting to a gloom without that direct glare, and blinked.

After a second, I focused, and I saw him. The boy who'd pushed Mr.

Owens into the lake so I wouldn't have to. The boy who'd left me to drown then dragged me back. The boy I'd kissed for luck.

Eric. He stared at me now, and somehow, even in the face of infinite glory—in the face of an indescribable perfection beyond anything I'd ever known—he looked beautiful. Maybe because of his messiness: in how his hand shook, in how his hair drifted in front of his eyes, in how his brown eyes squinted in a very human sort of worry. In how his voice cracked when he mumbled my name, his arms smudged with ash and cigarette burns.

"Ian... don't go there. Please." My arm leaked dark oil, but he held it tighter anyway, gripping on to what skin remained.

I stared back, not understanding. Didn't he see everything above us? Didn't he notice how beautiful it was? Didn't he want to go to heaven?

"It's perfect," I said, as if he needed help. "I can be perfect there. Why wouldn't I?"

He scowled harder, held tighter.

"I don't want *perfect*," he said, "I want *you*. I always wanted you."

I didn't understand. I couldn't understand. I glanced at him, at his hand, back.

"It's *perfect*," I said again, forcing the words through a throat too small and dry for everything in me, everything up there. I could feel myself crying, hot oil tears down my cheeks. "I don't have to live with myself there, Eric. Don't you understand? Nothing I did or was *matters* there. It doesn't matter that we killed Mr. Owens. It doesn't matter that I'm disabled and wrong and hurt. None of the pain or fear we went through will mean anything anymore. It's okay if it all falls apart."

I said this with rapture in my voice, hoping he'd finally understand... but instead, he only looked hurt. One last hurt in the face of the end.

"It meant something to me," he said.

I pulled at his grip, but he held fast, and I didn't *understand.* I couldn't understand. Why? *Why?* He glared at me with those brown eyes, more intense than the infinite, and I couldn't understand *why.*

Except... he wouldn't go to heaven, would he? I'd made him promise to keep living. No matter what happened, he'd said he'd never die.

So he wouldn't follow me into that blissful infinite, and the thought of that hurt, because . . .

Because it mattered to me.

It hurt because it mattered.

Someone grasped my other hand. I turned and saw Monica, her face whole again, holding a basket for a picnic I'd never gotten to finish having with her. A picnic I'd been trying to join since I was small. A picnic that wouldn't exist anymore in the face of that infinite. She stared up at me, eyes damp.

"I was hoping you'd stay behind for me," she mumbled. "I thought... maybe together, we wouldn't have to keep trying to be perfect enough to be worth it."

"I—we don't, Monica—" I trailed off.

It mattered.

Behind her I saw Angel, sitting on a truck roof with a worn knife in her hands, staring up at the stars. She was wearing my jacket, with all its little patches, and in the quiet of an empty town, she let herself breathe. A breath she couldn't take anymore, if the universe kept being too loud, too humming.

It mattered.

I saw Zoey in another truck, old bandages and derby stickers curled up by her shoes, tapping her fingers to the radio. Listening to Warren Buffett talk about how no one could care about the whole world at once, so we had to pick what we cared about and build our own worlds from it.

It mattered.

I saw Mom and Dad and Emma in a refugee camp somewhere across the state, eating stale cheeseburger casserole, laughing at inside jokes and arguing with one another.

It mattered.

Eric and Monica kept watching me. Kept holding my arms.

All of them were hurt and broken and wrong in some way or another. All their hurt and breaks and wrong choices could be drowned out in a beautiful infinite, turned into nothing more than a hum in tune with the universe.

But they *mattered.* The parts that hurt and broke mattered. They were small, impossibly small, before the weight of the rest of the world, lost before the weight of the infinite humming beyond that. The infinite that, fleeing from its burning gasoline self, had burrowed into the head of its last protective martyr. I couldn't possibly hold on to each of them and hold on to the infinite at the same time. They'd shatter.

So the infinite had to get out.

The walls shuddered again, the infinite reaching closer, all grasping hands and staring eyes and perfect warmth, but I shoved it back. And for a split-second, I swear it felt *angry.* It didn't feel angry in a human way, more like a swarm of insects and a screeching hiss at the edges of my head. They battered against my skull, pounding and harsh, and I screamed, flinching back...but it didn't hurt. It didn't reach any farther than that.

Because this was *my* head. It was battered and traumatized and liked to break down, liked to put me in and out of hospitals growing up, but all the medication and tests and seizures in the world hadn't kept it from being *mine.* Everything in it belonged to me, from the parts I loved to the parts that hurt to every part that fell somewhere in between.

And this thing had made the mistake of coming in here. All this belonged to me, selfishly, and it *wasn't welcome to take it.*

That *something* drove forward again, dropping everything else it had in favor of shoving *all* of itself into the cracks, all light and hums and overwhelming, infinite things—but then again, that wasn't anything new to me, was it? I'd died looking at a light I couldn't comprehend, and I'd woken up, anyway. I'd woken up from it a dozen times before, and I would again.

Something this flawlessly perfect, however? That couldn't survive in a place as messy and imperfect as this.

I squeezed my eyes shut and I clamped down on everything, on everyone, and too late the *something* realized this wasn't a welcome mat after all, but a vice. Too late it realized it'd drawn itself into a brain that was broken and prone to sudden self-destruction, and I felt it trying to writhe back even as I held it close, as I forced it to stay here with me as everything fell apart, not because of it, but because of *me.* It flailed, reaching for perfection and heaven and other ideas to escape into, and I yanked it down and forced it into something real. Something contained.

I smelled ozone and burning metal and fire, sharp tangs that settled in the back of my throat, and for the first time those scents made me smile. For the first time I turned my head and willingly stared into that flailing, flashing, panicking light. I grinned at it, all teeth.

"You want me to be a part of you?" I spat. "Fine, then. But you get to take *all of me.*"

And my brain, full of stress and death and grasping, hungry parasites who called themselves God, collapsed on itself, the mall's groaning walls at last snapping under their weight and crushing everything underneath into dust, then nothing at all.

TWENTY-TWO

I didn't expect to wake up. It didn't make sense to wake up, and that was okay. I'd set fire to heaven, and now I could drift easy through an afterlife made of half-dream fragments and nothing at all.

In one dream, I sat on the edge of the mall fountain, drinking flat pop. Mr. Owens sat to one side, blackberry thorns in his lap, and the Dairy Queen sat on the other, her uniform rumpled and ponytail loose. We were all together, watching the water rush over piles of spare change, listening to muffled mall music, and at peace.

In another, I stood on a picnic blanket with Monica's mom, her body turned away and her hands gripped around a shovel. She walked toward the hospital, and I knew without asking that she'd be busy clearing out the burnt debris for a while. I wanted to help, but I also didn't need to chase after her anymore—I could stay outside the hospital, on the picnic blanket, for as long as I wanted.

In another, I saw Angel and Zoey working on the truck, their hands smudged with oil, and when Angel slipped Zoey reached out and caught her by the back of her jacket, because Zoey always looked out for her girls first and foremost, and for once Angel didn't mind the company.

In another, I stood on top of a mountain with Dad and Emma, braced and unsure, but Dad patted my back and told me it'd be okay, the oil was gone and the water flowed clear again, and when I looked to the mountains ahead, I saw only drifts of snow and tasted winter air, and it was so quiet, I could finally breathe.

In another, I heard voices calling out to me. Not like the hum of the infinite, like *coming home*, but cracked and faltering and familiar.

Ian.

Please wake up.

We need you.

Come back, Ian.

Please.

I reached out for them, and I knew that once I got there I'd have to do everything I dreaded—I'd have to let my heart beat, let my lungs breathe, let myself live and fall and make all the mistakes and setbacks I hated myself for.

They called again, though, because they wanted me there. Because I was wanted, and I mattered.

So I reached out, anyway.

The worst part of seizures was the waking up afterward. Everything ached, my head rustling like a ball of cotton stuffing, and I tasted sour burnt plastic. Pins and needles danced on my skin like static off an old TV, and I felt at least a dozen new bruises and lumps to carry home.

I squinted an eye open into the bleak light. No sunlight or glaring fluorescents, at least. Nothing that would turn that cotton-stuffed headache into an immediate migraine. Instead, I saw distant chandeliers and dim afternoon sunlight, shining well overhead in beams and dust motes across a wood-raftered ceiling.

What . . . ?

Something soft underneath me. A bed? A couch. Felt like suede and stiff wooden backing. And something sticky, across my lips and hands and on the cushions. Blood? Tasted like blood, but sour. Oilier.

A shape blotted out the light. Round. Moving. A figure. A paramedic? I bit back a groan. I hated it when people called the paramedics. Paramedics always wanted to ask a bunch of questions, shine a bunch of lights, maybe even drag me on an ambulance trip, and I was *fine*, really, this happened *all the time*.

"Ian?" a voice called out. Familiar. Worried. I squinted up until I saw tufts of dark brown hair, brown eyes, a squarish face and a flat nose and stubble. Eric.

I shuddered out a breath. Drew in another. Finally, I gave him a shaky smile. "Still kickin'."

A blur of motion. I felt myself moving, and suddenly I was in Eric's arms, my entire world muffled down to fabric and shaking breaths and a warm chest hitching with tears.

"Thank God," he mumbled. Then: "Shit, goddamn it—you scared me, asshole."

I laughed back, winded and faint. "Scared me, too."

Another noise, this time a *whoop* of pure joy. I pulled back in time to see Angel standing behind Eric and flapping her hands like tiny bird wings. She slapped them in a rapid drumbeat against my legs until I pulled them away, wincing.

"Ow, ow, good to see you, too, Angel." I blinked, glancing around. "Where's—?"

I stopped, then, because I saw Monica. She stood a few steps back, next to Zoey, her hands clasped behind her back and her mascara hopelessly smeared. Zoey kept a hand on her shoulder, but once I caught her eye, Zoey dropped it, giving me a casual thumbs-up instead—though I swear she blinked a little harder, bit her lip a little more. Another of those distant things that weren't caretaker things, not really, she would *never*.

For now Monica stepped forward, and I reached out a hand to

her. That broke it; her eyes, already watering again, spilled over with new tears, the ugly kind that made her face redden and her nose run and her brows scrunch up like a baby. She wheezed for breath, sniffling wildly, and when she spoke up, the words came out cracked and stuttering.

"You look better," she mumbled.

I raised an eyebrow. "Better? Wait—" It all came rushing back to me at once, fragments of broken memories and bizarre dreams, lights and parasites and grasping things—and soon I was grasping, too, digging in my pocket for my phone and flipping the front camera on.

I saw my own face staring back.

And my eyes looked...still dark, but more alive. Still far too porcelain-doll wide, still lined with bags and worry marks, and I had a feeling those would never entirely go away—not after what I'd seen, not after that thing burned its away across my pupils and changed everything I saw in the world.

But they were mine.

That reflected version of me shook, distorting as my tears dripped onto the screen, as my fingers shook, and finally as I dropped it entirely, letting it scatter along the rug. Then Eric and Angel and Monica were there, hugging me close, and I hugged back, leaning into them, all of us crying like toddlers and none of us caring at all.

"It's okay, Ian," Eric murmured. "It's okay, it's gone. It's gone. We burned all the bodies we could find up there. Wasn't even hard—all it needed was one shitty old Bic tossed in, and the whole place went up. It's over."

I wanted to ask a dozen questions, about him and about what happened and if that was really his favorite lighter—but before I could start, something rustled. Everyone was here—Eric and Monica and Angel and Zoey—but something rustled beyond them, anyway.

I listened close. Beyond the lobby, down the hall toward the guest bedrooms, I couldn't hear a hum anymore. Instead I heard a dozen other noises: clattering silverware, rustling fabric, muttered voices... and somewhere underneath it all, the hum of classical music from a battered pink boom box.

Living noises.

And even as I watched, something moved ahead—a man in a dirty sweatshirt and jeans, shuffling down the hallway ahead and outward, scratching at the back of his neck. His eyes looked black, but also bright, tired, and confused. A small child tagged along after him, chattering about wanting to watch *Paw Patrol*...and then a new thought occurred to him, and he tugged on the man's sleeve and asked where the bathroom was.

People. And people I recognized, too, ones from the clearing.

At least a dozen humans, waking up and existing in Kittakoop.

I thought of that and I started laughing, a dry and not-entirely-sane noise, pressing a hand to my head and leaning back with it.

"Oh my god," I breathed, once I had enough air to do so. "I'm alive."

It took a second for it to click, but then Eric rolled his eyes and Monica laughed, while Angel stared between them in bald confusion. Zoey pressed a hand to her face, but between her fingers, I saw the hints of a smile.

Quarantine's over. The sickness is done. Everyone can go back to living, now.

I turned my head, staring out the window. Outside, the sun hung low on the horizon, casting long shadows across the hills and **CLOSED** signs, ending another day I'd managed to live through, despite everything. The breeze wafting in through the mesh smelled crisp and clear, like pine needles and grass.

It was a nice summer evening. Maybe one of the last summer evenings left before autumn rolled in and buried everything in crisp leaves and cold wind. Like Kittakoop, the weather felt stuck in suspense: always long, long summer days and dry summer nights, a held note of cicadas and mosquitoes chirping on and on before autumn closed it out.

Somewhere in the hallway, someone called out for a towel. Someone else called back that they were coming over. Someone asked if there was any hot water out here, because they were covered in this oily junk and needed a damn shower. Someone else griped about phone reception. Countless normal, human noises, layered over one another until they felt like music.

How long would that last? We'd all still died at some point. We still had the scars and marks of that. Would we still rot and fall apart from them? Would the things that were supposed to kill us still kick in eventually, or had we been given a free pass after seeing something infinite and weird enough to drag us back to life? What would we *eat*?

If I'd spent so much of my life preparing to die, then I didn't, what was I supposed to do with myself now, still braced for an end that could happen at any moment, without any future plans?

I didn't know. I couldn't predict the future.

So I decided, for now, to live in the present. One day at a time, one moment at a time, I'd push on ahead.

I'd learned how to die already. Now I needed to learn how to live, instead.

Eric reached for my hand, and I took it and squeezed. Monica took my other, and we sat there as a cozy little group, the former last kids in town—in an empty ski resort now buzzing with reluctant, confused, disoriented life. A town full of people who'd been dying, then came back, and had to remember how to exist again.

A town that would one day, with effort and patience, turn back into a home.

ACKNOWLEDGMENTS

Hey look, I made it! Believe me, I'm as surprised as anyone else. If you're reading this, that means you made it, too. Congrats!

There's no such thing as a lone wolf Renaissance man, though; pretty sure even da Vinci had someone doing his laundry while he drew. As such, thank you to my brilliant editor at Holiday House, Della, and my clever agent, Bibi the Human, for steering this book through contracts, formatting, and all the nuts and bolts that go on behind the scenes. If anything came out polished, thank them. For the rest, blame me.

Thank you especially to Luna, who put up with the earliest drafts, gave wise feedback, and reminded me to un-shrimp my spine from sitting too long. You are, and always will be, my problematic favorite. And thank you to our cats, Miss Kitty and Bibi the Cat, for reminding us both to go to bed on time.

Thank you to my mom, for answering all my two a.m. text messages and Facebook posts about writing, even when they didn't make sense.

Thank you to the Seattle NaNoWriMos, the #HopefullyWriting Slack group, my AMM mentor, the Friend Menagerie, and the Writing OCT Squad for your constant feedback and moral support. Y'all rock.

What happens to these characters from here? I don't know! For now, that's in the hands of the fanfic and fanart and fan theory writers. As for me, I'm gonna get a vitamin water and take a nap.

Take care, and hope to see you next time,

Natalie "Leif" Leif